A SUMMER DUET

A Secret Treasure: When pretty, passionate Eve Burnett meets the dark intriguing Julio Falcone, she is torn. As a man, Julio is powerfully attractive. As a policeman, he is bound to be a Fascist. Her brother, David, is connected to the Greek Partisans who wish to liberate Rhodes. Eve realizes that she may be forced to choose between the man she loves and the safety of her family.

Holiday in Bologna: When Heidi Manelli arrives outside the Italian villa in Bologna, she encounters charismatic Stefano. Is their developing relationship a holiday romance, or something deeper? Is her holiday in Bologna going to change her life forever?

A SUMMER DUET

A SUMMER DUET

by

Lindsay Townsend

Magna Large Print Books
Long Preston, North Yorkshire,
BD23 4ND, England.

British Library Cataloguing in Publication Data.

Townsend, Lindsay
    A summer duet.

    A catalogue record of this book is
    available from the British Library

    ISBN   978-0-7505-3664-6

First published in Great Britain in 2010 by
www.BookStrand.com

Cover illustration © Jill Battaglia by arrangement with
Arcangel Images

The moral right of the author has been asserted

Published in Large Print 2013 by arrangement with
Lindsay Quicke

Magna Large Print is an imprint of Library Magna Books Ltd.

Printed and bound in Great Britain by
T.J. (International) Ltd., Cornwall, PL28 8RW

DEDICATION

A Secret Treasure

To my mother, Joan, with love.

A SECRET TREASURE

Chapter 1

Eve was hanging washing in the small courtyard when she heard the knock. She dropped
the clothes pegs and ran across the searing
cobbles to the black door in the high stone
wall. She wanted it to be her brother David,
because he was missing and she was afraid.

Her heart raced as she opened the door
and the scent of fresh bread, herbs and coffee wafted in from the street. Disappointment seared through her as she realised at
once that it wasn't David. Outside, in the
narrow alleyway, squinting in the fierce
sunlight, stood two men. Eve recognized the
shorter, fatter one as Luigi Grassi, one of the
fascist henchmen of the Italian governor of
Rhodes Island. His early morning appearance at her parents' house in the Old City of
Rhodes Town, filled her with horror. Her
mouth went dry, her heartbeat stampeding
afresh. Had these men come to tell them
that David had been found injured or dead?

'*Si, signori?*' she asked, unable to prevent
the wobble in her voice. She had reported
David's disappearance four days ago and
Grassi had dealt with her then, all smiles as
he rudely appraised her blonde, slender

13

figure. He was a blackshirt bully, and she was wary of him. These closing years of the 1930s were anxious times, especially on Rhodes.

'May we come in, little English *signorina?*' Grassi answered his smile widening. He removed his fedora hat and stepped through into the yard without waiting for Eve's permission. 'There's no need to be alarmed. We've had no news of your brother. This visit is merely a courtesy.' He nodded to the shirt which had dropped from Eve's suddenly nerveless fingers. 'You've lost your washing.'

Eve reluctantly stepped towards the thick-set Grassi, but the man with him was ahead of her, plucking David's best shirt from the cobbles in a single, smooth movement. He held it out, his deep-set eyes full of sympathy.

'Thank you.' Eve blushed as the stranger looked at her. In her entire nineteen years, she could not remember being scrutinized with such care.

Boldly she stared back at the tall, long-legged man, who looked as if he belonged in uniform instead of his light summer suit and boater. Unlike the balding Grassi, he had thick dark-brown hair, with black brows and lashes. His handsome face seemed full of a contained energy that might be ardent, Eve thought, but might also be cruel. She frowned and took the damp clothing from him, bundling it into her wicker basket. 'Follow me.'

She hurried across the yard, disconcerted when the stranger fell into step beside her. 'There's been no news?'

'None from our end,' said Luigi Grassi. Catching up, the fascist official put an arm through hers, smiling as she flinched. He patted her hand. 'But David is a man, and English. You should not worry so much, *signorina*. We know that he is not involved in any trouble – yet. So far, you English have understood laws, and empire.'

Walking on her right side, the stranger cleared his throat. 'I am very sorry,' he said, with a sincerity Eve instantly believed. 'I hope that you will soon have news of your brother's safe return.' He ducked under the washing line as they marched, three abreast, past Eve's pots of basil and flowering marjoram, towards the arched stone doorway of the ancient town house. 'I wish to help. Signor Grassi has asked me–'

The young man broke off as Eve pushed open the house door and entered first, stepping into the shuttered calm of a small tiled foyer.

'Please,' she gestured them in.

He cleared his throat. 'You are the housekeeper here, no?' he asked, speaking for the first time in careful English.

Grassi gave a bark of laughter, muttering something in an Italian dialect which Eve was glad she did not understand. 'Yes, in a way,' she replied to Grassi's more sensitive partner.

It was true. She washed and cleaned and shopped and cooked and had done so from an early age, bringing a little order into her parents' cheerfully chaotic household. Her mother had no taste for 'domestic drudgery' as she called it and was unable to do more than dusting because of the onset of rheumatoid arthritis. Once active, now, during bad flare-ups of the disease, Philippa Burnett became bedridden. Eve was grateful that her clever mother remained free in her mind, continuing her studies despite her pain.

Eve's father, George Burnett, was also a scholar. In the twenties, he and Eve's mother had taken part in archaeological digs in Turkey. Now, in 1937, semi-retired to the congenial climate of Rhodes, George pursued an interest in the former knights of the island. Although English, Eve and her older brother David had been brought up amidst the classical ruins of Troy and Greece. David, a schoolmaster, shared his parents' passion for antiquity and chuckled at Eve's dream to go to England to study nursing. 'Face it, Evie,' he'd said, 'You're a bright little thing but scarcely university material.'

Remembering, Eve's face burned at his unfair comment as she opened the double doors to the lighter, airy sitting room where her parents spent much of their time and where they were now.

'Forgive the interruption,' she told them in English, 'But these gentlemen have asked to speak to you.' Seeing their instant alarm, knowing they were concerned for her brother, as she was, she added softly, 'There's no news yet of David.' She tried to smile a re-assurance, feeling her lips tight in her taut face.

Philippa Burnett recovered first. Covered by a light paisley shawl despite the early summer heat, sitting in her armchair close to the half-opened courtyard window, she looked as calm as an empress. Regally, she waved the two men to a couple of straight-backed chairs opposite the circular table where she and her husband were reading. 'Of course. Would you bring us some lemonade, please?' she asked Eve.

'Yes, Mum.' Eve withdrew, but not before she heard her father remark dryly in English 'Naturally, we're always extremely keen to hear from our Italian overlords.'

Eve chewed her lower lip in alarm, rushing to the kitchen to complete her task as rapidly as possible. Her father and David were idealists, outspoken in their criticism of Mussolini, the Italian dictator.

Her father's wry comment about overlords was true: for several years the Greek island of Rhodes had been controlled by the Italians. Under the fascist rule of Mussolini, that control had become harsher, with corrupt officials like Luigi Grassi harassing Eve's Greek friends and neighbors. As resident alien English, she and her family had so far escaped persecution, but Eve was worried as she prepared a tray of her home-made lemonade.

Was David involved with one of the Greek anti-fascist movements? Was that why he was missing? What had he done?

Hoping that none of these fears showed in her face, Eve checked her appearance in the antique mirror in the foyer as she left the kitchen. Her golden hair, pinned in its simple pleat, was reassuringly neat, but her mouth was pale, her gray eyes haunted against her peach tan. Conscious that the tall, considerate stranger – who knew English – would miss nothing, Eve rubbed her lips with a work-roughened hand and willed herself to walk slowly.

In the high-ceilinged sitting room, she found Grassi strutting to and fro on the rag rug. In Italian, lately the official language of Rhodes, he was hectoring her parents about David's 'undesirable' friends.

'Your son has fallen into wild company: vandals, petty criminals, the kind who daub political slogans on this island's public buildings...'

'Sounds rather as if you're speaking from personal experience,' George Burnett remarked in English, polishing his gold-

18

framed spectacles.

Eve laid her tray on the book-strewn table, wishing her father would be quiet for once. Locked into their study of the distant past, her mother and father seemed perilously unaware of the present. A protective rush of feeling overwhelmed her. Longing to stay, but aware that neither of her parents considered her grown-up enough to take part in a discussion with two fascist officials, she turned to go.

'Please – stay.' The tall stranger rose from his straight chair and offered it to Eve. He glanced at her parents. 'With your permission?' he asked them in English. 'This concerns your daughter also.'

George Burnett nodded and Eve sat down, detesting her own fear. Grassi was pugnacious but stupid: she knew he was interested in her and she felt reasonably sure that she might be able to use that interest to distract him. The man standing before her was different, sharper. There was a honed, muscular quality about him that his cream suit failed to hide. She wouldn't stand a chance against him physically, and Eve had the uncomfortable foreboding that he was more than her mental match.

Perhaps sensing her as the easiest target, the stranger seemed to address his remarks almost exclusively to her. His voice was low, calm, his English clear, but Eve remained on her guard. If David was involved with the Greek resistance, this man was her enemy.

A faint spasm of regret ran through her, but not for long. The fellow was too inquisitorial.

He began innocently enough. Declining Philippa Burnett's offer of a lemonade, he stood beside Grassi on the rug to introduce himself, since it was obvious that his associate was not going to.

'Good morning, I am Julio Falcone, a *carabiniero*–'

An armed policeman.

'I am on holiday here in Rhodes, when Mr. Grassi asks for my help with this missing person case.'

'Excuse me, but is David considered missing?' Philippa Burnett did not sound alarmed so much as bemused. 'My son, Mr. Falcone, has also been on holiday: a two-week cycling trip around the whole of the island.'

'For five days longer than the end of his vacation, Signora Burnett?' inquired Falcone with deadly gentleness.

George Burnett removed his spectacles again, giving them an unnecessary polish on the lapel of his neat dark suit. 'It's unlike David not to be in touch, now and then,' he observed thoughtfully. 'And it has been five days since he was supposed to be back.'

'Yes, Dad, but there aren't many places here with telephones – we're the only ones in our street – and David's not much of a letter writer,' Eve said quickly, glossing over her brother's lack of contact. She had hoped that the authorities would begin a search, and find him, before their mother began to be worried.

Philippa Burnett might appear calm, but she was not a strong, or a well woman.

Wanting to reassure her mother now, Eve continued, 'I think he's probably decided to extend his trip. School's finished and David's a dedicated cyclist.'

'Indeed?' said Falcone, glancing round the whitewashed sitting room, tilting his head on one side to read the titles of the books on her parents' many tall bookshelves. 'Italians are keen cyclists, so we shall have much in common. I'm a member of a cycling club in Parma, where I live. But this cycling trip of your brother's...' He fixed Eve with a pair of bright hazel eyes. 'He was alone, no? There were none of these "friends" whom my colleague is worried about with him?'

Eve thought she heard amusement in Falcone's voice, but Grassi, who had gulped down a lemonade and was now staring with naked greed at a beautiful rose-colored Venetian glass vase, seemed oblivious to their exchange.

Heartened by this, she answered, 'David was alone.'

Falcone produced a paper with a typed list

of names. 'Andreas the butcher, the one called Red-haired Andreas, he did not go with him?'

Eve shook her head. Her throat was dry, but she made no move to pour herself a glass of lemonade. Her parents, too, were not drinking.

'They are said to be good friends,' said Falcone.

'Perhaps, Mr. Falcone, but Andreas couldn't have gone with him.' Eve smiled as she delivered her decisive thrust. 'Andreas is making up a meat order for me today at his shop.'

'You are sure they did not set out together?'

'Of course I am!'

'Eve,' said her father, disapproving mildly of her tone. Under his and Falcone's combined stares, Eve felt herself starting to blush. She dropped her head, not facing her interrogator as Falcone went on.

'The route that he took. Did he leave word with you?'

'David is adult, Mr. Falcone,' put in George Burnett. He and his wife exchanged glances, something Falcone was quick to pick up on.

'But it's clear you're uneasy. Why? Why be concerned for a grown man adding a few more days to a round island cycling trip?'

Eve was quickly revising her first favorable

impressions of this over-zealous policeman. She had also noticed that his English had markedly improved. He was a sly one, she thought. He had been trying to catch them out.

'Shouldn't you be asking more pertinent questions?' she demanded, pleased to hear Grassi bring his jaws together in a snap at her sharp tone. 'Don't you want to know what David was wearing, Mr. Falcone? What kind of bike he has? Don't you want his photograph?'

Eve sprang from her chair, her cork sandals soundless on the mosaic floor as she crossed to the dresser. Lifting David's most recent picture in its leather frame from the polished oak wood, she thrust it at Julio Falcone, surprised by her own vehemence.

He was standing quite still, looking down at her. Beside him, Grassi scratched the side of his fleshy nose and added in a loud aside, 'That Greek butcher, always a problem to us.'

His comment went unheeded. Close to the shuttered window, sitting stiffly in their comfortable armchairs, Eve's parents stared at their usually placid daughter, their refined faces blank with astonishment. Falcone shook his dark head.

'You've already given a very full description to my colleague,' he said. 'A photograph would be welcome, however.'

He smiled at her, transforming his darkly handsome features into a younger, far less forbidding face. 'I give you my word that your brother's picture will be returned. I will bring it myself.'

He walked over to her and took the photograph. 'Thank you.'

He towered over Eve by more than a foot, but strangely, this close to Julio Falcone, she felt no sense of threat, as she always did when dealing with Grassi. He stepped back at once and gave her an almost courtly bow.

'We will leave you now,' he said, solemn again.

'If your son reappears, he should contact my office at once,' said Luigi Grassi in Italian. Striding past a narrow sofa to a low table, he ran a dimpled hand over the neck of the Venetian glass vase, murmuring, 'Bella, bella.'

Eve could not suppress a shudder.

Falcone said quietly, 'We shall see ourselves out.'

She responded to their farewells without looking at either man. Relieved that they were finally going, she was worried again. Wanting to be sure they had actually left, she followed them out and closed the yard door tightly after them. Her stomach churned with anxiety. Where was David? Was he safe and unhurt? Was he somehow involved with the butcher?

'I know nothing!' she burst out. 'He tells me nothing!' What had happened to David? *I am going to find out,* she decided.

Chapter 2

The instant she heard the outer door close on the two Italians, Eve tried to talk to her parents. George and Philippa Burnett remained suspiciously hearty, claiming that, as an intelligent young man of twenty-four, David was well able to take care of himself.

'I'm sure he's safe,' Eve agreed, 'but what do you think? That new officer, Julio Falcone; he seems very keen to me.'

'He was keen on watching you, certainly,' remarked George.

As he and Philippa exchanged a knowing look, Eve's thoughts flashed to the tall, handsome Italian. Julio disturbed her. He made her feel alive. He made her want to rebel against the narrow confines of her life. He made her aware of her mouth and body in a new way. *What would it be like to kiss him?*

'Can we not talk about this?' she asked, her mind fixing on the obvious fact that he was one of the occupying forces on Rhodes.

'About Julio?' Philippa asked coyly.

'About David and what he has been up to!' Eve found herself tugging at the skirt of her dress in sheer frustration. 'I am nineteen!'

'Two years from your majority,' her father

pointed out.

Then Philippa said, 'You ought to be setting out for the butcher's, Evie, or lunch is going to be very late.'

They wanted to talk privately, she thought. Disappointed and aggrieved at being left out again, as she had been throughout her teens, she ran upstairs to collect her shopping basket.

Outside, in the narrow alleyway linking their house to scores of other Rhodian homes within the Old City, she began to feel better. She was going to the butcher's, and Andreas was a major contact in the Greek community. If David were caught up in any resistance movement, Andreas would know.

The scents of the early morning, when she had risen to scrub the washing, were almost gone, but enough of the light and smells of her favorite time of day remained to put a spring back into Eve's step. Breathing the lingering perfume of honeysuckle and camomile, she turned up Homer Street and climbed steadily along the needle-slim cobbled road. David *must* be all right. They would have heard something, otherwise. Andreas would surely have come to them if there was any really terrible news.

Telling herself again that everything would be fine, Eve nodded to a girl playing hopscotch in the alleyway. The girl, a neighbor's daughter, was wearing a smocked dress that

Eve had made for her. Around them, the office workers scurried through the little squares towards Mandraki harbor or the town hall. Somewhere on the city ramparts a donkey brayed a single protest, then fell silent.

Eve jumped over a pile of donkey droppings in the middle of Homer Street and passed under three arches, two with hanging lanterns. The sunlight was increasing the nearer she came to the wider Street of Pythagoras, where she would cut down to the Jewish Quarter and Andreas' shop.

Weaving round the wooden jetty of one of the overhanging balconies, Eve heard a sharp cry behind her. She looked back, ready to help, and saw an old woman sweeping her whitewashed step with a twiggy broom. Under the widow's black headsquare, the wrinkled eyes were bright and aware, motioning towards a deeply shadowed archway.

Eve saw him then, the Italian policeman Julio Falcone. He had failed to duck under one of the many carpets hung out to air from the ancient wooden balconies, and had dragged a striped hearth-rug down over his broad shoulders. He must have been trying to extract himself from the heavy wool folds, but now he was utterly still, frozen in the shadow of the arch. Only because her eyes were good and she'd had the old woman's warning did Eve know the man was there at all.

The shock that Falcone was actually following her – and trying to disguise it – made Eve light-headed with alarm, but then her natural instinct for self-preservation stirred into action. Whatever this man suspected her of, she wasn't going to make it easy for him. She certainly wasn't going to bring Falcone within a hundred yards of Andreas' house. She would pick up her meat order and talk to the butcher later, when she had lost her irritating 'shadow' and could be sure of not being watched, or overheard. Mr. Falcone might well be fluent in Greek, as well as English.

Curiously exhilarated as well as uneasy, Eve marched back the way she had come, towards her unwanted escort, smiling to herself as she imagined his consternation. Just at the last moment, she stepped beneath a wooden-reinforced, half-ruined gate into Sophocles Street. Darting down the ochre steps, she made for the noisy road junction beside the Ibrahim Pasha mosque, whose dome and scaffolding-enclosed new minaret she could now see clearly. Swinging her shopping basket and increasing her pace as the flagged street opened out, she dropped towards the long bazaar. Eve thought she heard a drumming of footsteps in the road behind her. Disgusted by her own nervous giggle, she stopped by a leatherworkers' shop, pretending to be mesmerized by the workers' busy treadling of sewing machines.

Think! Eve told herself. Her parents said she was an intellectual lightweight, a bit of a fool, ready to be seduced by any beggar or hard-luck story. This time she had to do better than that: she had to lose Julio Falcone.

Above her head she heard a light breeze shifting in the plane tree close to the mosque, an eerie sound which made her shiver, despite standing in full sun. From the street of the long bazaar, she caught the badgering chant of one of the Turkish residents selling hibiscus flowers, and she wished fiercely that Falcone would go away. She knew she ought to confront him but shrank from the encounter, shy of accosting a virtual stranger.

I must, she thought. *Think of David. Do it for his sake.*

She turned and, as before, walked straight towards the Italian. 'Are you lost?' she demanded.

He stalked out of the shadows, his face showing a perfect surprise. 'Why should you think that?'

'If you aren't lost, why are you following me?'

'Am I? Perhaps we are merely going in the same direction.' He pointed further along the street. 'Shall we go together?'

Infuriated by his obvious lie, Eve stayed where she was. 'Admit it. You were following me.'

'So? Perhaps it is my job to follow you.'

'I thought you said you were on holiday.'

'And also to help Signor Grassi with the case of your missing brother.'

'So what about David? Why are you not looking for him?'

He shook his dark head. 'Do you not think I can do more than one thing at once?'

'Why are you following me?'

'Because you interest me.' He looked her up and down and smiled. 'Why do you think?'

His frank admission made her forget altogether that he was a stranger, or a threat. At that moment all she wanted to do was beat him at his own game.

'Fine!' she snapped. 'Then see if you can keep up with me!'

She spun round, catching him off-guard and walking so swiftly that she was almost running. Ignoring his warning, 'Wait!' she moved even faster, clutching her basket tightly and chanting in her mind, think! Think!

Then she saw a way out. Darting into a nearby shuttered alley, full of musty shops and strutting pigeons, she saw a gaggle of boys crouching over a game of marbles. She called to them softly.

'Have you got a ball?' she asked the eldest urchin in the sing-song Rhodian dialect.

'For sure!' came the reply.

Careful that the coins did not catch the by now glaring light, she showed the boys a handful of change. 'Yours – if you play ball along by the mosque steps.'

'For sure!' The eldest boy snatched the coins and roared off in the direction of the washing fountain of the Ibrahim Pasha mosque, his gang in rapid pursuit. Moments later, kicking a ball about the paved street, their yelling, boisterous figures soon surrounded the tall, light-suited foreigner, who could not move or see past them for several vital seconds.

Seconds were all she needed. Eve pelted down the dingy street where the boys had been playing. Soon she was hidden amongst the bustle of crowds, motorbikes and donkeys moving along Socrates Street, home of the long bazaar and, more importantly to her, one of the roads leading out of the Old City.

I've done it, she thought. *I've beaten him.* She grinned and swung her basket, telling herself she was glad, while part of her wondered when she would see him again.

Under one of the ancient windmills on Mandraki pier, Eve haggled for red mullet from a local fisherman. She bought bread and vegetables from one of the markets in the New Town, carefully slipping into the side streets whenever a group of Italian sailors, or shipyard workers bound for their new harbor at Akandia, marched out of the haze towards her.

None of these dusty, tired workers was Julio Falcone. Confident that she had indeed lost him in the maze of alleyways in the Turkish Quarter of the Old City, Eve now returned to the Old City through the nearest gate.

Checking over her shoulder, scolding herself whenever she started at looming shadows, Eve discovered that she had drifted into the Knights' Quarter, several streets away from her intended destination of Andreas' shop.

'Idiot,' she muttered, pausing by a stone cannonball stranded in the middle of the street, one of the hundreds left over from the famous siege of Rhodes in 1522 by Suleiman the Magnificent. The problem was that she loved the Old City with its huge, encircling medieval walls, its grand inns and palaces, where knights from the whole of Christendom had lived and prayed, its icon-rich churches, its mosques, its tiny squares and plane trees and palms. She could wander here for hours and frequently did, driven at times by a discontent that she did not want to admit to.

Reorientating herself, Eve looked about.

She was in a run-down part of the city, close to the former Palace of the Grand Masters of the Knights of St John, the holy crusading order which had built the castle and city walls of Rhodes Town. The palace was semi-ruined; trees and scrub grew in many of its former rooms, but Eve had heard a recent rumor that the Italians were planning to rebuild it as a summer home for Mussolini.

'Good morning, Eve.' Stella, one of Eve's Rhodian neighbors, called down from the balcony of her nearby house.

'Good morning!' Eve returned in Greek, waving to the buxom figure of Stella's next-door neighbor Penelope. Before the Fascists banned the Orthodox religion, Penelope used to help the Greek priest to sweep out the tiny shrine in the cellar of her dilapidated house.

Turning, Eve continued to walk towards the old palace, stepping round scaffolding that surrounded part of the last house, set beside the junction of two streets.

Glancing up the longer, straighter of the streets, Eve saw Julio Falcone before he knew she was there. He was strolling down the famous Street of the Knights, turning his dark head this way and that – clearly still looking for her, and clearly not looking for David.

Eve stepped back behind a palm tree and a single, antique wall topped by michaelmas daisies. Relieved that he had not spotted her, she found herself drawn into watching him through a crack in the wall. Head erect and straight-backed, his boater set at a jaunty angle, Falcone moved with unconscious grace. She would have liked to see him run, or dance. *With her.*

Where did that come from?

She frowned and shook her blond fringe, annoyed with herself. She should be making for Andreas' shop, while there was time. Tearing her eyes from the crack, Eve realized she had to stay where she was for several minutes. Falcone was too close. He had crossed the street and was closing on the last house, near her hiding place.

One of the ramshackle pieces of scaffolding on the balcony creaked ominously. Eve heard it, but the Italian policeman, calling a Greek 'Good morning' to Stella, missed the snapping sound.

Further along the street a group of workmen yelled a warning and pointed.

'Help!' Eve shouted in Italian, as a metal pole detached itself from the cat's-cradle of beams and scaffolding and plummeted towards the tall figure.

Julio leaped back, losing his boater, and the pole bounced on the cobbles, rolling into the middle of the road with a discordant clanging.

Hands over her ears, Eve saw Julio look up

immediately, his arms outstretched as if to catch something. Had he thought someone had burst through the scaffolding?

She had no chance of further reflection, or flight. His face, which had bleached marble-white, now became flesh and blood again as he raised an arm in thanks to the warning shout of the workmen. He scooped up his hat and walked over to Eve's sheltering wall.

'I am glad we have found each other again,' he remarked in English, standing on tip-toe to look down at her behind the blocks of stone and michaelmas daisies. He sounded calm, but surprise and something more, perhaps satisfaction, perhaps even pleasure, showed in his crinkled hazel eyes. 'Are you all right?'

Overhead, Eve heard Stella snort and go inside, slamming her balcony door.

'Yes, thank you.' Smarting at being discovered, for shouting when she needn't have done, Eve picked up her basket and made for the middle of the road. There was no point in hiding now. 'I would move that metal pole, if I were you,' she called over her shoulder.

She hurried off, determined not to watch as Julio Falcone no doubt casually recovered the pole, but he caught up with her after a few paces.

'Please...' He sounded a little breathless, for which she was glad. Not understanding why she did it, Eve stopped.

36

'Are you all right?' she found herself asking.

He nodded. 'But when I hear a young lady call help– '

'I couldn't remember the Italian for "Look out", that's all.' Although she was telling the truth, she could not meet his eyes.

Ignoring her small protest, Julio took her shopping basket from her with a, 'How do you think I feel, marching along beside you, unladen? Now, please–' He held the basket almost teasingly out of her reach '–Allow me to buy you a *caffè* and one of those sticky Greek cakes. As the least of thank yous.'

Julio smiled, and again Eve was struck by how much a smile transformed his brooding good looks. She was relieved, too, that he seemed to bear her no ill-will for having gone out of her way to 'lose' him.

'I–' She cast about for an excuse, tempted to accept his offer but wary of becoming more involved. Julio was different from the boys she had walked out with, the wiry Rhodian youths who had strolled with her through the streets, their hands scarcely touching. When her and Julio's fingers had collided over the basket, that brief, casual touch had made her tingle from her palm to the crown of her head. She had scoffed at romantic movies, where the hero and heroine had appeared to be dazzled by the slightest embrace, but now she had experienced it for herself, finding it both disturbing and exhilarating. 'Perhaps another time,' she finished lamely.

'Why not now?' he asked with another smile, offering her his arm. 'Did you go to the butcher's, by the way?'

His abrupt question reminded Eve that she was dealing with a policeman. She did not take his arm. She raised her face to his in seeming frankness. 'I have,' she said, praying inwardly that she would not blush. 'But forgive me. I must really be getting home. I have lunch to prepare.'

'Ah, yes, in your role as housekeeper. My mother and sisters would appreciate your lack of time. They often scold me for adding to their work.'

'I do the same with David.' Eve knew she was lingering, delaying the moment when she would ask him to return her basket. A shiver of dread ran down her spine. What if he were to rummage in the basket and realize she had lied to him? What if their hands touched again? Would she tingle all over? Would her feelings of confused delight show in her face?

'What do you do to annoy them?' she asked quickly, covering herself.

'My sisters would tell you I'm a nuisance with the washing. My cycling clothes, for example. I often–' Julio stopped suddenly, as if deciding that talking about clothes was too personal. He pointed a muscular arm to the ruined Palace of the Grand Masters. 'Is that the old Turkish prison?'

'It is – and the former palace of the grand masters of the Knights of St John, and beneath that, a temple to the sun god, Helios.' Grateful for the change of subject, Eve grinned at his raised black eyebrows.

'You're very well informed,' Julio said. Still carrying her basket, he looked up and down the street. 'May I escort you home? That is, if you can turn me in the right direction for your house.' He gave her a wry smile and a very Italian shrug.

Eve giggled, then wished she hadn't. She was nineteen, for goodness' sake, not a silly schoolgirl! Aiming for sophistication, she inclined her head, then spoiled the effect by starting when Julio tucked her hand through his arm as they began to stroll down the hill towards Socrates Street and the markets of the long bazaar.

'It's all right,' he said reassuringly. With what seemed a deliberate effort to put her once more at ease, he asked, 'Are there any remains of the temple of Helios? I have an interest in ancient things.'

'You should talk to my father,' Eve said, distracted by the feel of his warm, muscular arm cradling her own and not wanting to claim knowledge which was not hers. 'As my family will tell you, I'm no scholar.'

Thoughts of her family brought her back to her missing brother David. What had happened to him? Anxiety made her tremble and at once Julio turned his aquiline profile towards her, his sooty eyebrows frowning. 'You have gone very red,' he said, misinterpreting her distress for simple sunstroke. 'Here, take my hat. You are too gold for this hot sun.'

He dropped the boater onto her head – her golden head, Eve corrected in her mind, flashing her companion a grateful smile from under the brim of her new hat. In truth, she loved the sun, but it was no hardship to wander these baking streets wearing Julio's holiday boater. He was telling her about his home in Parma, about his love of the opera there, and his single trip to Rome, when he had gawped at the Colosseum and wondered what it would have been like to fight as a gladiator in that amazing arena.

Eve shook her head. 'They were cruel games.'

'Yes, they were,' said Julio. 'Did you hear any of the Olympic Games in 1936? I listened to them on the radio.'

'Hitler's games?' Eve murmured, recalling them all too well. Did Julio admire such a man? Chilled at the idea, she listened intently, ready to condemn any admiring comment about Nazi Germany, but all Julio talked about was the amazing athlete Jessie Owen.

'I would love to shake his hand,' he was saying. 'My friend Levi, who is also a sprinter, says that Owen is the best runner he has ever seen.'

'You have a Jewish friend?'

'Of course! Why not?' He seemed on the point of saying more, then braced his arm for her as they walked back up the steps and under the ancient gate into Sophocles Street. 'Tell me about your temple to Helios. Was he the god whose statue was the original Colossus of Rhodes?'

'He was, and Rhodes was *his* island, his favorite place in the whole world.'

Guiding Julio along the familiar cobbles of Homer Street, Eve explained more: about the site of the temple of Helios and about the island folklore surrounding the rose, said by some to be the sun god's flower. 'Some say, too, that the statue of the Colossus stood in the ancient temple precincts, although no one knows for sure,' she concluded. 'My parents would love to dig there, although I think – '

Eve stopped, surprised that she had almost told him one of her more private thoughts. This Julio was easy to talk to, she decided, and a polite and charming escort. With a pang of disappointment, she turned into the smaller alleyway off Homer Street and noticed the tamarisk tree in her neighbor's courtyard, their walk home had been almost too quick. Or was his charm merely a pretense? Was he tricking her into being comfortable with him with small talk?

'I imagine the Rhodians would like to uncover their past,' Julio remarked. 'It is their history and culture.'

This was surprising from a fascist official, and so close to Eve's own opinion that she assumed he must have guessed her thoughts. Disconcerted, she took back her shopping with a dignified, 'Thank you,' then remained standing outside the black door into the yard. On their walk from the Knights' Quarter conversation had flowed, but now she was unsure what to do or say. She couldn't invite Julio in for coffee, that would alarm her parents.

'Thank you,' she said again and held out the boater. Now it was off her head, she missed both the hat and the warmth that lingered from his hand after he had placed it on her hair.

Julio shook his head. 'Keep it. I would like to see you again, anyway. Because of your brother, of course' he continued, as Eve felt her gray eyes widening. 'I will keep after Luigi, as you say in English, make sure David is not forgotten.'

Sensing another thanks would be too much, Eve wet her lips with her tongue, aware that her nervous action had drawn Julio's eyes to her mouth. 'Goodbye, Mr.

Falcone.' She put out her hand.

Falcone took it, smoothing his thumb, once, lightly over her work-roughened fingertips. 'I have enjoyed this morning.' He pushed the courtyard door open for her. '*Arrivederci.*' He gently squeezed her hand and then released her, stepping back and setting off in the same direction as they had come, turning before the corner to wave.

'*Arrivederci,*' Eve murmured, ducking through into the courtyard. She was so tempted to watch him leave, to see his graceful, purposeful walk as his tall, strong figure strode away. All in all, this had been an amazing morning, beginning in bitterness but finishing unexpectedly sweetly. The electric prickle of his final touch still lingered: she brought the hand he had caressed up to her lips, trying to smell his scent on her. Regretfully, she closed the outer wall door, attempting to gather her scrambled wits. Lunch must come first, she decided. The red mullet would not take long to fry.

'Thank God he's gone.' A croak, hardly more than a whisper, broke into Eve's cooking plans. Startled, she dropped the basket of vegetables and fish, running across the yard to where the sound had come from.

Huddled against the stout door of the house, swaying slightly on his feet, his face hidden by the curve of the arch, was her missing brother, David.

43

Chapter 3

Eve Burnett interested him, Julio admitted grudgingly, as he turned away from the alleyway where she lived. He had admired her courage from the first, seeing her face up to Luigi Grassi, and her subsequent passionate concern for her missing brother and parents was disarming.

She'd a streak of mischief in her, too – she'd led him a merry dance through Rhodes Town, leaving him exasperated and completely lost. But then, contradictory, just like a woman, she had warned him about that piece of falling scaffolding. He liked her for that, just as he liked her stubborn shyness, the way she lowered her eyes whenever he looked at her too closely. Her Italian was charming, almost fluent, and her voice sweet.

He liked to hear her talk, and her talk was interesting. Today, though, she had fallen silent whenever he interrupted, and he'd been forced to prompt her to go on. They had been conversing in English by then, so it wasn't a language problem. Perhaps at home she was accustomed to being over-ridden, her opinions dismissed.

Julio frowned at the idea and shortened

his stride, slowing down without admitting to himself that he was doing so. This jumble of streets where she lived was like Eve, he thought, mysterious and appealing. He wanted to know both better.

He thought she might be interested in him, or was that wishful thinking? Julio shrugged. He would have time to find out. He had told Eve and her family that he was on holiday, which was not the whole truth. After his three weeks vacation, he had been assigned to Rhodes for a further two months, by order of his ex-high school colleague from Parma, Luigi Grassi.

Grassi was his superior because Grassi was high in the fascist party, which controlled everything in Italy. Grassi had asked for him especially, and because Grassi had connections in the party, strings had been pulled. So he, Julio Falcone, formerly of the Parma *carabinieri,* was stuck here for the summer.

He hoped his mother and sisters would be okay without him.

There were compensations, however. There were the archaeological sites, and now there was Eve.

Julio stopped in the shade of a plane tree and closed his eyes. The bustle of the town and chatter of swifts fell away as his mind filled with images of Eve. Little, pretty Eve Burnett with her pert, trim figure and her hair the color of a saint's halo. He longed to see more of her shapely legs and those engaging dimples in her cheeks when she smiled. He wanted her soft gray eyes to look at him and only at him. He thought of her mouth and imagined what it would be like to kiss those pink, fresh lips into lush redness. Would she taste of English tea? he wondered, shaking his head at the idea. 'Of sugar,' he said aloud, and grinned.

Her slight, small fingers were a wonder to him and he admired her for the callus on her palms: she was a hard worker. He wanted to find her some handcream, offer to smooth some into her skin: a deliciously sensual idea that aroused and disturbed him together.

I should not be thinking of her in this way, he thought, as his guilty images of embracing Eve grew hotter and more elaborate. Daydreaming was one thing, but she was no doll, to be played with and discarded: she had feelings, and spirit.

'Plenty of spirit,' he murmured, with a chuckle, recalling how she had confronted him. She was a saucy creature, just asking to be kissed.

And her brother was missing. When he thought of that again, Julio frowned. He could only begin to imagine what she was feeling. If one of his sisters went missing, he would go crazy.

I must do what I can to find him, he decided,

starting off down the street again, this time in the direction of the police station.

What if David Burnett is involved with Greek partisans? What if his pretty sister is? What then?

I would have to interrogate her, he thought. *Torment her with a kiss on her mouth, and then on her stomach and then higher.*

Further thought was impossible. Wishing he could dive into Rhodes harbour and cool off, Julio lengthened his stride more, already planning how he could see his saucy English maid again.

David was wet and shivering. When Eve felt his forehead, he was burning. His clothes were muddy and he was limping.

Even so, Eve had a great deal of trouble coaxing him inside. In a series of tense, whispered exchanges, David insisted that their parents should be told nothing and Eve argued that they should. It was cruel to keep them longer in suspense and how would David be able to remain hidden, limping and with a fever?

'Later, then, if you must,' David hissed through chattering teeth. 'But not now, Evie. Dad will want to know what happened, every detail. You know how he is.'

'All right, later.' Eve hooked an arm around her brother's heavy figure. 'But as soon as you're in bed–'

'With hot milk.'

'With hot milk,' Eve repeated, pushing open the house door. Had she closed the sitting room door on her way out, or would her parents be greeted with the shock of David's enfeebled return? 'Now, hush.'

Her warning almost came too late. 'Eve? Is that you?' called her mother from the sitting room.

'Yes, Mum.' The sitting room door was ajar but luckily neither of her parents had stirred from their armchairs. 'I'm just going upstairs for a minute.'

'Be quick, dear. Your father is becoming dreadfully peckish. He says it's affecting his concentration.'

'I'll be as fast as I can,' Eve shouted, raising her voice to cover the sound of David's stumbling footsteps. Like her father, she had lots of questions, but these must wait.

David's clammy weakness alarmed Eve but she said nothing, guiding her brother to his room.

'Strip off and get under the covers.' She darted to her own room for the untouched tumbler of water beside her bed. When she returned to David's room, he downed the glass in a single long swallow, flopping back against the pillows.

'Who's the Italian?' he demanded, his light blue eyes bright with interest and fever.

'I'll fetch your milk, and Mum and Dad.' Eve gathered up David's scattered clothes and backed out. On the way downstairs she retrieved Julio's boater, which had rolled to the bottom of the steps. It had fallen from her head whilst she was helping David. Without really looking at the boater, Eve dropped it onto the umbrella stand and hurried into the sitting room.

David had sprained his left ankle and seemed to have the flu. Eve brought him warm milk and an aspirin, told her parents he was home but in bed, and took him some fresh soft bread and cheese. She was already planning to return to town as soon as possible to buy a boiling fowl for chicken soup.

Her brother ate lightly, but, tucked between crisp white sheets, he was already looking better than the bedraggled scarecrow who had hailed Eve on the doorstep. He had her delicate features, translated into more masculine lines, and a fair mop of curls that made him look younger than twenty-four. His strong, stocky body would recover quickly, Eve knew, if it was given the chance.

'How are you?' Philippa asked, settling on the bed close to David's pillow, ignoring the risk of infection.

'Glad to be home.' David gave his winning smile, although Eve, hovering behind her parents with a hot water bottle, saw how his face was deeply lined, with dark shadows under his eyes.

'What on earth happened to you?' George Burnett restlessly paced the bare floor. 'Did you take a tumble off your bike? Where is your bike? And why are you so late?'

'Won't this wait?' Eve began.

'George!' Philippa twisted on the bed to glare at her husband. 'He's home. That's all that matters. Now, why don't you go with Eve and see about some more hot milk.' She turned to her son, her elegant, rather imperious face glowing with love. 'You could manage another glass, couldn't you, my dear?'

'Yes, please,' said David, in a stronger voice than before. Like Eve, he was automatically protective of their mother, reluctant to cause her concern.

So was George Burnett. Behind his spectacles, his dark blue eyes were avid with curiosity but he retreated silently with Eve, a slim, black-haired, neat man with a very straight carriage and a penetrating stare. Eve was relieved that he had given up his questioning so easily. David needed quiet, good food and rest, and she was determined that he should have all three. She, too, was burning with curiosity, but for now that must wait. David must get well.

David slept all afternoon, watched over by his mother. In the evening he ate some of Eve's fresh chicken soup and seemed more his normal self. His face was still stained along the cheekbones with a vivid red but his eyes had lost their sunken look, and he said that he was ready to talk.

'Bring a chair, Dad. This is going to take a while.' David flapped the covers with his good leg. 'You can sit here, Eve. If you behave.'

Eve stuck out her tongue at her brother and sat down. David was much brighter, but she was anxious he did not over-tire himself. She was also uneasy. How and why had David been living rough these past few days? He had certainly done that. When she'd attempted to comb his hair for him, a few minutes earlier, the comb had snagged on bits of twig and leaves. There were his filthy clothes, too, soaking in her wash tub.

A dry cough announced George Burnett's return with a chair. The family settled on or close to David's bed.

'I'm sorry if you've been worried,' David began. 'And I know you've had visitors.'

Eve felt her face going red, but her parents assumed that David meant Luigi Grassi's visit and assured their son that they had seen that 'odious upstart' off.

'Really,' said David, leaning his head back against the pillows. 'That's irrelevant now, of course – except the authorities mustn't know I'm here.'

'Why not?' Philippa asked. She looked at

51

her husband, alarmed. 'Do you know any-thing about this, George?'

'No, my dear,' George Burnett said, as he glowered at his son, clearly caught between curiosity and anxiety. 'What's been going on?'

'David is trying to explain,' Eve inter-vened. 'Go on, David.'

The fever flush on David's cheeks crept over his whole face. 'I wasn't simply on a holiday, you see. I've been ... delivering things for Andreas.'

'That hot-head! Why can't he do his own delivering?' burst out Philippa.

'David knows what he's doing,' said Eve, wanting to support her brother, though keenly disappointed that he had not thought to tell her anything about this. 'Go on.'

'They've been letters, mostly, and the odd package. Ways for the group to keep in touch.' David held up a hand. 'Better that you don't know what group, then you can't let it slip out by accident in conversation.'

Aware that any group was probably a Greek resistance unit and that David's last warning was meant for her, Eve almost flared up, then reminded herself that her brother was still very weak. Annoyingly, he was also right. Julio might be charming, but wasn't that his job? What did she know about him, really?

David meanwhile was still explaining.

'My last package was very important. *Very.*' He took a deep breath. 'I was to meet someone at Monolithos – at the old crusader fort.'

Philippa gave an indignant snort. 'That's miles away, right at the other end of the island!'

'Yes, Mum, but that was the best ... the safest place, we thought. Except my contact never appeared. Then, when I started cycling back on the track from Monolithos, I ran into an Italian patrol.'

'So?' demanded Philippa.

'It was after curfew,' David explained patiently, 'So I hid.'

'Yes, but you're English!'

'Go on,' prompted Eve, tactfully ignoring her mother's protest.

'It was when I was hiding that I picked up the sprain. I got away that time, but they'd had their lights on me. So I decided to keep hiding.'

David slumped very slightly in bed. Beads of sweat had begun to gather along his hairline. 'I couldn't be sure, either, you see, what the Italians might have learned about me.'

'You mean, someone might have told?' asked Eve, revolted by the idea.

'Unlikely, I know, but possible. Whatever, I couldn't take the risk, especially not carrying this final package.'

'Where is it?' George Burnett asked, sliding forward on his seat.

David smiled. 'Hidden safely, never fear! No risk to us, either. The authorities could search this house until doomsday and not find it.'

'It's far away from your mother and sister?' George Burnett persisted.

'Dad, please. We're not made of china,' Eve protested.

'George, don't talk about us as if we're not here,' said Philippa.

George Burnett inclined his head to his wife. 'I apologize, my dear. David?'

'Don't worry, Dad. It's not here.'

David sounded tired, but convincing, so Eve wasn't sure why her brother's assurance seemed hollow to her. Not wanting to alarm her mother any further, she said nothing for the moment.

'I didn't return here straight away, in case the house was being watched,' David continued. 'I left my bike in a village close to the sea. I hoped that if it was found, it would convince the authorities that I'd taken a ship to Turkey.'

'Oh, David.' Eve knew how proud her brother was of his bicycle.

'Then, last night, I started to feel quite seedy, off-color.' David gave a shrug. 'It seems the outdoor life doesn't agree with me.'

He glanced at each of his parents, anxiety making him look almost boyish, his blue eyes and dark tan showing up vividly against his navy pyjamas. 'So if I could stay – at least until my sprain has gone? They won't be looking for a fully able-bodied man, you see.'

'David, of course you can stay! This is your home.' Philippa found her son's hand and clasped it. 'We've always told you to come home,' Philippa went on. 'Especially if you're in trouble.'

'Yes, right,' George Burnett agreed. 'You did the right thing.'

'That goes for you, too, Eve,' said Philippa, determined to reinforce this advice.

Eve nodded and rose from the bed, wanting to give her parents a moment alone with their son. 'Would you like more hot milk?' she asked her brother.

David coughed a 'Yes,' and she went downstairs to make it, feeling drained. Tomorrow, she thought, she must see Andreas, to collect her meat and to tell him that David was safe. Or did the Greek butcher already know?

You're playing a dangerous game, she thought as she stood heating the milk in the cramped, old-fashioned kitchen. Whether she meant herself and Julio, her brother, Andreas or all of them, Eve wasn't sure.

Returning to David's room, she found him alone, his only light a lantern which he had loved as a child and always kept as a kind of good luck charm. The room shimmered with shadows. Eve prepared to leave quickly, but David stopped her as she handed him the hot milk.

'You never told me who that Italian fellow was. I heard him chatting you up outside the yard wall.'

'He wasn't chatting me up, as you put it–'

'He sounded pretty keen to me, Evie.'

Eve rose, putting half-light between herself and her brother. She could guess what David was about to say and she felt wary of admitting anything, even a name. 'That was Julio Falcone,' she said slowly. 'He came yesterday, with Luigi Grassi.'

'Grassi's poison!'

'Yes, but Mr. Falcone isn't like Grassi. Not all Italians are fascists, you know.'

There was a silence, punctuated by the hissing lantern.

'Are you going to tell me the rest?' Eve demanded. 'Were you ever going to tell me?'

David looked startled by her directness. 'What do you mean?'

'Whatever you're hiding from our parents, David.'

David shifted on the bed. 'I'm hiding nothing.

'Nothing!' Eve's indignation boiled over. 'You call working for the partisans nothing! You do this without a breath of warning to the rest of us–'

'Because it's dangerous,' David broke in, looking at her as if he no longer knew her. 'Where has all this bad temper come from, Eve? This isn't like you.'

'You mean because I argue with you now?' Eve retorted, astonished herself as she answered him. But she had already confronted Julio, a policeman, one of the authorities. Speaking out against him today and, later, walking and talking with him, had revealed to her a confidence that she had not known she had.

'What is he, then, your Mr. Falcone?'

'A policeman from Parma.', Eve stared at the light until it hurt her eyes. 'Don't change the subject.'

'Eve, he's an official. He's bound to be a fascist. He'd have to be in the party to keep his job.'

Eve's chin came up. 'Not always.'

'God, I'm tired.' David sighed and put the glass of hot milk to one side, on the floor. 'I suppose he's good looking?' he said.

Eve refused to look David in the eye. 'I never noticed.'

'Are you sure?' her brother asked gently.

Reluctant to risk another quarrel again with her far from well brother, Eve stepped back from his bed. 'I'll leave you now, since you're tired.'

'Please, Evie,' David said quickly, 'I'm asking you to be careful.'

'As you've been?' Her heart hammering, feeling sticky and restless, Eve nodded stiffly and left the room, closing the door on the dim lantern and on David, whose unexpected homecoming had been both marvelous and disturbing.

Chapter 4

In the old town, Julio ducked under a final arch and some trailing flowers of bougainvillea, then caught the fresh scent of herbs. In the hidden courtyard beyond, Eve was watering her pots of basil, thyme and rosemary: he could hear the splash of water, followed by the rich swirl of released fragrance. She did everything with care, consideration – *cleverness* the policeman in him warned, but he suppressed the thought.

'Greensleeves is my delight...'

She had a clear singing voice, but not as strong as his mother's. Maria Falcone had trained to be a singer in America, the country of her birth. She had met her future husband, Julio's father, on a visit by her American choral society to Parma, and had stayed in Italy ever since. A proud Italian-American, Maria had raised her children to be bi-lingual, although Julio's English had been growing rusty through lack of use.

'...my lady Greensleeves.' Eve's song finished, and he heard her light step on the yard flags. He wished she would sing again – her voice was nothing like his mother's. It was warm and sweet and, as he listened, it coiled into him like the fragrant herbs and sunshine. Her singing reminded him afresh, though he needed no reminders, that Eve was a beautiful young woman and he was a man.

He listened intently, but she was sweeping now.

Suddenly both nervous and inspired, Julio decided to stop hanging around her house like a teenage Romeo. He was, after all, twenty-six. He knocked smartly on the courtyard door.

The door opened after a few moments. Was the delay suspicious, Julio wondered, or was he merely impatient to meet her again? He saw her tip-tilted nose first, and her astonishing hair. She wasn't wearing his boater, sadly, but the sight of Eve made him feel ready for anything.

'Mr. Falcone ... hello.'

'Julio. Or would you really prefer me to call you Miss Burnett?'

Her head came up at once, to check if he was laughing at her. Julio kept his face straight and was gratified when she said quietly, 'Of course not.'

Since he wanted to take her out he did not ask to come in but said quickly, 'I have found a hotel with a good piano player and superb coffee. Would you do me the honor of accompanying me there now?' He glanced deliberately at his watch. 'I believe there is time before lunch.'

Just like his younger sisters, she glanced down at herself. 'My dress–'

'Is lovely. Please say you'll come.'

He heard her take a deep breath and braced himself for a refusal, but instead she said, 'I must tell my parents.'

She closed the door, leaving him marooned in the alley. Perhaps that was simply the English way, he thought, but his instincts were telling him that Eve was different today, less relaxed.

Eve came with him for coffee that morning and all the following mornings for a week. Good days for Julio, who found her company delightful. If she was ever quiet, a small frown turning down the corners of her mouth, he thought of the missing brother, or parental pressure. He knew that the Burnetts disapproved of him. Eve never invited him in off the street, not even so far as the courtyard.

They talked about anything and everything. He was surprised she was Roman Catholic. 'I thought all English were Protestant.'

'No more than all Italians love Mussolini,' she replied with a smile.

'Do you like dogs?' she asked him one morning.

Was this one of her tests, he wondered,

aware of how many of their conversations had touched on the rights of man and politics. He was honest in his reply. 'Absolutely! Do you like cats?'

'Very much.' A dimple sneaked into the corner of her mouth as she tried to suppress a grin. 'How do you feel about snakes?'

'Pythons, yes: the way they grab and squeeze.' He lunged for her, playing at snakes, and she slipped away from him, laughing out loud.

On the seventh morning, arriving early for their meeting, as was his custom, Julio spotted Eve walking up Homer Street with another man, a big Greek with a full red beard, sharp black eyes and a head full of fiery, turbulent curls. She was talking closely to this off-duty Father Christmas and Julio felt a tide of black jealousy threaten to engulf him. It was as much as he could do to hail them civilly, in Greek.

'Good morning!' His voice seemed to bounce off the high walls of the alleyway. He was gratified when Andreas – it could be no other – jumped, then glowered at him.

Eve broke off her conversation, the smile slipping from her face. As her head came round, Julio was struck afresh by how pretty she was, her dress of soft brown wool a new one to him and a pleasure to see, falling sleekly over her slender curves.

'Julio, you are here already.' She never said

such things usually.

It was strange to hear her speaking Greek rather than English, he thought. There was a strained look to her warm gray eyes. As he closed on her, she turned back to her new companion, the red-haired Greek.

'Andreas, may I introduce–'

'Forgive me.' The butcher held up a hand and Eve was instantly quiet. The devil of it was, Julio thought, was that Andreas was impressive, right down to his deep, imposing voice.

'I must return to my shop,' Andreas continued, like a biblical prophet laying down holy laws, 'I have many other customers who need me.'

'Of course, Andreas. Thank you,' Eve said quickly.

She remained watching after him, shading her eyes against the brilliant late May sun, as the man strode past Julio with a grunted, 'Farewell'.

Julio knew he had interrupted something. 'Are you all right?'

She stared at him for a second, as if she didn't know him, and then shook herself. 'Sorry – a ghost walking over my grave,' she said in English. 'Does your mother ever say that? Is it something Italian-Americans use?'

'I forget,' Julio said. 'It doesn't matter.' He held out an arm. 'Shall we go?'

She did not hesitate to link up, which

made him feel both relieved and at the same time, even more suspicious. He had already told Luigi Grassi, in one of his earlier reports, that David Burnett had not returned and seemed unlikely to appear now, but his new boss was right. This family all needed watching, including pretty, innocent Eve.

Chapter 5

David still would tell Eve no more about the resistance group or the mystery package and where it was hidden. Andreas would not tell her any more either. David always met her protests with the sly, 'Still going for coffee with that policeman?' and Eve would instantly fall silent. She did not want David complaining to her parents about Julio and causing even more stress in the house. Her mother and father were already silently disapproving: Philippa's lips tightened each time they heard Julio's distinctive morse-code rapping on the outer yard door and George would raise his head from his books with a weary sigh. Eve knew they were waiting for her to stop seeing him.

'I can't do that,' she argued once to her father. 'We are already under suspicion from the authorities. If I keep seeing Julio it proves we have nothing to hide.'

This was not true for her, of course. She saw Julio because she wanted to, because he made her feel alive and special.

He loved to bring her things. Italian coffee from Parma. Posies of hibiscus flowers. Pink ribbons for the boater he had already 'loaned' to her and was now absolutely hers.

'I will fix them on for you,' he said and they sat close together under the plane tree close to the Ibrahim Pasha mosque, Julio steadily threading the ribbons through the straw rim of the boater while Eve was still wearing it. 'You must not get heat-stroke,' Julio had said, and she had readily agreed. To sit side by side, half-turning to each other, feeling Julio's long thigh lightly pressing against hers, had been a moment of unguarded delight. His fingers were gentle and warm, his touch shimmering about her head and face, making her feel as if she was bathed in an airy, floating light.

'All done.' He tied the ribbons lightly under her chin and kissed the tip of her nose and they had both laughed, utterly caught up in each other.

In return she told him about the famous crusader knights of the island. Once, hearing him mention how he loved apples, she managed to find two apples in the market and wrapped one in a twist of tissue paper and made the other into a toffee apple. That morning, hanging about the yard waiting for his knock, she had been as whirling and nervous as a swift, hoping he would like her tiny gift.

'For me?' he asked, when she offered her presents. In an instant, years had dropped away from his face so she could see the gleeful boy within the man.

'Toffee apples are a tradition in England,' Eve explained. 'I hope you like – *Julio!*' She was happily scandalized by his playful lunge for the apple and the big bite he took out of its shiny, caramelised surface.

'Mmm. Very tasty, thank you,' Julio remarked, winking at her. The grim policeman was utterly gone these days: he was as bright as the Rhodian sun.

But of course they could not always be playing. Increasingly, Eve found that she was forgetting to ask after the search for David. She longed to tell him about her brother, but dare not in case Julio turned against her, accused her of not trusting him. And how could she answer that?

Every day she spent with Julio, she was torn between her own happiness and the threat of David's discovery; between her own sense that Julio was a decent, honorable man and the dread that the dazzle of his charisma was blinding her to his real intent.

Andreas considered Julio a love-sick fool. 'We can use that,' he had told Eve, when she visited his shop, the dawn of the day after the big Greek met Julio in the street.

Eve had said nothing. She did not want to be duped herself, but neither did she want Julio used. More and more, her feelings for him had grown and the thought of him being hurt in any way made her feel sick.

She, David, their parents and Andreas and his fellow Greeks were still involved in a dangerous game. The 'package' David had mentioned, on the first night of his return, still needed to be recovered and passed on.

Eve bent over her rubbing board in the early morning heat in the courtyard, feeling increasingly beleaguered. Andreas had told her that her family must hang on to the package. His mother was sickening and looked likely to die, and he would be involved in the funeral arrangements, with no chance to move David's mysterious package into safer hands.

Also, as Andreas had pointed out, turning his bushy-eyebrowed face to Eve's, 'I'm a known trouble-maker to the fascists. So far, you and your family have not been under any great suspicion.'

'Grassi did call on us,' Eve pointed out.

'Once only – pouf – a nothing visit.' Andreas made light of the fascist official's interest in them. 'Has he called since? No! Only your puppy-dog admirer.'

'Julio is no dog,' Eve said quietly.

Something in her set expression and the steely glint in her usually peaceful gray eyes made the Greek butcher quickly change the subject.

'No matter! You are English and the Italians want to keep England on its side, so they will move carefully with you. For now, the thing is safest in your care.'

'What thing?' Eve had demanded. 'How long must we hold it? Where is it? David won't tell me.'

Andreas had grinned at her temper. 'Patience,' he'd advised. 'God will show us a way.' He winked a black eye. 'I have given you a nice rabbit today, good food for your ailing mother.' They both knew that the ailing mother was David.

Remembering their latest exchange, in the shadow of Andreas' shop awning before dawn that morning, Eve scrubbed harder at her father's shirt collar. Her parents were another worry. George Burnett had finally taken refuge in his studies and was no trouble but of little practical help, whilst Philippa had recently picked up a chill. Eve spent a good deal of time devising dainty dishes, tempting her mother's jaded appetite. So far at least, Philippa was still pottering about the house, often with one of her beloved books in her hands. Eve was glad to see this. She dreaded another bout of Philippa's arthritis.

Eve rinsed the shirt and wrung it out, adding it to the pile to be rinsed a second time. The next shirt she took was David's, and as she soaped and scrubbed she thought about her brother. She had found a note, written in Greek, in his shirt pocket.

On it was written the single word, 'Helios'.

'What is this?' she had asked him, dropping the note onto his bed.

'Part of a crossword,' David had replied, but she could tell it was a lie. 'Don't fuss, Evie.' He lay back in bed and closed his eyes to prevent her asking more questions.

Meanwhile, her brother had rapidly lost his limp and for the last few days his temperature had been almost normal. He seemed well on the road to recovery, including being irritable and bored. He had Eve running up and down the stairs with drinks and cards and books until she longed for her oasis of peace and gentle teasing with Julio. During coffee yesterday, they had told each other Christmas stories – presents, lights, Italian cribs, church services. Sometimes coffee with Julio was the single thing Eve looked forward to.

The shutters of David's room opened and closed, opened and closed: the signal that her brother needed something. Eve finished wringing out his shirt, then went inside and upstairs.

David was lying on top of his bed, curled over on his side. He lifted a wan face to her. 'My chest hurts,' he whispered.

Eve knelt by him. He looked feverish again, and he had a nasty dry cough that she didn't like at all. 'Where's this come from, eh?' she said gently. When she had popped her head round his door earlier he had been sleeping soundly.

'Sorry, Evie.'

The apology made Eve want to cradle her brother but he needed nursing, not sentiment. She dropped a blanket over him.

'After I dressed, I came over rather queer.' David coughed again, drawing his knees closer to his stomach. 'Maybe I've picked something else up.'

'Overdone it more like,' Eve said firmly. 'I thought you got out of bed far too soon last Friday, when you insisted on coming downstairs.'

'Had to.' David was breathless. He touched his breastbone. 'Hurts to breathe,' he muttered. 'I'm sorry.'

'That's two apologies in less than a minute. You need a doctor.' Dr Manoli would come and surely he would not give David away? Eve shook her head: David's new illness meant that she had no choice. Whatever the risk, Dr Manoli must see him.

Dr. Manoli expected to see Mrs. Burnett, but tended his new, unexpected patient without comment. Telling Eve he would see her downstairs, he closed the bedroom door on her, leaving Eve standing bereft on the landing. She paced up and down, her head feeling as if it might explode with anxiety and tension as she waited for his verdict.

The minutes seemed to crawl by before he reappeared and joined the family in the sitting room.

'How is he?' Philippa asked, her light brown eyes bright with alarm. Her plump, sagging figure was encased that day in a severe navy two-piece. It was as if her mother needed the support of that stiff cloth, Eve thought, wishing for a selfish moment that David had not come home until he was properly well.

The usually cheerful, wiry doctor shook his head and ran a hand through his pewter-colored hair. 'It is good that you called me,' he began. 'David has pleurisy. Steady, Mrs. Burnett,' Dr. Manoli went on as Philippa stifled a cry. 'He is young. He will recover. I will leave you a prescription and your daughter will be able to poultice his back, yes?'

Philippa and George Burnett looked at Eve, who nodded.

'A linseed oil poultice, every two hours, until further notice.' The doctor asked for his hat and waited for Eve to walk him to the courtyard door.

'Your mother is not strong,' he said. 'She must not be allowed to nurse her son.'

'I'll look after David,' Eve promised.

There was a familiar knocking on the courtyard door.

'I will leave you.' Dr. Manoli nodded to Julio in the street outside, and Eve was left alone with her Italian policeman.

She couldn't look at him. She was panicking about David, about making linseed poultices every two hours, about keeping her mother away from David and most of all about whether Julio had heard her mention her brother's name.

'Is it your mother, little one? Is she not well?'

Julio stepped through the doorway into the courtyard and Eve sagged against his broad chest in sheer relief. He had not heard!

'Eve?' His arms came round her, gathering her closer.

His embrace almost made her break down completely, but she couldn't afford that. Clenching her hands into fists, Eve heard herself say, 'I'm sorry, Julio. Mum isn't right. So – so I can't come for coffee with you today. Not today, or for a long time.'

Her chest hurt as she spoke and she wondered for a mad second if she had caught David's pleurisy but she knew it was disappointment. Disappointment and fear. Suppose Julio thought she was using her mother's illness as an excuse to be rid of him?

Why should that trouble you? He's a fascist, her conscience goaded, and all the time she remained in Julio's arms, her head in the crook of his shoulder. She wanted to stay there forever, safe in his arms, inhaling his scent of coffee and his own particular musky, masculine tang.

'Eve.'

She felt his hand on her head, tender and comforting. His fingers smoothed down her cheek to her chin and raised her face.

His green-flecked eyes were hard to read but his mouth smiled reassurance. 'I will come tomorrow,' he said. 'And the day after. And the day after that.' He gripped her chin lightly for a second. 'Be careful for yourself, little one. No going... Crazy? Is that the word?'

At her tense nod, he bent his head and kissed her lightly on both cheeks, then he stepped back into the street, leaving Eve staring after him. For a wild moment, even with David so desperately ill, she had wished that Julio had stayed longer, that he had brushed his lips against hers.

The next few days were hard for Eve. She grew sick of the smell of linseed, and guilty of refusing to allow her mother to set foot in David's bedroom. Some days she ran down to the long bazaar and back for basic shopping. Once, she had asked her father if he could go to the baker's.

'I couldn't possibly,' George Burnett said. 'The neighbors would make me a laughing stock if I strolled out of here with your shopping bag.'

Eve was too weary to argue. Instead, when

Julio appeared on his daily brief visit, she asked him if he would go.

'Of course,' Julio said at once.

He was quite dark with the sun by now and looked, if possible, even more handsome. Burnished, Eve thought, as she waved him off and then ran upstairs to warn David to make no sound.

'When Julio comes back, I'm going to ask him in to the courtyard for coffee,' she told her brother. 'You'll be all right, won't you?'

Propped up on pillows, in fresh pyjamas, David managed his first real smile in days. 'You don't want the odd theatrical cough?'

'Be serious.'

'You don't have to fuss, Evie. I'll be as silent as the grave.'

'Don't!' Eve shuddered at the analogy.

For Julio, coffee that morning in the courtyard with Eve was not a success. For some reason, her father had joined them and he then proceeded to dominate the conversation.

'Are your parents well-to-do?' George Burnett asked in careful Italian.

'My Dad was an engineer,' Julio answered in English. 'And my mother is a singer.' He smiled at Eve: this was old ground for them. 'She's American.'

'American. How interesting,' said George Burnett dryly, still in Italian. He removed his spectacles and gave them a brisk polish on the lapel of his jacket before saying to his daughter, in English, 'Will you put my sugar in my coffee?'

Julio saw the flush of temper on the back of her neck as she slowly obeyed her father. He would never have dared to speak to his sisters in that way, and now, in a silent gesture of support, he pressed his foot gently against hers.

Eve flashed him a quick smile, then, noticing her father watching, she hid her face behind her cup. Under cover of the table, with that streak of mischief he always enjoyed whenever she showed it, she teasingly tapped his knee.

'How is your mother?' he asked, trying to be serious whilst what he was really tempted to do was tickle her all over, really make her laugh.

'Getting better, thanks,' she replied, the glow fading rapidly from her face as she suddenly shook her head at her father.

Puzzled by her action, Julio was even more astonished when George Burnett pursed his narrow lips and burst out with, 'Don't you have things to do, Signor Falcone? Like finding my missing boy?'

'Of course.' Julio flung back his chair and rose to his feet, tempted to tip his half-finished coffee all over Burnett's neat black hair. He would have stayed for longer, just for the hell of it, but he didn't want to make things any harder for Eve than they plainly already were. 'Forgive me, I have to leave. I have another appointment.'

As he let himself out of the yard, Julio's anger gave way to renewed suspicion. He remembered Eve's warning head-shake to her father: what had that been about? But then he thought of her quick smile for himself, the way they had united against the crusty English scholar, her playful knee-pinch.

I know she likes me, he thought, striding away, making as ever for the police station to find out if there was news of David Burnett. *I know she likes me, so what is going on in this house?*

It had to be parental disapproval of their relationship, he told himself. *What else could it be?*

'He's probably gone to make a report to his boss,' David said later.

Eve stood up from her brother's bed.

'I'm sorry, Evie.' David caught her arm before she stalked from his room. 'I was wrong to say that.'

Once, Eve would have brushed the matter aside, but meeting Julio had given her confidence. She looked David square in the face. 'Yes, you were,' she said.

Amazingly, under his mop of fair curls,

David was blushing. Still sitting up in bed, he half-turned to the shuttered window. 'I've been wrong about you,' he mumbled. 'You're a good nurse. I think you're right to want a career in nursing.'

'Thank you.' Astonished at praise from her always superior older brother, Eve settled back on the bed. 'You are looking brighter again, but we've been here before.'

'I know.' David wet his lips with his tongue. 'Eve, I need to talk to you, and Mum and Dad. I don't know how long my wretched lungs are going to take to heal and there's something–'

He broke off, coughing, the longer than usual speech tiring him. He waved aside the glass of water Eve offered. 'I'm feeling relatively reasonable, so will you fetch our parents?' he asked. 'The longer this goes on, the more danger, and you all should know what it is we're hiding.'

He meant the package. Eve ran downstairs to ask Philippa and George Burnett to join David in his room.

Philippa insisted on sitting close to her son. 'He is much better, and so am I,' she declared, when Eve tentatively mentioned Dr. Manoli's warning. 'Don't fuss, Eve.'

Bringing a second chair for himself, George Burnett asked, 'Are you going to tell us everything now?'

'Yes.' David's bright blue eyes seemed almost steely in their determination.

Eve positioned herself against the longest wall, opposite to the window. Through the chink in the shutters she could see an alley cat lounging on top of their courtyard wall, a welcome piece of normality in these tense days.

Suppressing a yawn and stretching her aching back, she was aware that it was almost time for her to prepare another linseed poultice, but she didn't want to leave and miss anything. Besides, David had geared himself up; in his sturdy body, which even a bout of pleurisy had not diminished, she could sense the tension pouring out of him. His tanned face gleamed with scarcely-contained excitement.

'Eve,' he said, when their parents had sat down by his bed, 'would you go downstairs—'

'I won't leave, David,' she said firmly.

'—and look at the courtyard wall behind your pot of basil. Bring whatever you find there, please.'

That was why David had dragged himself downstairs last week, before he had even begun to recover from the flu! He'd been hiding something. Eve ran down to the courtyard, almost forgetting in her haste to make sure that none of their neighbors could see.

It was the work of seconds to move the basil and worm her fingers into the tiny cavity revealed behind the herb pot, to lift out a small, heavy package. Replacing the basil, Eve marveled at her brother's cunning and foresight. He must have found this hiding place before he set out on his supposed cycling holiday, an insurance in case he had to keep the package, instead of passing it to whoever should have met him in the south of the island. A wise and very necessary precaution, Eve thought, as she hurried upstairs.

She handed the object over to David. He laid it in his lap, touching the folds of brown paper carefully, as if the package were alive, and smiled up at them.

'I don't know what, if anything, Luigi Grassi knows about Andreas' resistance group,' he said, 'but Grassi and his cronies would go mad if they knew what we've taken, right from under their noses.'

'Could you not begin at the beginning, David?' George Burnett asked.

David coughed, rasped a few times and shook his head. 'I'm all right,' he told Eve and his mother. He looked down at the parcel. 'When is the beginning? That's the problem.'

George Burnett sighed, crossed his legs and folded his arms. 'Just do your best.'

Perhaps that was the prompt David needed, for he began to tear at the brown paper. Without raising his eyes from what he was doing, he said, 'I was with Andreas' cousin Demetrios when Demetrios found this. Andreas knew I could be trusted with it, because he knows me well, and you, Eve. We knew the fascists had their eyes on Andreas and his cousin, so I was the one chosen to go to Monolithos, to meet the Athenian contact who could take this back to Greece, where it belongs.'

The last of the wrapping paper fell away and David placed the mysterious object upright on the palm of his hand. 'Look,' he said.

Philippa and George Burnett were stunned, their faces completely still. After a moment, Philippa reached out a hand to touch – a single fingertip only, quickly withdrawn.

'Is that solid gold?' George Burnett whispered reverently.

'Solid gold,' said David. 'Do you recognize what it is?'

Too shocked to speak, Eve nodded. David, intent upon the gold resting on his palm, did not see the gesture and continued to explain.

'This is a piece of Greek art. It belongs to Greece. It's a sacred statuette, in solid gold, of the Greek sun god Helios, ancient patron of the island of Rhodes.'

'It's the spirit of the island,' said Eve,

81

speaking for the first time. Leaving her place by the wall, she crouched beside the tiny golden sun god and wondered at its excellence. 'This is what that note in your shirt pocket meant: Helios.'

Nine inches high, the figure was of a beautiful, nude young man wearing a head-dress which looked like a sun-burst, the sign of his god-head. The statuette appeared perfect, as perfect as when it had first been made.

'How old is it?' she asked.

'Fourth century BC, I believe,' said David. 'Around the time Alexander the Great was alive.'

'It's flawless.' Her breath misted the smooth planes of the statuette, and she felt as if she had committed an irreverent act.

'And it belongs to Greece,' David repeated.

'Of course it does.' Eve understood his insistence. The fascist officials of Mussolini had plundered archaeological sites from other Greek islands, claiming that they, as modern Romans, represented the true guardians of classical culture.

'Where did Demetrios find this?' she asked.

'I wonder if it's a copy of the original colossus of Rhodes,' remarked George Burnett. He removed his spectacles and polished them vigorously.

David took several breaths. He was tiring, but Eve knew she could not stop him yet. It would be unkind even to try.

'It was in the ruins of the palace of the Grand Masters of the Crusader Knights,' David said. 'Demetrios and I often go there to talk – if we're stopped by the fascists, we can always say we're searching for old cannon balls, or the foundations of the lost temple of the Sun God. Something even the fascists can't complain about.

'An erosion gully had opened up under a collapsed staircase,' David continued, 'and Demetrios suggested that we should shine a torch into the gap.'

'When was this, David?' Eve asked.

'About three weeks ago. Just after my pupils had broken up for their early summer holiday.'

'I see. Go on.' She dismissed as irrelevant her hot spurt of anger at David keeping this whole matter from her for so long. Anger and frustration were luxuries she could not afford now, with this golden treasure in the house.

'We shone our torch and straight away spotted something. So we marked it with a little pile of white stones and then came away before Luigi Grassi or any of his henchmen caught us poking around.' David smiled, then it turned into a frown. 'You know there's a rumor going round that the fascists are planning to renovate the palace of the Grand Masters? Knowing that, we didn't want to run into any officials.

'We went back late that night.' David was speaking quickly, his breath coming in staccato gasps. 'We found the gully and dug it with our bare hands. The earth was dry; it didn't take long. The statue was lying so close to the surface that another heavy rainfall might have washed it out altogether, for anyone to steal.'

'That's unfair, David,' said Eve.

David shook his head. 'This statue is unique. We couldn't afford it to be lost – or taken by someone like Luigi Grassi.'

Eve looked at the statuette again. A beam of light through the shutters caught its halo and the whole figure was bathed in a dazzling pool of fire. She felt its beauty, its rareness, and was afraid.

How long could such a treasure remain hidden? How long would her family, as keepers of this treasure, remain anonymous, and safe?

Chapter 6

The following afternoon, Dr Manoli called in and pronounced himself satisfied with his patients. Philippa was more lively, and David was considerably improved.

'No more poultices for you, Eve,' Dr Manoli said, fingering his sleek, graying moustache as she walked with him through the courtyard to the street door.

'Thank you!' Eve was grateful and relieved. She watched the doctor's spry, dapper figure disappear down the alleyway and for that moment forgot the danger her family was in. Happy to share the good news, she ran upstairs to her brother's room.

'It's official, you're cured,' she called out on the stairs.

'So it would seem.' David was up and dressed and walking about the house to build up his strength. Meeting her on the top step, he strolled downstairs with Eve. 'I'm glad to be out of that bed.'

'So am I!' Eve gave his arm an affectionate squeeze. 'Do you fancy anything special for supper?' she asked. 'Time for a celebration.'

David thought a moment, reflectively scratching his throat. 'Retsina. I haven't had a glass for ages,' he said at last. 'And some good Rhodian tucker. I'm tired of slops.'

Eve grinned at him, happy that he had recovered his banter. 'I'll see what I can do,' she promised, and then, unable to resist a tease, added, 'something nice and squishy. Octopus?' David hated octopus.

'You dare!'

David chased her into the sitting room, where he had to catch his breath on the sofa. Leaving him with their parents – who had missed their studies over the last few anxious days and were once more bent over their books – Eve slipped out into the city.

Rhodes Town was stirring after the siesta. Men played tavli in shady corners, women crocheted on doorsteps and shopkeepers were taking down grills to reopen their shops. Greeting neighbors, Eve went down to the market close to Hippocrates Square. She bought the retsina, some salad and a leg of goat. Roasted goat was David's favorite dish.

Relaxing a little for the first time in days, Eve did not hurry over her shopping. Taking time to enjoy the bustle and life of the city, she watched other women milling in the square, their shopping baskets laden with fruit or cheeses, whilst children played under the plane trees. She avoided looking at the caged birds, which she always felt sorry for, but smiled to see the city walls lit by the lowering sun, the ancient ramparts gleaming as if dusted in gold.

Gold reminded Eve again of the statuette in their care, the spirit of the island, and she shivered, the evening no longer so carefree.

'Good afternoon, miss,' called an Italian voice overhead.

Glancing along the length of the massive retaining city walls, Eve spotted Luigi Grassi and Julio, strolling along the walkway on the wall top.

They walked as if they owned the place, Eve thought angrily. She waved but did not answer.

'Come up, miss.' Luigi Grassi leered a welcome. 'Join us.'

Eve felt she had no choice but to obey: she did not want to arouse any more suspicion by refusing. As she found the nearest staircase to the city walls, she remembered Grassi's greed, and his staring at her mother's Venetian glass – and, more uncomfortably, Julio's supposed 'interest' in archaeology. He had talked to her as if each country should be left to deal with its own history, but did he truly believe this? Or was he, like Grassi, another cultural rapist?

The Rhodian statuette was now returned to its niche behind her pot of basil. *They'll not get the spirit of the island,* Eve thought, stepping out into the sun's glare on the wall top.

Luigi Grassi nudged his companion. 'Is this not a splendid sight?' He nodded at the approaching Eve. He added more, in an Italian dialect. Eve caught the word 'taming' and blushed with anger. Hating Grassi, disliking Julio being in his company, she planned to say her goodbyes at the earliest opportunity.

'How are you today?' Grassi tried to insinuate an arm around her waist but Eve deftly avoided him, glad that the city ramparts were five feet wide. Before Grassi could move again, Julio put himself between Eve and his boss.

'Falcone!' Grassi motioned Julio aside, but the bigger man did not stir. When it was obvious that Julio would not move, Grassi was forced to peer around him to direct his remarks to Eve.

'You are an inspiration to women, my dear. Such a charming, simple dress.'

'Thank you,' Eve said, wondering why Grassi was asking her no questions about her brother. She glanced at Julio. Standing beside her, shielding her from Grassi, Julio was unusually quiet. He seemed preoccupied with the view from the battlements, and he stared across the city to the ancient citadel of the knights and the ruined palace of the Grand Masters.

Why was Julio looking there? Eve gripped her shopping basket handle even tighter. She wanted to distract him, and she also wanted to call Grassi's bluff, ask him if he had heard anything about her missing brother.

She stepped out of Julio's protective shadow. 'Any news of David?'

Grassi waved a casual hand, dismissing her question, while Julio silently shook his head. Then Grassi cleared his throat.

'I would like you to attend my next party, Eve … I may call you Eve?' He leaned against one of the crenellations, his fleshy, full-lipped face glowing like a mask in the late afternoon light. Even his beautifully cut dark suit could not disguise his thick-set limbs.

Eve was glad he had made no attempt to take her hand. She glanced again at Julio, sensing his unspoken protection and concern, then wondering for a horrible moment if she was wrong about him.

'Eve? My next party?' Grassi had asked a question and the fascist official was not used to being kept waiting.

Julio cleared his throat before Eve had chance to speak. 'Would your fiancée, Donna Maria Scartoni, welcome her?' he asked mildly.

Not caring where it fell, Grassi kicked a loose pebble off the battlements. 'Maria understands my mission,' he said stiffly. 'We must show the benefits of greater civilization to others, Falcone. How else is modern Rome increased?'

If Grassi was 'civilized', Eve thought, she

wanted no part of it.

Julio did not enter that argument, he merely said, 'Believe me, Maria Scartoni would not understand.'

Grassi's ponderous jaw set. 'Who are you to tell me– ' He broke off with an effort, perhaps sensing Eve's wide eyes, and possibly aware that he was making a spectacle of himself.

To their left, along the battlement, came the sound of pounding feet. An Italian soldier, hot and out of breath, stopped in front of them, saluted and handed Grassi a note.

Eve's breath stopped. Was the note to do with David? Had he been discovered? Had the statuette been found?

'*Bene.*' Grassi crumpled the note and waved the soldier away. 'It seems I must leave you, my lovely English girl,' he said. He tried to smile but was clearly too angry to do so. 'We shall resume this discussion another time. Falcone?'

'I am going the other way,' Julio said imperturbably, giving no more reasons and – despite Grassi's glare – no apology.

'Farewell.' Grassi gave the fascist salute, clearly expecting one in return. Julio responded with no more than a curt nod and the shorter, fatter man stumped off, the sun lighting up his bald crown and sweating neck.

'An urgent appointment,' Julio remarked,

when Grassi had gone. 'The note said that his Turkish bath and massage were now ready.'

Without looking at each other, he and Eve started to laugh, causing several roosting pigeons to flutter off the battlements in alarm.

'Forgive me.' Julio wiped his eyes, the brief moment of levity passed. 'But I would not have you attend Grassi's parties. They are altogether *too* Roman.'

Piqued by his possessiveness, Eve said, 'That would be my choice.'

Julio rested his forearms on top of one of the crenellations. 'Grassi likes to hold his soirees, as he calls them, in the mineral hot springs at Thermai Kallithea.' He looked down at her. 'The men wear togas, the women rather less.'

'Oh.' Eve bit her lip, not wanting to ask what she thought.

'No, I have never been to one of his parties, but I have heard a great deal about them.' Julio smiled at her now, his eyes beguilingly tender. 'May I escort you home?'

They stayed on the battlements for part of the return trip, Julio again carrying her shopping. Without Grassi, Julio seemed as charming as ever and Eve almost felt herself tempted to tell him about the gold statuette. After all, how would she feel if the positions were reversed and he did not mention it to her? She would think that he did not trust her.

Of course, she did not speak. Even for Julio, she could not risk the safety of her brother and family. She had to be sure that her Italian policeman would still support her and her family and she was not sure yet. He had not declared any part of his feelings to her.

'That's a long face,' Julio teased. Then, growing serious, he said, 'Or are you thinking of your brother? I am sure he is safe. We have heard nothing to the contrary.'

'No,' said Eve, tempted now to confess about David.

'And you mustn't allow Grassi to upset you. He's a village bully really, nothing more. If you stand up to him, he collapses.'

'Easy for you to say. You're one–' Eve broke off.

'One of them, you were going to say?' Julio asked, with raised black eyebrows. 'One of the dreadful Italians who have built roads here and helped to improve the island's agriculture? We are not all like Grassi.'

Eve looked over the battlements at one of the city mosques, restored by the Italians. 'I'm sorry,' she whispered.

Julio took her hand and clasped it. 'I have a favor to ask,' he said. 'I have already asked your mother.' A quirk of humor tugged at his mouth. 'I telephoned from my hotel. She agreed with me that since she is now improving, a trip for you into the countryside would not be impossible, and would do you good.'

Her mother was no doubt eager to have David to herself for a while, Eve thought, relieved that Julio had telephoned rather than calling in unexpectedly at her home. 'Thank you,' she said, a little awkwardly, wishing even as she spoke that Julio had asked her first. 'That was very considerate.'

'But?' Julio asked.

'My mother is not strong,' Eve began, thinking of David. Surely she needed to stay and make sure her brother was not caught?

'She told me she was as fit as a flea.' His hazel eyes brightened with humor. 'A most curious English phrase. Or is it that you do not want to spend so much time with me?'

'No!' Eve burst out and, catching his smug expression, she clenched her free hand into a fist and snapped, 'But you should have asked me first! I don't like your going behind my back. It's dishonest.'

If Julio was startled at her sudden resentment, he did not show it. Still holding her hand, he stopped and faced her. He rubbed his forehead before speaking, an unusual action for him and one Eve guessed was down to nerves.

'Please, would you come with me to

ancient Kamiros? I have the loan of a motorbike, and we can picnic in the ruins by the sea. Have you ever been there?'

Eve shook her head. 'Are you sure?' she asked, already mollified by Julio's 'please' and beginning to feel intrigued. 'It's a long way, over twenty miles.'

'Which is why I have borrowed the motorbike. What do you say, Eve? An excursion from the city tomorrow, beginning at dawn?'

'Maybe,' she said, determined not to reveal her feelings again so quickly.

'It would only be a day. A single day.' He smiled and swung her hand in his, letting her feel his easy strength. 'A sweet truancy.'

His enthusiasm was catching. As she imagined riding pillion with Julio, visiting the famous classical Greek city of Kamiros, Eve knew that her mother, and especially her father, would have given only grudging permission – to avoid suspicion they would feel they had no choice but to agree – but for her it was different.

She suddenly found that she wanted this day with Julio, wanted to escape from Rhodes City and the worries over David, her mother and the gold statuette. Why not? It was just a day.

'Yes, please,' she blurted out, laughing as he gently squeezed her fingers.

He came for her in the pre-dawn twilight.

Her father saw them off, and Eve, still tying her headsquare, sat cautiously on the motorbike behind Julio. With her face pressed against his shoulder and her body close to his back, she felt the heat from his body and the closeness of her hips to his. Locked into this embrace, she tingled with new sensation; a strange fluttering in her stomach and lower, in her loins. Wondering if Julio was experiencing the same things as she was, she tensed, feeling shy as they rolled down Homer Street, coasting to save petrol and let the neighbors sleep.

Rhodes Town was eerily quiet, full of prowling cats and shadows, with the sound of a cock crowing in the darkness. Eve could hear the hum of the electric lighting and, below that, the sound of the sea. The crown daisies were closed up like tiny umbrellas, but there was a jasmine-like scent wafting through the deserted alleyways.

'The houses look like Minoan houses,' Julio called over his shoulder. 'From ancient Crete.'

'Yes, they do,' Eve agreed. The two-story houses in the old city, all unpainted stone and brown doorways, looked older than classical ruins. She watched people begin to meander slowly from these houses, quietly, with no greetings or eye contact. She felt very high, riding pillion on the great bike, and very proud. She and Julio, knights together, sweeping out into the country. She shouted to him.

'This is how the Templar knights would ride, two together on one horse!'

'Have you your sword?' he called back. 'Should I be quaking in my shoes?'

'Hardly!' She hugged him tight, happy to seize the legitimate chance to do so. He was so powerful and muscled: his stomach was as hard as a stone. Stripped, he would look like the gold statuette, she thought, and blushed at her own imagination.

'I think you're prettier than any knight,' Julio hollered. 'Hang on!'

He swept them low round a corner, the track skimming beneath them in small gray clouds of dust.

'Are you warm enough?' Julio called out again. 'You are welcome to wear my jacket.'

'I'm fine.' It was cool, but colors and shapes were flooding back with the rising sun and, as she and Julio passed the checkpoint at the southern city gate and took the road south, the crown daisies were beginning to open.

They made good time along the coast road, passing red hibiscus hedges, rocky scrub, tiny churches and roadside shrines. Hay was being turned in some of the fields, and Eve waved to the black-garbed women, feeling a little guilty that she was enjoying herself while native Rhodians were working.

'Hey, no glum face,' Julio said, twisting round at that moment and seeing her small frown. 'Today is your holiday.'

'Our holiday,' Eve corrected him, laughing.

'Look.' Julio pointed out a windmill close to a small-holding. 'I'd like to make a carving of that.'

'You sculpt?' Eve was astonished.

'Only wood-carving. It started when I made a Christmas crib for my sisters, the year our father died.'

Knowing already that Julio's mother was a widow, Eve felt sorry again, especially for Julio and his sisters, Teresa and Bianca. Then the pleasure of the moment raced in her afresh as, giddy with happiness, she bowled along with Julio, her man, who thought she was pretty.

A few more miles passed, with the wooded mountains swinging away into the distance as the bike droned across a large plain. Then, suddenly, they saw the sea again, and Eve gasped.

'What is it?' Julio called.

'The sea. It's so blue, Sometimes I forget how blue.'

Julio looked round and grinned, his teeth dazzling in his tanned face and in the shimmer of daylight. It was so warm now that they had stopped a moment for Julio to remove his jacket and Eve her cardigan, although she had kept her headsquare on so that her whipping blonde hair would not blind her or her companion. When they sat together she felt even closer to him, almost skin against skin. She traced the contours of his flesh through his cotton shirt with her fingers, pretending to brush away dust from his tensed shoulders.

'Tease,' he grunted, accelerating so she clung to him tighter still, inhaling his warm salty-sweet scent, the whiff of fresh cotton and tang of engine oil: a powerfully masculine combination. Her heart pounding, Eve laughed in return, reveling in being a tease.

The sun was high and the cicadas shrilling loudly when Julio drove the motorbike into an olive grove on the slope leading to ancient Kamiros. He offered Eve a hand to help her from the bike.

'Thank you.' Glad to accept his assistance, Eve scrambled off the bike. His long, strong fingers felt cool against her skin and his hand lingered perhaps a little too long but she no longer cared.

Straightening and smoothing down her full-bottomed dress, she almost buckled. Her legs had become stiff on the drive down the island.

'Careful!' Julio caught her in his arms before she tumbled onto the track. He waited a moment, both of them laughing and breathless, until she had regained her footing, then he released her, giving her elbows a final squeeze. 'Shall we go?'

He held out his hand again, for her to take.

'Yes.' Clasping his lovely strong fingers, Eve allowed Julio to draw her after him. They walked along a track edged with mallow and wild oats, with mountains on three sides, and a view of the sea beneath.

Ancient Kamiros, a ruined Greek city abandoned long before the crusader knights had built their walls and citadel in Rhodes Town, had been described by Eve's father as, 'The Pompeii of Greece.' Walking through its recently-excavated streets, Eve understood why.

'You can almost imagine a Greek shopkeeper watching from one of these doorways,' she told Julio. 'Isn't it marvelous, walking where the people who lived here must have walked, hundreds of years ago?'

Julio nodded, pointing out a fig tree growing in the ruins. Then he said, 'I wonder if there are guards here, usually.'

Eve felt as if he had just thrown a dash of cold water into her face. 'I presume you mean Italian guards?'

Part of her was instantly appalled at what she had just said, aware that she might insult or hurt him, aware too that she was here alone with him, miles from anywhere. But suddenly she wanted the truth, once and for all. Was Julio another Grassi, or not?

'Do you mean Italian guards?' she persisted. 'Since the primitive Greeks would not be capable of taking care of such classical remains?'

Julio stopped in the middle of Kamiros' ancient main street. 'What?'

'Nothing!' Eve turned her back on him and stalked a few steps. Breathing fast, she stopped, glaring at a sheared-off column of a Doric temple without really seeing it.

For an instant, there was no sound but the wind, as it blew across Eve's fringe and rocked the branches of a nearby pine wood.

'Do you really think I believe that?' Julio sounded cold, remote. He seemed to have moved further away from her.

Eve shrugged. 'How am I to know what you believe?' Her doubt was tearing her in two. She longed to think that she could trust him with her knowledge of the golden statuette, and it frustrated and hurt her to have to keep silent.

'Eve!'

She sighed at the indignant cry. 'How do I know?' she repeated, without turning. 'You seem to be Luigi Grassi's friend.'

'Friend!' Julio gave a bark of laughter. 'Are you crazy? I loathe the man. I'm only here because he knows I'm a good policeman, and honest. Most of his cronies take bribes.'

'But you're too dedicated, or too proud to do so?' Eve dug her fingernails into her hands as she waited for the answer.

'Are you saying I should be corrupt?'

'Of course not.' Eve whirled about, startled to find that Julio had come closer – close enough to shoot out his arms and encase her in an iron grip.

'Now,' he said, bending his head to her. 'Let's talk about what you really mean, shall we? You're worried I'm a friend of Grassi's, that I came to Rhodes as a favor to him. Not true! His forces are bungling and corrupt and so he sent for me–' Julio stabbed his breastbone with stiff fingers – 'to bring some order and some fresh ideas. Because he's a party man, I was commanded by the fascist authorities back in Italy to holiday here and then stay on. As a fascist favor to Grassi. It was an order I couldn't refuse. Once this week is finished, I shall be at work here.' His head came lower. 'I was sorry to leave my mother and sisters,' he said softly, 'but not sorry to meet you, Eve.'

His breath was close enough to stir her fringe. 'I would love to find your brother for you, little one,' he murmured. 'Once Grassi gives me access to the files and I have men to command, I will scour this island.'

'Don't,' Eve pleaded. Julio's long, passion-

101

ate speech made her feel guilty and alarmed at the same time, and his vow to find David made her ashamed of her continuing deception. She flinched as he drew the head-square down off her hair.

'Look at me,' Julio commanded gently.

Ashamed of her own fear, Eve raised her face.

'Luigi Grassi is a party man, *but I am not.*'

His unflinching stare and solemn, ardent expression convinced her, even before he added, sheepishly, 'I did once pay a bribe. Back in Parma. It was to one of my superiors in the *carabinieri*. He fixed it so that I looked to be in the fascist party, but I've never had to go to any of their meetings.'

'You're not a fascist?' Eve was trembling: with relief and with the strength of her own feelings.

'No,' Julio said. He touched her lips with his hand. 'Friends?' he asked.

Eve nodded, although for some strange reason she still felt disappointed, almost tearful. 'Friends' didn't seem quite enough. She didn't want Julio treating her like a younger sister.

'Good,' he said.

He smiled, gathering her tightly to him, and kissed her.

Chapter 7

A week later Julio returned to work as a uniformed officer of the *carabinieri*, this time posted in Rhodes Town. Another two weeks passed, with Julio and Eve spending part of each day together. They visited mosques and churches, and walked the city walls and the Street of the Knights. She helped him select presents for his mother and sisters in the long bazaar.

It was a time of delight for Eve – she had never been so happy – but also a time of anguish. Despite her growing closeness to Julio, she could not tell him about David or the statuette. Sometimes, when Julio met her during his office siesta, downcast again because there was still no word at headquarters of the Englishman, David Burnett, Eve could hardly bear to look at him.

Ashamed and guilty, she would play her part, pretending anxiety for her 'missing' brother, hating herself, until at last Julio's smile returned.

She told him nothing. She was afraid to. Every day that passed made confession harder. It would seem to Julio that she did not trust him. And perhaps she didn't – not completely, anyway. It was a betrayal of him.

The matter was complicated, yet simple. She loved her family and she cared for Julio. She loved their times together. She didn't want to pierce that feeling of lightness and fizz of anticipation which came over her whenever she saw him. With Julio she was happy, in their own private world.

'I'll tell him everything, when he says he loves me,' she found herself confiding to her pot of basil as she watered the peppery-scented herb each evening.

The statue hidden in the niche behind the pot of basil was still in its brown paper packaging. David was still hidden at home. Eve carried messages from David to the butcher, Andreas. That David was now recovered. That the package was secure. That David had heard nothing from any other members of the Greek resistance.

Andreas listened and said little. As he had predicted to Eve, his own mother was very ill. Over the same three weeks, whilst Eve was so guiltily happy, Andreas lost weight. New wisps of gray appeared in his red hair and beard. Finally, when Eve sped to his shop in the Jewish Quarter one early morning to relay a stark question from her brother– 'How long before the package is removed to safety?' – she found the butcher's closed and shuttered.

'Andreas left last night, for Monolithos,'

Andreas' neighbor called down from her balcony. 'His mother died yesterday evening, and he has many relations in Monolithos, many arrangements to make. His wife is in, if you would like to see her.'

'Thank you. I will,' Eve called up from the street. She was very sorry for Andreas' loss, but also aware that Monolithos was the place where David should have met his Athenian contact, the one who never appeared.

Perhaps as well as informing his family in Monolithos, Andreas would take the opportunity to arrange the safe passage of the statuette.

'Please let him do so,' Eve prayed. She was horribly uneasy with the gold treasure hidden in their courtyard. Once it was where it should be, with the Rhodians, surely that would clear the way for her with Julio?

Eve put that thought aside as she visited Andreas' wife to give her condolences. She stayed longer than she had planned, and as she hurried from the Jewish Quarter she was breathing hard. She could hear the noonday bell ringing out over the city and moaned aloud.

'Oh, no.' She had walked down to the butcher's shop at seven that morning. Now it was twelve and she had no shopping yet for lunch. Briefly, she considered telephoning her parents, to explain that she been delayed, but where in the city was there a public phone? It would mean going out of her way to find one. Better to go straight home.

In the nearest available shop she bought oranges and cheese, and hurried on. As she crossed the busy road junction beside the Mosque of Suleiman, she heard a car horn. Startled by the unusual sound, she stopped outside the mosque and looked around. Within or outside the city, cars were rare.

'Miss Eve!' Grassi thrust his bullet head through the open rear window of a black Fiat Balilla sedan.

In a squeal of brakes the car pulled up, its long, gleaming bonnet parked diagonally in front of Eve, cutting off one avenue of escape. She turned, but Grassi had already lurched out of the back passenger door. His bulk prevented Eve from leaving in that direction. Fighting down panic, she backed against the warm stones of the mosque's high surrounding walls.

'Move those people on,' Grassi snapped at his driver. It was his own car blocking two street entrances at the top of the long bazaar, Rhodes Town's busiest street, but Grassi's driver leapt from behind the wheel to harangue the waiting carters and mule drivers.

Ignoring the buzz of angry voices, Grassi held out a hand to Eve. 'Miss Eve, charming as ever,' he said. 'You will come with me, please.'

'I'm sorry, I can't,' Eve said quickly. 'My parents are expecting me, and I have my duties–'

'Oh, but my dear, I insist!' Grassi reached her in three strides and grabbed her arm. He bundled her round the open back passenger door and into the car.

Pushed onto the back seat, Eve almost lost her footing, but she managed to scramble to the other side of the Balilla to snatch at the door handle. Grassi seized her wrist.

'Mr. Grassi!' She twisted round to glare at her oppressor, attempting to sound like her mother at her most dignified. 'What is going on?'

He grinned, making her wait before he answered. Trapped and tense, perilously close to tears, it was hard for Eve to remain still on the slick leather seat as the fascist official released her wrist.

He lounged on the seat beside hers, his knee insolently pressed against her calf, almost daring her to make another attempt to escape. Had Grassi heard something? Did he know about David, or the statuette?

Luigi Grassi made himself completely comfortable in the back of his official car, then patted her knee. 'I am merely concerned about you and your little family, my dear,' he remarked. 'As a lone foreigner in this place, you are naturally vulnerable.'

'Why naturally?' Eve demanded.

Without asking her permission, Grassi lit a fat cigar, nonchalantly puffing smoke into the car to escape where it could through his and the driver's open windows.

'You ask me that, when my associate Falcone is plainly ensnared by you?' He looked her slowly up and down. 'I must admit, that until he began his hunt, I was not so intrigued – no more than when considering any other pretty girl – but lately I have realized that you have hidden depths for one so young.'

Eve wafted cigar smoke away from her face. Mention of Julio made her more afraid, reminding her that this time, unlike her previous encounter with Grassi on the city walls, Julio was not here. She and Julio looked out for each other, she realized in that instant. He had protected her on the city walls just as she had saved him from the falling scaffolding, but right now, trapped in this car with Grassi, she was on her own.

'Please state your business, Mr. Grassi,' she said coldly. 'I have errands to run.'

'For Andreas, the trouble-maker, perhaps?' Grassi scratched at his black stubble and drew hard on his cigar. 'Would you care to explain your business with him?'

'I buy meat from him,' Eve said.

'Every day? You have been seen in the Jews' quarter every day.'

Eve stopped herself from asking if buying

108

daily meat was a crime. 'Yes,' she said, facing Grassi but really staring at a point somewhere beyond his right ear.

Grassi gave a grunt of amusement and barked to his driver, 'Move, man! I am sick of being gawped at by these peasants.'

The driver started the big car and it rolled down the sloping street of the long bazaar, going further away from Eve's home. Sitting with her shopping perched protectively on her lap, Eve felt relieved that Grassi had not offered to take her home. What if he decided to barge in there, frightening her mother, maybe even catching David?

Alarmed at the prospect, it was several moments before Eve began to feel uneasy for herself. With the driver using the horn and ruthlessly nosing the heavy car through the throng, they had almost reached the end of Socrates Street. 'Should you not be letting me out, or taking me back?' she demanded. 'Where are you taking me?'

'To an office in Mandraki harbor,' Grassi told her pleasantly. 'Somewhere informal, where we can be private.'

'Why?' Eve's heart was racing as she fought to keep her composure. 'Somewhere informal' meant that Grassi was taking her to a place where there would be no other officials. If she once set foot in the building, she would be lost to the outside world – no one, not her family, not even Julio, would know where she was.

Squashed into a small, tight huddle in the back of the Balilla as it sleeked its way through the city walls and turned towards the harbor along the road that ran by the sea, Eve admitted that she had under-estimated Grassi. She had considered him a greedy fool; a man to be avoided. Trapped in his car, he was a much bigger threat to her. He was dangerous.

She clasped her hands tightly together in her lap, to avoid him seeing them shake.

Grassi leaned towards her, smiling as Eve instinctively shrank away. 'So vulnerable, you English, caught up in your ridiculous sense of fair play. Fair play!' Grassi snorted. 'What rubbish! The strong survive and rule. We modern Romans are born to rule. We understand it.'

'I see,' Eve whispered. At this point, even a fascist political speech would be welcome, she thought grimly. Anything to keep Grassi busy. She dreaded him touching her again, afraid that she would scream.

Grassi threw the stub of his cigar out of his open window. 'Look at your family,' he scoffed. 'A brother who has no doubt fled to safer, softer climes. A mother who is always sick. A father who looks like a twig.'

'Leave my family alone!' Eve flared, unable to keep silent under these insults.

'Or what, Miss Eve? Will you kick me with

your sandaled feet? Throw oranges at me, perhaps?'

Don't tempt me, Eve thought, staring down at the oranges in her basket, wondering if she could use them, or the basket, as weapons. She had to get out of this car. Could she haul the door open? No, Grassi would be on her in an instant. She heard him chuckle and clamped her arms by her sides. She was beginning to feel sick with anxiety. A glance towards the sea showed her the windmills of Mandraki. Wherever it was, they were closing on Grassi's lair.

'Here we are,' Grassi remarked, savoring the moment.

His driver brought the car to a stop outside the monumental Post Office – built by the Italians. Looking towards the end of the harbor, Eve scowled at the statue of the she-wolf, balanced, by the Italians, on top of the more seaward of the two tall columns guarding the harbor entrance.

She wondered if she could possibly dash into the Post Office. Surely even Grassi would be stopped if there were witnesses?

'Come along, Miss Eve,' Grassi drawled.

His driver had stepped from the Balilla and was blocking her door with his long, scraggy body.

Eve hung back. 'I'll report you to your superiors,' she threatened. She pointed to the Venetian-style Palace of the Italian

111

Governor, set just across the street, next to the red-tile roofed cathedral. 'I don't have far to go.'

'Report me for what?' Grassi was openly derisive.

'You've kidnapped me, threatened me, insulted my family–'

'Me?' Grassi widened his eyes and spread his hands in a gesture of mock-innocence. 'I have been a model of restraint, as my driver will testify.' The gaunt driver nodded, his hard face never losing its sour expression, and Eve knew it would be their word against hers.

Grassi insolently clicked his fingers, and Eve had no choice but to shuffle along the back seat towards him. She ducked out of the car, squinting in the bright sunlight, looking about for some means of escape. Clutching her shopping basket, she saw herself running out of options.

Except for one idea, ironically supplied by Grassi himself...

Grassi took her arm, and Eve allowed herself to be steered across the street towards the new cathedral. Every step brought her closer to that sanctuary and lulled Grassi into believing her cowed.

A group of male office workers, striding smartly towards them, gave Eve her chance.

'My bag!' she cried, dropping her basket of shopping.

Oranges spilled everywhere. In seconds, the Greek office workers were scrambling to retrieve them for her. Grassi let go of her elbow to motion to the office workers to stay back, and Eve stepped out of his reach.

'Here, miss. Here is your bag.'

'Here, miss—'

The office workers crowded round her, coming between her and Grassi and ignoring the puce-faced official as they offered the oranges and her basket. Eve took the basket and oranges, thanked them all and walked smartly into the cathedral. Behind her, hemmed in by the helpful and now talkative Rhodians, Grassi could not follow for several vital seconds.

Fleeing along the long nave, aware of Grassi now hurrying after her, Eve looked about wildly for a priest, but found herself staring at Julio.

Chapter 8

Julio had slipped into the cathedral to think and to pray. Walking slowly up and down the nave, half-hoping, half-dreading that a priest would approach him and ask what was wrong, he had been considering his life

Even before he met Eve, he had been uncomfortable with the fascist regime in his country. Now, several weeks into his posting on Rhodes, witnessing how certain officials bullied the native Greek population, he had decided he could no longer go on pretending.

He was a proud to be a policeman, but not under Mussolini, not as one of the authorities who, far from protecting their people, seemed intent on oppression. Creatures like Grassi relied on informers. Julio had quickly realized that his presence in Rhodes was only for show. Grassi wasn't interested in looking for Eve's missing brother, for instance, or in the opinions of an honest detective. Julio had been brought in simply to make Grassi look good – a man with contacts.

Rapidly disillusioned, Julio had already written to his mother in Parma, and sent money, with the suggestion that she and his sisters go on 'holiday' to America, to visit their relatives. Julio hoped that his mother had read between the lines of his letter and understood his real aim – that she and his sisters remove themselves from Italy before the situation became worse. Signs of a coming war in Europe were increasing daily.

Then there was Eve. Julio sensed that she was in some kind of dilemma and he longed to help her. Eve had been preying on his mind. However uncertain the future, he wanted to be part of hers. He wanted to restore her brother to her, make her smile, make her laugh even more.

Make her his.

Ashamed of having such possessive, earthy thoughts in church, Julio turned for a final time in the long, candle-lit nave, striding for the exit.

He had been thinking of Eve and now, amazingly, she was here, rushing up to him, pale and breathless, plainly distressed. *'Cara,* what is it?'

The endearment was almost wrung from him. He had never seen her look so frightened. She was whiter than paper, her pretty floral dress was creased and fluffy tendrils of hair spilled from her usually immaculate pleat.

'Nowhere else. Seemed the best place,' Eve panted, looking round over her shoulder.

Julio had already seen the rotund figure in

pursuit. The thought of bloated, corrupt Grassi pursuing Eve, terrorizing her, made him furious. Had they not been in church, he would have struck the man. He wanted to flatten Grassi, lay him out on the ground.

Julio stepped in front of Eve, his feelings wrung again as he saw her trembling and sway slightly. Without thinking about it, he drew her to him for an instant, then put her gently behind him, to deal with Grassi.

'Falcone!' Out of breath, Grassi marched up to the uniformed *carabiniero* and tried to face him down. 'Why are you here?'

'To meet Eve,' Julio lied, too angry to say more.

'That's right,' Eve said quietly behind him.

Grassi's eyes were furious little slits. 'You said nothing about this!' He jabbed a finger at Eve.

'You didn't ask.' Walking silently on the rich flooring, she came to stand beside Julio, offering her support rather than leaving him to tackle Grassi alone.

Did she really think he couldn't cope? Julio was torn between pride and exasperation. Glancing down at Eve's tiny, slender figure, pride won: he marveled at her resilience and courage.

He was about to ask her permission to escort her home, but she anticipated his request.

'Will you take me home, as arranged?' she

asked. Looking up at him, her face appeared serene but her gray eyes remained bleak with fear.

What had Grassi been doing to her? Julio glared at the dark-suited fascist, who was staring at Eve.

'I will come, too,' Grassi announced. 'The driver can remain here in Mandraki. The Balilla will not pass through your shabby little back streets.'

Julio longed to wipe Grassi's evil grin off his smug face, but he knew he wouldn't be the one who suffered retaliation. 'Very well,' he said, with a calmness he did not feel. He and Eve would have to put up with Grassi, but he would see Eve home, safe and unmolested.

'Here we are.' Julio thumped on the courtyard door. His mother would have taken the heavy knock as a warning, but would Eve's?

'You surprise me, Falcone,' Grassi remarked with malice. 'I would have thought you strolled straight in here.'

To reinforce his point, Grassi twisted the door handle and barged into the courtyard. 'My, my,' he said, his voice oozing satisfaction, 'we seem to have caused a stir.'

Stepping onto the hot cobblestones after Eve, Julio took in the scene. There was an overturned deck chair in the middle of the sunny yard, with a glass of half-finished retsina stranded beside it. The main door beneath the stone arch was ajar, and Julio's sharp ears heard a rapidly closing door somewhere inside the house. Conscious of Eve's shocked, sickened look and Grassi's gloating delight, he schooled his expression into a careful blankness.

'That the people living on this island are uneasy with us should hardly be a surprise,' he remarked. 'We have not made ourselves popular.'

Grassi stuck out his double chin and pot belly, which his skillfully cut suit could not quite disguise. 'Strong leadership is not about popularity,' he snarled. 'These Greeks need civilizing.'

Julio clung onto his rising temper. 'This is an English family,' he pointed out. 'Do you not recall how you asked me to come with you to this house, because of my good English? That was one of the supposed reasons why I was posted here from Parma.'

'Thank you for reminding me of that, Falcone!' Grassi thrust his legs wide apart, mimicking Mussolini's favorite pose as George Burnett appeared in the doorway. 'You can tell this English lord we are going to search his house for contraband and evidence of anti-fascist activities.'

Grassi's soft shoulders began to shake. 'You see, Miss Eve,' he roared between gusts of laughter, 'It isn't wise to cross me!'

Chapter 9

Eve felt as if her stomach had dropped to her feet. She knew Julio would have no choice but to take part in the search.

This is my fault. If I hadn't thwarted Grassi, if he hadn't seen Julio with me and realized that we care for each other, then none of this would be happening.

Grassi is jealous!

Where was David? Where could he hide? What if Grassi found the statue? Not daring to consider what would happen if the official found him, or the spirit of the island, Eve joined her father in the foyer.

Grassi strutted indoors, shouting, 'Stay where you are! Anyone who tries to escape will be shot!'

Striding alongside Grassi, Julio looked grimmer and fiercer than the fascist official, if that was possible. Hurrying after Julio, horribly aware of his pistol and gun belt – something she had always disliked – Eve automatically cried, 'No!' as Grassi kicked open the door to the sitting room.

Sitting at the table, with books piled high around her armchair, Philippa Burnett dropped her pen. 'George? What is going

119

on?' She tried to stand to face the intruders, using the table as a brace. She rose a little and then sank deeper into her seat, the effort plainly too much.

'George,' she murmured, one hand plucking anxiously at the long paisley shawl still draped over her legs.

'Mum!' Eve started towards Philippa but Grassi stopped her.

'You,' he said, pointing at George Burnett. 'You stay here with your wife.' He dragged painfully at Eve's arm. 'You – upstairs. You can show me the bedrooms. Falcone, you search downstairs!'

With Grassi hard on her heels she stumbled upstairs, taking each step as slowly as she dared.

'Hurry up!' Grassi pushed her sharply in the small of her back with the flat of his hand. He smirked at her shocked expression. 'That's only the beginning.'

Beginning of what? Eve escorted Grassi about the upper floor, opening doors and cupboards in response to his barked orders. Downstairs, she could hear no voices, no protests, only the terrible, heavy tread of a man systematically combing through the kitchen and sitting room.

How could Julio do this to them? How could he be part of this? If he found David, would he betray him to Grassi? Eve became hot, then cold, at the idea.

'This room.' Grassi pointed to David's bedroom. He had scarcely glanced around her room, contenting himself with pointing at the bed. 'Lift the coverlet,' he'd said. He had done the same in her parents' room. Eve had the feeling that he enjoyed ordering her about.

Grassi didn't really believe that David was here, which was just as well. But where was her brother? Walking into his room, Eve discovered that her hands were visibly shaking.

Entering after her, Grassi sat on the bed and leaned against the headboard, folding his arms above his head. 'Open the wardrobe door.' From the kitchen immediately below David's room Eve heard the scrape of a chair leg. She was glad it wasn't Grassi down there, pawing through her pots and pans, but the thought of Julio searching made her squirm. In that instant, she felt ashamed of him. She opened the wardrobe door with an angry jerk, turning on the bare floorboards to face her tormentor.

'You see? There is nothing here.'

'So it would seem.' Grassi clicked his tongue. 'What a shabby suit,' he said, glancing at the meager contents of David's wardrobe and then at his own expensive dark clothing. 'Is there anything missing? Put your hands in there, girl. Stir around and see.'

Smarting at the 'girl', Eve did as she was told.

'Enough!' came a self-satisfied voice.

What next? Eve thought.

Grassi turned his head a fraction, his heavy jaw opening slightly, possibly in surprise. 'Why are there fresh flowers on that clothes chest?'

Eve walked to the simple vase of camomile, brushing a finger across one of the small daisy-like flowers. 'As I'm sure you've noticed, I put flowers in every room,' she said.

'Oh yes, the good housekeeper,' Grassi scoffed. 'Open the shutters and then strip the bed.'

He swung his legs off the mattress and strolled to the newly-opened window. 'This is a better view than I have,' he remarked accusingly.

Eve moved quickly out of Grassi's way and set to drawing off the bedcovers. She had no sense that David was under the bed – surely her brother would have discounted such an obvious hiding place? *I may be wrong, though.* Her breath stopped in her chest. She felt clammy all over.

'Wait! What's this?' Grassi demanded.

Eve looked to where Grassi pointed and almost sagged in relief. She rapidly folded David's blue pyjamas and dressing gown and put them with the top sheet.

'It's only David's night clothes,' she explained, blushing as she spoke of such things to Grassi.

'Ready for your brother's eventual return,' observed a different voice.

'That's right,' Eve said, holding Julio's gaze with her own. He had come upstairs, and she had not heard him above her own racing heart.

From the landing, he gave her such a cold look that Eve almost cried out. His deep-set eyes flicked over her and he turned to Luigi Grassi. 'There is nothing downstairs,' he said.

Striding into the room, Julio took in the partly-stripped bed in a single glance. 'Have you checked the chest and drawers?' he asked Grassi.

'We were coming to that.' Grassi pushed a shutter to its fullest extent and murmured, 'Amazing.' He rested his forearms on the windowsill to stare out over the roof-scape.

'I will search,' said Julio, stepping around Eve as if she was no more than a wooden chest or arrangement of flowers.

He did, too, deftly, impersonally, as if he was in a stranger's house. Eve's face prickled with alarm as she watched and tears threatened. Why did Julio not glance her way? Why did he seem so suddenly remote?

Above her head, Julio's eyes met Grassi's and he opened both hands in a negative gesture.

'So there is nothing here,' said Grassi.

'Nothing,' said Julio. 'Except a pretty girl.'

He caught hold of Eve and pulled her to him. Before she could speak, his mouth came down on hers.

He had kissed her on the day they traveled together to ancient Kamiros, but this was different. This was hard, greedy, his mouth and hands seizing what he wanted. She felt a blaze of heat in her lips and face, a fire spreading throughout her slender frame as her body responded. Her lips opened under his, her tongue exploring as her fingers ached to do the same. He had clamped her so tightly to him that Eve could feel the hard long lines of his body. She wanted to feel more, but now she could also feel that his left foot was moving, seeming to kick something away.

His odd action broke the spell. Finally, she struggled to free herself and was abruptly released.

'Get out.' Shocked at her own passion and furious for giving in to it, Eve stalked out of the room and then immediately walked back in. 'Go,' she said, in a low, hard voice.

'Yes. I think we'd better, Falcone. We appear to have outstayed our welcome – or rather you have.' Grassi marched past Eve, tipping her a mock-salute. 'Until the next time, Miss Eve.'

Julio said nothing, even when Eve turned away from him, and his face remained as impassive as a cast of bronze. She listened to him going downstairs but did not watch through the gaping shutters as he and Grassi finally took their leave. Instead, Eve remained where she was, standing quite still.

After a moment she touched her lips with trembling fingers, reliving that kiss in her mind. Why had he done that? Why had she?

Slowly, as if waking from a daze, Eve knelt at the end of David's bed. Carefully, she drew out the object that Julio had kicked under the mattress, hiding it from Grassi.

It was David's identity card, the one every citizen of Rhodes was supposed to have on him at all times. It had fallen close to the bed leg, and she had missed it. Grassi hadn't spotted it either, but Julio had seen it and taken steps to prevent its discovery.

On her knees, with the battered card gripped between her fingers, Eve started to cry.

Chapter 10

'Eve? Evie, what's wrong? What's the matter?'

David dashed up the final three steps of the staircase, finishing on the landing where Julio had been. The sight of him safe and well made Eve stop crying for a second, and then she started crying harder than ever.

'Evie.' David ran into the room and knelt on the floor beside his sister. 'Evie, it's all right, they've gone.'

'I know!' Eve sobbed.

She felt her brother's arms go round her and wept afresh, wishing they were Julio's. 'This is such a mess.'

'Steady on, sis, it's not so bad.' David rocked her, smoothing her hair. 'Don't cry, Eve. It really is all right. Mum is safe and Dad is making lunch...

'There!' David exclaimed as Eve raised a tear-stained face out of his neck. 'I thought that would surprise you. Bread and cheese and some real English tea. Pep us up, somewhat.'

Eve felt over his arms and shoulders, touching him as if to convince herself he was real. 'You're here. You're safe.'

'That's what I've been telling you, silly.'

'How? Did you manage to go next door, over the wall, perhaps?'

'Nothing so energetic! There wasn't time, although that policeman of yours certainly hammered on the door. We knew straight-away that something was wrong, even Dad.'

David leant back a little and burrowed in a trouser pocket, producing a clean hand-kerchief. 'Here, dry your eyes.'

'Thank you.' Eve tried to do so but the tears kept coming. She knew now that Julio must strongly suspect that David was living with them and that she had not told him. He would think she didn't trust him. Worse, he might even consider that she had gone out with him for no other reason than to ingratiate herself, to throw him off guard. Yet he had kissed her...

Eve gulped and tried to focus on her brother. 'Where did you hide?'

David grinned. 'I'll show you when we go downstairs,' he said, and then added in a more serious tone, 'Mum thinks we fooled them but I'm not sure. Grassi, certainly. He was more interested in our glassware. He actually took that Venetian rose glass vase – claimed it was contraband.'

'No!'

'He did. Mind you, your policeman had moved the vase to a very attractive setting on the low table by the sofa, far away from the main table and my hasty hiding place. As if he intended it to be a deliberate distraction.'

David lowered his head to stare into his sister's face. 'What do you think?' he asked.

Eve hid her eyes in David's handkerchief. 'You're saying that Julio knew where you were? That when he was searching, he knew?'

'I think he did, yes. You see, he asked Dad to move from the table, but not Mum. Hello! What's that?' David pointed to the object lying on Eve's lap.

'Your identity card. It was on the floor and Julio kicked it under the bed, perhaps by mistake?'

'What?' David laughed, 'Your policeman, doing something by mistake?'

'I wish you wouldn't call him that.'

'Ah, that's better. You're getting your fight back. Now, before we go down and join the parents, suppose you tell me what was upsetting you so much when I walked in a few minutes ago.' David brushed a lingering tear off Eve's long lashes. 'Was it that bully, Grassi?'

'He kissed me!'

'Grassi?' David's hands bunched into fists.

'No, no, Julio! Julio kissed me, and he thinks I don't trust him and now he'll just despise me...' Eve started crying again.

Leaning against her brother's chest, she

felt his laughter. 'Is that all?' David asked.

Eve drew back. 'What do you mean?'

David was shaking his head. 'If a little blonde had made me feel rather an idiot, I think I'd have kissed her, too – a good long smacker of a kiss.'

'David!' Eve batted him with a hand. The kiss Julio had given her had indeed been long and more than that, passionate.

'Mind you,' David added judiciously, 'your policeman is a proud man. He may object strongly to being duped, or kept in the dark.'

'Yes,' Eve said softly. 'He may.'

'And he does work for the fascists.'

'Yes,' Eve said, even more softly.

'So it might be wise if I think about moving on. Myself and the statuette.' David sighed and scrambled to his feet, holding out a hand to help Eve up.

'Come and eat,' he said. 'Things will look better, once we've caught our breaths.'

First Eve closed the shutters in David's room, remade his bed and then returned to her own room. Her parents would not have heard her soft crying from downstairs, and she didn't want them to know just how upset she had been.

Her mirror showed a pair of over-pink eyes and swollen lips, which she would pass off as the start of the summer cold. She didn't want questions from anyone.

'Come on!' David called from the landing.

'Okay.' Eve rubbed at her cheeks and went out to face her family.

Downstairs in the sitting room, David was keen to show off his hiding place. 'Can we show Eve what we did?' he asked their mother.

Away in the kitchen, Eve could hear her father pacing up and down, opening cupboard doors in his search for plates. Marveling that George Burnett had even set foot in there, she found herself standing near the sitting room sofa. The low table, without its missing vase, drew her eye like iron to a magnet. Tears pricked once more and she dug her short fingernails into the palms of her hands, impatient with her own weakness.

'You're not looking.' David's face wore a hurt expression.

Eve raised her head. 'Sorry.'

David walked over to where Philippa Burnett was sitting, surrounded by stacks of books, and moved two of the stacks close to her feet. Deftly, he inserted himself into the gap between the armchair and table, crouching where the leaf of the table hid him from view. He drew back the two book stacks, and Philippa shook out her paisley shawl, floating a large patterned corner of fabric over the gap between her armchair and the tiled floor, covering the view of David's legs and feet.

Eve tried to enter into the spirit of their disguise, walking the length of the sofa and back, staring all the while at the armchair, table, piles of books and veiling shawl. 'Very ingenious,' she remarked, hoping her voice carried sufficient enthusiasm. She didn't want to spoil her mother's triumph.

Sitting in her armchair, Philippa was smiling broadly, clearly pleased with herself.

Although her face hurt with the crying, Eve forced her features into a grin. 'Well done, Mum.'

'Yes, that's what I think,' Philippa agreed. 'Your father is convinced that Mr. Falcone didn't do a very thorough job of searching.'

Philippa drew her shawl back across her legs, unaware that she had just exposed David's feet, which could be glimpsed through the legs of her armchair.

'He certainly made enough noise,' she went on, 'and that odious Grassi made off with my vase.'

'I never cared for it.' Carrying a tray piled with cups, plates and a steaming teapot, George Burnett appeared in the sitting room doorway. 'How do you negotiate that gloomy corridor from our foyer to the kitchen, Eve?' he asked his daughter. 'I know I've done it before, but you manage it several times daily!'

His spectacles were steamed up, Eve noticed, and despite her private misery, she could not suppress a tender smile. Poor Dad had tried, she thought, but domestic arrangements really weren't his forte.

'Our hallway,' Philippa corrected him.

'It's a corridor.' George Burnett placed the tray on the low table and dropped onto the sofa. 'Oh, do come out of that ridiculous hiding place!' he ordered his son. 'I think you're mad, the pair of you. The only reason that David hasn't been dragged off to jail is because Grassi was too greedy and Falcone too lazy to conduct a proper search.'

George Burnett wiped his spectacles and looked his daughter straight in the eye. 'Or perhaps that *carabiniero* had other interests, eh? I'm beginning to wonder if I wasn't mistaken about our Mr. Falcone. He's certainly more than your average bully-fascist.' He patted the cushion next to him. 'Why don't you come and sit by me and pour the tea, Eve? I think we're all ready for a drink.'

They ate a bread and cheese lunch while sitting around the low table. Eve was sorry but also relieved when her father said to David, 'Where will you make for, Turkey? It's less than a day's sail from Rhodes and there are plenty of trustworthy fishermen who would take you, and gladly.'

Philippa paused in her slow, careful

peeling of an orange. Her light brown eyes were sad. 'Do you think that is necessary, George?'

Her husband leaned across the low table and touched one of her still hands. 'You already know the answer to that, my dear.'

Philippa's shoulders drooped. 'I know,' she said quietly.

'Facts must be faced.'

'Yes,' said Philippa and Eve together, but Eve was certain they were thinking of different things. As a mother, Philippa would naturally be concerned with David's safety. So was Eve, but Julio remained in the forefront of her mind. Even whilst they discussed ways and means of moving David safely out of Rhodes Town, sneaking him and the gold statuette through the various Italian checkpoints, Eve was haunted by 'her' Italian policeman. Julio, who was so proud, and who had told her that he prized honesty above all things.

Who now knew that she had lied to him.

Eve spent the rest of the day on edge, starting whenever she heard anyone walking past in the alleyway, whenever she heard a motorbike gunning along Homer Street. She did not expect Julio to return with soldiers or other armed police, but supposing she was wrong? Exhausted after several tense, unhappy hours, she fell into bed and slept quickly, oblivious to the whine of mosquitoes beyond the net draped round her bed.

She dreamed of Julio. In her dream he was a Roman centurion. She was brought to him in chains, by unseen forces, and he struck off her chains, but he did not kiss her.

She woke, missing his kiss, and lay awake for the rest of the night, watching the stars fade in the approaching dawn.

She had lied to him. His little English maid had lied and lied. Julio understood why, but he was also disappointed. Did she not know him yet? Did she not recognise yet how he felt about her?

How can she, stupido, *when you have not told her?*

Standing in a shabby Greek bar in the middle of Rhodes Town, having a much-needed glass of ouzo, he scowled and gnawed fretfully on another onion ring. Maybe he should not have kissed her like that, but she had looked so pretty and saucy and plain naughty he had not been able to resist. She had kissed him back, too, very thoroughly.

So what now? Where did this leave them? What should he do next?

Rising early, Eve knew that it was up to her to put the first part of her family's plan into operation. Once it would have astonished her that her parents and older brother

134

would trust her with such responsibility, but they had seen her grow up in the past few weeks.

Walking again through the dusty Rhodian streets to Andreas' shop to see if the Greek butcher had returned from Monolithos, Eve felt like an old woman. She had the bitter certainty that she would not see Julio for a coffee or a stroll today.

She did not know if she would ever see him again.

Andreas was back in his shop. He grinned broadly at Eve, bold as a pirate, and nodded his red maze of curls at one of the joints hanging from a meat hook.

'I have some wonderful mutton for you today, my girl,' he boomed. 'When you make lamb stew for the family, tell them to thank Andreas!'

'They always do.' Eve handed across her basket for Andreas to drop a portion of mutton into it.

Even at this early hour, his shop had many customers, but Andreas and Eve were old hands at silent, non-verbal communication. Before he brought his cleaver down on the meat, Andreas slightly jerked his head towards the little square opposite his shop.

Eve glanced that way and saw two men lurking beside the fountain in the square. Neither were in uniform, but Eve knew instantly from the cut of their suits that they were Italian.

So Andreas' shop was now being watched even more closely.

The Greek butcher handed Eve her basket across the counter. 'The stew bones you asked for are wrapped in the newspaper.'

'Thank you.' Eve had not asked for bones but she knew better than to question Andreas in public. She paid him and bade him goodbye.

She hoped she might see Julio on her way back but saw only another *carabiniero,* strolling past the mosque of Ibrahim Pasha. Missing the Greek church bells of her childhood – such bells were now banned on Rhodes by the fascists – Eve continued along Sophocles Street and home.

Unwrapping the 'bones' in the kitchen, she found a note from Andreas.

David, who read written Greek better than she did, translated it for her.

'Andreas says that he's set something up for us – those are his exact word – outside the city, but that getting through the city is something we'll have to do ourselves. Andreas says a boat will be waiting at Kritika to take us to safety. It will be waiting from tonight for three more nights.'

'Three days!' Eve paused in chopping onions. 'I never expected it to be so soon.'

'It has to be,' David told her. 'We have to take the statuette out of the fascists' reach.

Every day that passes increases the chances of it being discovered.'

David, who was helping Eve, laid his knife and half-peeled potato on the well-scrubbed kitchen table. 'You do realize that you and Mum and Dad will have to come, too,' he said quietly. He threw Andreas' note into the oven and the smell of burning paper filled the room. 'Mum and Dad have decided. They talked it over again whilst you were out shopping this morning. With what happened here yesterday, and all the recent news of Hitler and his Nazis rearming Germany they feel that it's time they went home to England.'

Eve, staring at her board of neatly diced onions, could hardly believe it. 'So sudden,' she whispered.

'You can see why, though?'

'Of course,' Eve said. 'But to leave here in only three days or less...' The thought of leaving Rhodes and not seeing Julio again, perhaps not even being able to say any kind of farewell to him, overwhelmed her.

'Are you all right, Eve?' David asked, his even, boyish features racked with concern. 'You look almost in pain.'

'Onions,' Eve said quickly, wiping away a treacherous tear.

Somehow she prepared the lamb stew. Later, she even forced some down, but eating whilst her throat was tight with grief was a hard thing to do. 'Leave the washing up until later,' David told her, as she prepared to make her escape and go walking along Homer Street in the vain hope of seeing Julio. 'We all have to talk.'

Talk they did, too, the whole family, around the table where they had eaten their meal. Eve cleared the plates and brought in small demitasses of Greek coffee and a tin of lemon-flavored Greek delight and listened whilst David outlined what must happen.

The family would leave the city separately. George and Philippa Burnett would leave tomorrow morning, with the cover story that they were spending the weekend at a friend's villa on the east side of the island. Eve and David would follow on the next evening, under cover of night.

'It must be this way,' David stressed, waving aside the tin of sweets. 'I can't be seen here, obviously, because I'm still officially missing, but if Eve were to go with you, even the fascists might suspect that something was afoot. The family's probably being watched, so you can't all go together.'

'I'll make sure I'm seen around Rhodes tomorrow, then,' said Eve. 'If I'm here, the authorities will believe that Mum and Dad's weekend trip is simply that: a trip. Not that they're going for good, or that I'm leaving, too.'

Eve stumbled a little on the word 'good'

but managed to keep her face under control. Philippa leaned anxiously across the table towards her, but George Burnett touched his wife's arm.

'It's for the best, my dear,' he said, watching Eve as he spoke.

Eve knew that her father meant her leaving Julio. Everything in her heart and mind told her that was not true, but time was running out.

The siesta passed, and the long evening, and still Julio did not come.

Soon there would be no time left.

Chapter 11

Eve spent her final day on Rhodes packing and cleaning and walking through the Old City. She wandered along the Street of Knights but did not see Julio. She hurried to the New Market in the New Town, but saw no sign of his tall, long-legged, handsome figure.

Passing Andreas' shop, the butcher's wife called to her from the doorway. 'Come and look at this embroidery.'

When Eve walked over to admire the delicate, intricate work on a tablecloth, Andreas' wife whispered fiercely, 'Andreas is sending a guide for you tonight and he will also be with you for part of the way. No questions! Those pigs of fascists are straightening up by that fountain: in another moment they will be crossing the square to spy. Say farewell now!'

The embroidered tablecloth was whipped away and Eve waved and said goodbye, her voice not quite steady as she knew that she would never see Andreas' plump, graceful wife again.

That was how the rest of the long day went: Eve visiting favorite places, longing to stay, and hoping each time she turned another street corner that Julio would be striding towards her, his ardent face full of love.

Maybe he doesn't really care, Eve watched a basking lizard in the family courtyard, envying the creature its simplicity. *Perhaps for him I was only one of many girls.*

Her heart told her that was not true, but how could she be sure?

By sunset, when Eve was watering her herbs for the second time that day, Julio had not called or phoned. Neither had her parents and although Eve knew that there were no telephones at the tiny northern fishing village of Kritika, she wished she could hear something.

'Please let them be safe,' she prayed.

Neither she nor David felt like eating much, and Eve could not face cooking on that final day. They shared a silent, dismal meal of stale bread and olives, washed down by coffee. At times, when she chewed on her crusts, Eve had the strange sense that Julio was close, perhaps even in the alleyway outside the house, but when she left the sitting room and darted across the courtyard to open the yard door, there was never anyone out there.

Twilight came and the slender new moon rose. 'It's lucky it's not a full moon tonight,' David said, peeping through the sitting room shutters.

'Yes,' said Eve. She did not feel anything

was 'lucky' at the moment.

'I'll be glad to be moving about freely again.' David stretched his arms above his head and cracked his knuckles. 'I was getting to feel pretty cooped up, hiding in this house all day.'

'Yes, I imagine you were.' She wished she could stay here and hide. At least until she had seen Julio again. She wanted the chance to explain, if she could.

David glanced at his watch. 'Almost nine. Andreas and the guide will come when the streets are quiet. Are you ready, Eve?'

Eve nodded to the small suitcase by her feet. She had been able to take only a few basic clothes and scarcely any mementoes. She wished again, fruitlessly, that she had something more of Julio's than the ribbons she had cut off the boater, some more lasting token to keep. All that remained otherwise were memories.

In another moment, Eve knew, she would start crying again. Hating the idea of David seeing that, she walked rapidly across to the sitting room door. 'I'm going out in the courtyard,' she said. 'When are you going to collect the package?'

'When Andreas and the guide have come.'

She did cry in the courtyard, silently weeping until her eyes felt like red slits and her head ached. Then she was glad of the deepening darkness, because when Andreas and their guide slipped into the courtyard it was all business.

'This is Yiannis.' Andreas introduced their guide, a dark, skinny man who seemed all head like a spider. He moved like a spider, too, keeping always close to the walls and silent as a shadow. He nodded to Eve and David without speaking.

'He will take you out of the city,' Andreas said. He thrust a bundle of clothes at David. 'Change into these. You are too English in those trousers and jacket. If you are spotted by a patrol or the *carabinieri* in such clothes, you cannot claim you were not breaking the curfew, merely slipping to a neighbor's house for some cigarettes, *neh?*' Andreas gave a deep belly laugh.

Eve was also given a bundle and told to go upstairs and change. Back in the sitting room in her new costume, she was instructed to completely cover her head with a dark blue headsquare trimmed with red zigzag braid.

'Especially that blonde fringe,' Andreas warned.

Moments later, Eve and David saw themselves transformed into two very fair-looking Rhodians in traditional island dress. Andreas grinned and tugged at Eve's swirling dark blue skirts.

'Very good!' he said.

It was hard for Eve to lock the house door and leave the key under her pot of rosemary, so she did it quickly. Whilst she was doing that, David recovered the package from its niche behind the pot of basil. He handed it out to Andreas, who looked at the brown paper without offering to take it.

'We would like to see the sun god,' Andreas said quietly.

Eve did not want to look at the statuette again, not when it was the cause for David having to flee the city under cover of darkness, and not when it was one of the secrets between Julio and her. She kept her head down as the parcel was unwrapped but knew by the sharp intake of their guide's breath and Andreas' startled exclamation that the gold sun god had been revealed.

'It was to see this that I took the risk to come tonight.' Andreas touched the sun god's tiny halo with the tip of his index finger.

'Has it been worth it to you?' asked David.

'It is a moment without price,' said Andreas, then he turned aside abruptly. 'Put it away. We must go!' He lifted Eve's suitcase from the courtyard flags.

Following Yiannis, their guide, through the empty streets reminded Eve of her pre-dawn trip with Julio on their way to ancient Kamiros, but how different were the circumstances! Here every moving shadow was a potential threat. The hum of electric wiring set Eve's nerves on edge as they hurried along the alleys in single file. She thought

144

she knew the Old City as well as anyone, but they crossed and recrossed squares and doubled back on themselves so often that she became quite disorientated.

'Yiannis knows his business,' Andreas whispered at one of their frequent stops, whilst their guide went on a few steps alone to ensure that the way was safe. 'He will bring us clear of checkpoints and patrols.'

They were gliding along the city walls now, passing the entrance to a tiny shrine in a medieval tower. Below them in the city, less than the beam of a torchlight away, Eve could hear two or three Italian guards stamping their feet against the increasing cold. She trembled, wanting to run but knowing it would be fatal. She glanced at her brother and saw his profile as if it were molded in glass, the tension naked in his face. Her face felt stiff and unyielding and when the guide Yiannis beckoned them, it was hard for her to move her feet.

Soon they were off the medieval walls and at street level, moving, Eve thought, towards the sea. She could taste salt on her lips: the salt of the sea, or fear, or tears

'Stop! Papers! Show your papers! Stop!'

The rough Italian voice and the brilliant lightning-flash from searching torches had them all running, scrambling over the cobbles to the nearest dark alley. There was no time to look round. Eve ran with the three men, her lungs burning as they dashed up another narrow street. Ahead, Eve could see palm trees and tamarisks in a tiny square, somewhere perhaps to hide.

'This way!' came an urgent whisper in Greek from the top of the alley, before the street opened out into the square. 'Not there – patrol there. Come!'

Ahead and to their left, a narrow torch beam flashed on and off once, a beacon to guide them. Eve, David, Andreas and Yiannis launched themselves down the almost invisible turning, running a few steps and then finishing at a blank high wall. In the square with the palm trees Eve could hear the sound of splintering branches, heavy feet and cursing as fascist forces turned their torches fruitlessly over the area. Then another hue and cry went up and the whole pack was off again, pounding away down the streets, until they no longer heard anyone behind them.

'They've gone!' David gasped, when he had breath to speak.

'For now,' agreed the new voice, this time speaking in English.

Catching her breath, leaning against the alley wall, Eve felt as if the ground had shifted under her feet, as if she was in the midst of an earthquake. Half-hoping, half-fearing, she raised her head to face the man who had saved them.

He caught her up in his arms and held her

tightly against his chest. The other three men remained frozen against the wall.

'Julio,' Eve whispered, plucking at his sleeve. The instant he embraced her she had known it was all right, but David and Andreas and their guide would not know.

With one arm around Eve's waist, keeping her close, Julio extended a hand to David. 'I have been searching a long time for you,' he said softly.

'Julio, I'm sorry– ' Eve began.

'Hush, little one. Let your brother speak.'

David stepped forward into the middle drainage channel of the narrow alley and briefly took Julio's hand. 'Thanks for the warning there,' he said in Greek. 'Or are thanks premature?'

Julio gave a grim smile. 'As you all now realize, I also speak Greek, but not so well, so I will change to Italian. It will be quicker for me to explain.'

'You need to explain,' Andreas said, in Greek.

Julio nodded once. 'This may make things simpler,' he said. Taking out his fascist party card, he held it up for all to see and then tore it in half and then quarters, letting the pieces fall onto the cobbles.

Andreas jerked his bearded chin towards Julio's gun-belt. 'Give me that and I might be convinced.'

'Very well.' Julio unclipped his gun, hand-ing it to Andreas butt-first. The Greek butcher and resistance fighter weighed the gun in his hand and glanced at it. 'You have removed the bullets?'

Julio grinned. 'I am to show my trustworthiness, not my folly.'

Andreas stepped back into the shadows, beckoning to David and the guide. Whilst they whispered together, Julio squeezed Eve's middle.

'You have been very brave – and foolish,' he said in English. 'Your brother is very like you. Like his picture, too. I have his photograph here for you. I did promise to return it.'

Even in the gloom of the alley, Eve could feel her cheeks burning. 'I was going to tell you about David – '

'So why didn't you?'

'I was too happy,' Eve whispered.

It was the truth, but in that instant, her words sounded feeble. Worse than feeble, an insult.

Julio touched her hot face. The tips of his fingers ran gently under her eyes. 'You have been crying, a lot.'

'I thought I'd never see you again.'

'See me?' Julio chuckled and lifted her closer in his arms. 'I could not come earlier, otherwise I would have been missed at police headquarters, but I have been watching you very closely this evening, especially tonight.' He kissed the tip of her nose. 'This time you did not lose me in all these back streets.'

'You've been following us!'

'Of course,' Julio said. 'Grassi may have seen nothing in your house but a vase he fancied, but I knew at once, after my search, that you and your family would have to leave, and quickly. I was going to make myself known once you were out of the city, but then you were spotted. I know how the leader of that patrol works and knew he would have his men comb the trees. He always does. I couldn't let you all be trapped and taken.'

His strong body shuddered and Eve tightened her grip, comforting him. 'We're safe,' she whispered. She wanted to kiss him, felt a moment of her old, diffident shyness and then did so, kissing him tenderly on his mouth. 'Thanks to you.'

Julio lowered his head and kissed her in return, a long kiss, like the one he had given her in David's bedroom. 'I've wanted to do that for days, hours, every minute,' he said, when he finally drew back a little. 'Especially when I saw that identity card. How could you have been so careless?'

'You did hide it from Grassi,' Eve murmured. 'When you kissed me. You knew then about David.'

Julio snorted. 'I'd already spotted your brother's feet under the table downstairs!

And it was as well for you that I'd already had my suspicions about him. His crazy hiding place gave me quite a start.'

He shook his dark head. 'When I marched upstairs, I was so angry with you then, for not trusting me, but even so, I only wanted to kiss you, *cara*. To prove to you that you could trust me.' He chuckled softly. 'I had to do something too. Give you the chance to tell Grassi and me to get out, something Grassi would believe. The kind of thing he would do. I meant to startle you a little, but never frighten you.'

'You didn't,' Eve whispered. 'Not because of that, at least. When you didn't return—'

'I've told you why I couldn't come before.' He brushed her cheek with his fingers. 'But you should not have carried the burden of hiding your brother alone.'

'I'm sorry,' Eve said, marveling at what Julio had told her; that he had already suspected that David had been hiding at the family home. 'Tonight,' she said, 'I thought I sensed you sometimes, but then I wasn't sure.'

'I would be a poor policeman if I could not follow without being spotted.' Julio stepped sideways slightly, to look her up and down. 'As you know, I was only caught out in that way once.'

'When you baldly admitted you were interested in me!'

'I couldn't help it.' Julio grimaced. 'I thought you the prettiest thing I had ever laid eyes on.'

'Thing!'

'Thing,' Julio repeated with relish. 'And horror, for causing me so many sleepless nights.'

'I'm sorry,' Eve said automatically, then recalled that she, too, had suffered sleepless nights. She gave him an impish grin. 'Serves you right.'

'*Basta!* Enough!' Julio made a cutting downward motion with one hand. 'Your brother and his friends have finished their talk: we should go.' In contradiction of that, he ran a hand up her spine. 'The costume suits you.'

He turned before Eve could respond, protectively standing in front of her as Andreas approached.

'We have decided to trust you,' the Greek said. 'Because we have no choice, and because Eve trusts you. But we do things our way, or not at all.'

'Agreed,' said Julio.

'We will split up,' Andreas said. 'You and the girl, Yiannis, David and I. She will tell you where to make for, once you are through the city.'

Eve made no protest about Andreas' brusque speech. They were at risk, lingering here in this alley, so time was of the essence.

151

Andreas' plan also made sense. If they separated, it would give any trackers two trails to have to chase instead of one. And David had to escape, with the statuette. The golden spirit of the island had to be put out of reach of the fascists. Going their separate ways, she and David would meet up again and reunite with their parents at the boat. Yiannis and Andreas would go to ground on the island: possibly go to mainland Greece later.

But then Andreas did a shocking thing. 'Here.' He gave Eve the brown paper parcel of the statuette.

'But–' Eve tried to protest.

'No argument!' Andreas enveloped Eve in a swift bear hug. 'I'll miss you, English girl,' he said in Greek. 'Take care of yourself.'

'You, too.' Eve could no say no more, her throat was thick with tears.

David clasped her arm. 'I'll see you later, Evie.' Picking up the suitcases, he glared at Julio. 'Take good care of her.'

'I will,' Julio promised.

'If you do not,' Andreas said, speaking in Italian for the first time to underline his intent, 'You will answer to me.'

'Stop it!' Eve whispered, her vision blurring. She heard Andreas instruct Julio to wait a few moments and then leave the city by whatever gate he felt best. The Greek returned Julio's pistol with a gruff, 'God go with you!'

They left then, David, Andreas and Yiannis, vanishing into the shadows. Overcome by so many brutal partings, Eve could not speak or think clearly. She felt Julio's arms close around her once more and fought against a sudden, almost irresistible desire to sleep.

'It isn't safe here,' she reminded him. 'Come on, I'll guide us out.'

Walking helped Eve return to life, and of course Julio was with her now. There were no more shadows or secrets between them as they stole, hand in hand like errant children, towards the closest city gate. Once, far off, Eve thought she heard the drumming of flying footsteps, but no one accosted them.

'What's that?' Julio asked after a time. He pointed to the brown paper parcel gripped in Eve's white-knuckled hand.

The time for secrets was long past. Taking a deep breath, Eve blurted out, 'It's a solid gold statuette of the Greek sun god Helios and we're carrying it to safety.'

Julio cocked a black eyebrow. 'Away from the rapacious Italians, eh?'

'Not all Italians,' Eve shot back.

'No, only the fascists,' Julio agreed. 'May I hold it?'

Eve handed it to him at once, only aware of what she had done when she had done it.

'Thank you,' Julio said softly. He handed it back, saying, 'What it is like?'

'Very beautiful. A nude, like Michelangelo's David, but with the sun god's halo,' Eve explained.

'A very special symbol, then, for the Rhodians and Greeks,' Julio observed. 'I remember you telling me that Rhodes is the sun god's island.' Eve nodded, relieved that he had understood.

Julio unwound his fingers from hers. 'We're approaching the south gate of St. John.'

'Yes.' In the last few hundred yards, Eve had begun to recognize the street again.

'It's quieter than the Amboise Gate,' Julio said encouragingly.

Less massive, too, thought Eve, bringing to mind the huge towers and vast walls close to the Amboise Gate. In another way, it was oddly appropriate, for they would be passing close to the section of medieval walls that had once been defended by her countrymen, the English knights of the former knights of Rhodes. She could already see the windmills on top of the English section of the crusader walls.

Ahead was the gate of St. John. Italian guards milled on the stone bridge thrown across the deep dry moat running between the inner and outer curtain walls.

'Let me do the talking,' Julio warned.

Eve gripped the brown paper parcel of the

priceless statuette in a way that she could use the parcel as a weapon, if need be. Could she hit someone? If they threatened Julio, yes, she could, she decided. Apprehensive and wary, she heard her blood buzzing in her ears as she followed Julio into the light of the guards' sentry box.

She could no longer smell the sea but hay and other earthy scents, the smell of the land outside the walls, where she and Julio would be free.

She did not glance at the guards, nor protest when Julio clasped her shoulder. She lowered her head and eyes and pretended to be mute, ignorant of Italian.

'Pretty islander. Unusual coloring,' remarked one of the guards, paying more attention to her than a uniformed officer of the *carabinieri* or the bureaucratic details of Julio's papers.

'When you've finished questioning her,' the guard added, 'let me know. Maybe she can help me with my Greek. Eh, *bella?*' He loomed a few seconds more in Eve's path, breathing out a mixture of garlic and wine.

'She doesn't understand you,' Julio said, steering Eve rapidly round the guard and across the stone bridge.

Eve did not take a proper breath again until they had passed through the second checkpoint and were striding quickly towards the suburbs that had grown up around the ramparts of the old city.

'Where are we going?' Julio asked.

'To Kritika, an old Turkish village on the Monolithos road, going south,' Eve explained. 'It's about two miles from Rhodes Town.'

'Three kilometers,' Julio translated to himself. 'Not much of a distance, but we will be conspicuous, walking at night. I'll see if we can "borrow" a mule, or bicycles, from one of the houses we pass.'

They walked in silence for the length of a street before Julio said, 'Today, I received a letter from my mother, who tells me that she and my sisters are spending some time in America. They have already set out for a long holiday over there, staying with family.' He stressed the word 'long'.

Julio shook his head sadly. 'I am sure Mamma and my sisters are sorry to leave Parma, but I am relieved they have done so.'

'My parents are returning to England,' Eve said.

'And you will go with them,' Julio said, a statement, not a question.

'I have a cousin in England,' he went on, when Eve nodded reluctantly. 'He works in a woolen mill in a place called Bradford. I have often considered taking up one of his frequent invitations for me to stay with him.'

'A holiday?' Eve asked, not daring to presume more.

'Perhaps longer.' Julio gave her a look that stopped the breath in Eve's throat. 'Eve.' He took hold of her free hand. 'Will you–'

There was the sound of a powerful car turning into their street. Eve dragged Julio into a house doorway.

'I think it's Grassi!' she panted, starting as she heard the familiar growl of the Fiat Balilla's engine. She tried to press Julio back into the shadows of the shallow doorway, praying that the family inside would not hear, or open the door and frame them with light.

'I'm darker than you.' Julio transferred her firmly into the corner, near the door hinges, and covered her navy skirts and top with his own blue uniform. About to argue as Julio's uniform had a red stripe running down the side of his trousers, Eve found the breath knocked from her by Julio's shielding body.

'Sorry, little one. Now be still.'

The approaching car shot past their doorway, leaving standing clouds of dust.

'It's gone,' Julio said, as the Balilla's head-lights receded into the distance. He lifted Eve off the doorstep and right off her feet.

'Julio, put me down! There's no time,' Eve said, spoiling her serious warning by giggling. 'This is mad,' she said, her head against his shoulder.

'But we must do it.' Julio set her down lightly and took her hand again. 'I do not think we shall see Grassi again tonight,' he said.

They walked a mile, seeing no more cars or patrols. Reaching the road to Monolithos, Eve pointed to the ink-black sea. 'Our way out,' she said.

'Are you sad to leave?' Julio asked.

'I am.' Eve frowned. Even the hope that she would soon be reunited with David and her parents failed to lift her spirits.

Julio put an arm around her shoulders. 'You're weary,' he said. 'When we reach the next house, I'm going to see if we can borrow some bicycles.' He touched a finger to her lips. 'I did say borrow, not steal. I'll even leave a note.'

By now, the homes had become more spaced out along the coast road. Eve wandered on the verge, listening to the soft rustle of the sea on the narrow pebble beach. On the landward side, they were passing a dense pine wood, but with her head turned north, towards the brooding presence of Turkey, she did not see the gap in the trees, or the high gates.

Eve missed the private entrance to a wooded country villa, but Julio did not.

He shook her arm gently. 'Wait here.' He pointed to a low wall where she could sit. 'I'm sure this place will have some kind of transport we can use. I won't be long.'

Eve sat on the cooling stones, resting her aching feet. Pulling off the navy headsquare and making an impromptu bag out of it to carry the brown paper parcel, she watched Julio slip between the iron gates. She heard him running down the track towards the pine-shrouded villa.

Julio was going to ask me something. She smiled at what it might be, hugging the knowledge to herself.

Again she heard a car, driving along the Rhodes-Monolithos road. Suddenly its headlights came full on and she realized it was far closer than she had first thought. With the lights dazzling her, Eve flung herself off the wall and onto the rough grass verge, desperate not to be seen.

The car accelerated and she relaxed, listening as it streaked by her.

'Eve? Eve!' Julio must have heard the car. She could hear him pounding back up the gravel path, sprinting to check she was safe. 'Eve!'

'I'm fine!' She rose to her feet from the grass and waved, showing him that she was unharmed. 'It's gone!'

Julio grinned, his teeth showing very white in the dim light, waved in return and laughed when a donkey, grazing somewhere close, began to bray.

'I go, I go!' he called, over the bellow of the complaining beast, lifting both hands in defeat as he pelted back down the driveway.

Eve settled on the wall again and the donkey continued to bray, long, loud wheezing moans that seemed to have no end. She peered into the darkness, wondering where it was, and then heard, too late, the distinctive crunch of car tyres on the road.

Eve leapt to her feet. In a squeal of brakes, the Balilla stopped only a car's length from her. Sleek and black in the night with its headlights off, its return had been masked by the country darkness and the ear-splitting brays of the donkey. The driver turned its headlights on again and re-started its powerful engine. The passenger door swung open and Luigi Grassi called out, 'I see my informant was correct. One of the English Burnetts is indeed traveling towards Monolithos tonight. With a great treasure, I'm told. Now come and join me, Miss Eve. Or shall my driver fetch you?'

Chapter 12

Eve knew she could not out-run the driver. Julio was still somewhere in the villa grounds, unaware of this new danger.

Please, God, don't let him come back to check on me now! His gun had no bullets, she remembered, and even if he had ammunition on him, both Grassi and his driver were armed. It would be two against one.

These cold, clear calculations flowed through Eve's mind in a rush. Beneath them was fear. To her horror, she discovered she was rigid with shock and fright. Determined not to scream or plead, she realized, too, that she could not move, even though she wanted to.

With an angry curse, Grassi's driver left the car. Somewhere off in the night the donkey was still braying, as if adding to her own silent protest and rage. She was hauled towards the Balilla. Moving, she came alive again and tried to drop the headsquare and its priceless brown paper package amongst the tall grass, but the driver found that, too.

Trying to kick the man and struggle free, her silent writhings softly applauded by Grassi, she was shoved into the back seat and the heavy door locked behind her.

'You are not good at disguises, Miss Eve.' Grassi tossed the headsquare out of his car window and placed the package ostentatiously on the seat between them. 'Do not try to escape, or I will be forced to restrain you.' He stroked the package, then flicked it, smirking as she flinched. 'Where are the others, eh? I know you will not be alone.'

'We split up.' Eve forced herself to look straight at him, compelled her voice to be clear and steady as she deliberately opened her eyes wide and lied. 'There is no one else with me.'

She heard the driver put the car in gear. She felt it move and could not suppress a wave of panic. She trembled violently and could scarcely sit still. Aware that Julio must have heard the car by now and sprinted back to the road, she did not look back for dread of alerting Grassi or the driver. She forced herself to speak. 'How did you know to come here?'

'As I said earlier, I was told, Miss Eve.'

'How can you trust informers?'

Eve could not quite disguise her disgust, and Grassi was onto that in an instant. 'Very easily!' He laughed. 'It is merely a question of applying payment or pressure, or sometimes both.'

Grassi smoothed out a crease in his suit jacket. 'For the most part I find informers almost worthless, but tonight–'

He broke off, heightening the tension by pretending to be absorbed in the land and sea-scapes flashing by as the car hurtled on its way. 'Tonight a drive from Rhodes Town along the coast road towards Monolithos was no great hardship,' he went on, addressing Eve's reflection in the darkened glass of the passenger window. He turned his head to look at her directly. 'And my informant's brief, befuddled "tip" has netted me a great prize.'

Pity at the unknown informant's terror and her own revulsion at having to share a confined space with Grassi threatened to break Eve down completely. Her clammy hand brushed against the brown paper package. Feeling the crumpled paper and string, she realized that she had to keep hoping, keep striving. Otherwise, David's and Andreas' and Julio's efforts would be for nothing. The golden spirit of the island would be stolen by Luigi Grassi.

The idea of such a man even touching the sun god statuette gave Eve the anger she needed to resist him.

'Where are we going?' she asked.

In the mirror, the cadaverous-looking driver scowled, as if he had not expected or wanted her to speak out so bluntly, but Grassi answered, in tones of some surprise. 'To Thermai Kallithea, naturally. I have people there who know what I like.' He traced a finger along one of the grooves in the leather seat. 'We will have a celebration, and I shall decide what will be done with you, Miss Eve.'

He reached across and flicked a strand of Eve's hair. 'Even that fool Falcone could appreciate your potential.'

'Where is he?' Eve thought it better to ask. If she said nothing, Grassi might become suspicious.

The man shrugged his rounded shoulders. 'Patrolling. Rounding up petty thieves. Whatever. Falcone is a very provincial fellow, of limited tastes and abilities. He has been a disappointment to me.' Grassi's mouth twitched with remembered amusement. 'You were right to throw him out that day. Now if I had kissed you...'

Eve bit her lip on a furious retort. Grassi took her blush of anger to be a flush of confusion and shyness. He chuckled.

'I look forward to instructing you,' he said casually, and Eve flinched. He fingered the string around the brown paper. 'Would you like me to unwrap this?'

'As you wish.'

Grassi seemed amused by her impudence. 'Later,' he said. 'For now you may divert me by giving an account of how you came to be on this desolate stretch of road, at such a ghastly hour. Did your very proper English parents not object?'

'Didn't your informant tell you?'

'Now, Miss Eve, no cheek, or you will regret it later. Now, who else was with you?'

Eve shivered and shook her head.

'Nothing to say?' Luigi Grassi's voice boomed in the car. 'Fear not, Miss Eve. Before the night has ended you will speak.'

Eve turned away from his mocking laughter and tried to think of escape.

The Fiat rolled swiftly over the coast road. To Eve's mingled relief and consternation, they passed the tiny settlement of Kritika without even slowing down. Luigi Grassi's terrified informant had obviously not passed that vital piece of information on, or had never known it. The big car turned inland, traveling across the northern tip of the island, and soon the lights of the famous thermal springs came into view.

Eve was given no chance to admire the spa's 'Arabian-Nights' style of architecture. She was taken directly from the car to a room close to several open-air mosaics, and locked in.

'Patience is a virtue!' Grassi called back as Eve tried to open the door and then the window. 'You will not be forgotten, Miss Eve!'

The small, square room contained nothing except a Roman-style dining couch draped with towels. Avoiding anything that Grassi might have touched, Eve sat huddled on the floor tiles. Her ears strained to hear the slightest sound, especially the return of any footsteps, but she heard only a light breeze in the palm trees, a distant murmur of voices, the faint clinking of glasses. *Was there a party going on somewhere?* Forcing herself to move, she stumbled to the door and shook it. She remained locked in, but there was the window to try again.

Then a wind-band started up, playing jazz. Even as part of Eve's mind registered surprise that Grassi would have such 'culturally decadent' music at his party, the main thrust of her thoughts was that locked window. She had to get out of this room – and the jaunty drums and whistles would cover her escape.

Seizing a towel, she looked at the couch again. There were no pillows she could use but beneath the couch, put there as an aid for someone like Grassi to heave himself onto it, was a small wooden stool.

Thank you! Now please, please let Julio be safe.

Eve snatched up the stool by one of its three legs and quickly, before she gave way to a thousand doubts, she raised it one-handed over her head. Listening to the band gather itself for another shrilling, thrilling climax, she approached the glass.

A thunder of drums and a thunder of

blood in her ears and she smashed the stool through the window, smashing the pane over and over, wielding the stool like an axe. The window shattered in a mass of shimmering fragments and fell away into the dark garden.

Eve flung the towel over the windowsill and launched herself out into the darkness, clinging onto the ledge until her arms ached like toothache. Finally she let go and dropped four feet down, landing straggle-legged on top of a lavender bush. Trembling, a thread of laughter bubbling on her lips, she rolled out of the bush and began brushing chips of glass from her clothes, before she realized what she was doing.

I'm out! Now get to those trees. Move for cover

She ran across a tiled floor and then froze, spotting a shadow flitting from the trees. Had she been heard, after all? Who was it? Who?

She shrank back – then ran forward, her feet almost soundless as she skimmed the warm stones and tiles without pause, without looking back, running towards Julio. He had come for her. He had followed and come and now she was going to him, the man she loved.

'*Cara!*' He threw his arms about her and kissed her.

'Julio!'

'I saw you at the window just now, back-lit against the electric light, with that stool raised like a sword.' He playfully tugged her hair. 'My little Viking.'

'Hush! We're not out of danger yet.'

With both of them laughing softly, they moved through the spa, passing its domed great hall and its loggia, gleaming a soft dove-gray by starlight.

Hand in hand, they fled across the beautiful mosaic floors. 'In the roadside villa where we stopped and separated, I found a motorbike in their barn,' Julio explained, as they ran down a staircase. 'Luckily, someone also left the ignition key in it, or I wouldn't be here.'

'Julio, how did you know to come to these springs?' Eve began, when a roar from the great ball and a sudden stop in the music rooted her to the spot.

'No!' Grassi's loud voice was almost a shriek. 'What is it? A can of mosquito repellent!'

Shocked by the revelation Eve automatically turned back towards the main hall.

'Quickly!' Julio tugged at her arm. 'Grassi will be after you next!'

That threat was more than enough. Eve started to run again. Hand in hand with Julio, she pelted with him from the hot springs as fast as they could go, zigzagging around palms until they reached the ornamental park, where Julio had left the motorbike.

They left Thermai Kallithea in clouds of smoke and petrol fumes, whilst black-shirted officials scoured the grounds in response to Luigi Grassi's increasing incoherent commands. 'Find her! Don't tell me she isn't in the room, find that English girl now! Find her!'

When Julio was certain that no one was following them, he cut the engine.

'I followed Grassi's car,' he told Eve, as the bike gradually coasted to a stop. 'I was too late to prevent them from grabbing you, but I saw their lights, so I left my own headlight off and followed. I hung back far enough for them not to notice me.'

The wheels of the bike were no longer turning. Julio dismounted and gathered her close. 'I thank God that you escaped and that we found each other in time,' he said.

They remained standing in each other's embrace, both too moved to speak. Finally, obviously reluctant, Julio kissed the top of Eve's head and looked up into the night sky.

'We should go, little one,' he said. 'Your brother and parents and new life are all waiting for you at Kritika.' He touched her cheek with gentle fingers. 'I would like to be part of that new life, Eve.'

'Wonderful! That's wonderful,' laughed Eve, seizing his hand and kissing it, then standing on tip-toe to fling her arms about him and kiss him on the mouth. In that moment, she hardly cared if any fascists were still looking for them or not.

'*Cara! Bellissima, cara!*' Julio swung her right off her feet and kissed her again, a long, lingering, sweet kiss. When they broke apart, he shook his head at her.

'You can make me forget everything!' He grinned. He took her hand, to help her back onto the motorbike.

'Julio, wait,' Eve said quickly, before her nerve failed. 'I've something to tell you.'

In as few words as possible, she told him why Luigi Grassi had been so furious. 'The gold statuette I told you about. I thought Andreas had given it to me, but he must have given me a fake, perhaps as a deliberate blind or diversion, and chosen to keep the real thing–'

'Because he wasn't entirely sure of me,' Julio finished. 'A shrewd move, and one I understand.'

Eve also understood, but she felt aggrieved. 'Andreas could have warned me. I thought I'd lost the spirit of the island to Luigi Grassi!'

Julio shook his head at her. 'Is it not better this way? The Greeks have the golden sun god, which is theirs, and Luigi Grassi gets mosquito repellent?'

Eve thought a moment, smiling at the idea of the mosquito repellent, but still not entirely convinced.

'Your brother knew nothing of the statuette's substitution. But he also did not know that Andreas had given you that brown paper parcel.'

'How do you know that?' Eve asked, astonished.

'Because David had gone to the end of the alleyway with that other Greek when Andreas put the fake parcel into your hands.'

'And Andreas did carry my suitcase for a time, which contained the mosquito repellent, and he didn't want me to argue,' Eve said excitedly, catching on to what Julio was saying.

'Indeed he did not! That would have alerted David, and your brother would most surely have refused any idea of your carrying the parcel.' Julio held up a hand. 'As I would have done, had I not been going with you.

'I'm happy your brother chose to trust me with your care,' Julio went on. 'In an odd way, I feel that I know him already.'

'I'm sure David feels the same.' She shook a teasing finger at Julio. 'Are all older brothers this over-protective?'

'I imagine so.'

Eve scowled, although she was glad that David had known nothing of Andreas' cunning sleight-of-hand. It was one thing for Andreas to have ruthlessly seized the moment to increase the chance of keeping the golden statuette. After all, the Greek had no reason to trust Julio. It would have been quite another had her own brother been party to a deception that might have led to her being put at risk.

'Andreas still let me go with you,' she said, hurt at the idea that the Greek butcher, her friend since childhood, could have been so calculating.

Julio threw back his head and laughed. 'Could you imagine him stopping you?' he asked. 'You don't know, little one, how determined you can look! But you should not misjudge your old friend. He is beset by troubles. As we now know, a single informer, a few careless words in the wrong ears, can cause great difficulty! Knowing who to trust is hard. I believe he was sure enough of my feelings for you, but not at all sure how I might react when faced with a treasure of solid gold.'

He squeezed her band, raising it to his lips. 'Andreas must have thought that he was merely removing temptation from my way, but he was wrong. The treasure I want is right here.' Leaning down closer to her, Julio kissed Eve's soft, open mouth.

'Come.' Taking advantage of her startled silence, he started the motorbike again.

With Eve riding pillion, they returned to the coast road and the hamlet of Kritika, where a fishing boat was moored ready to take them to safety.

'Look, there's David. He escaped!' Eve waved wildly at her brother, who raised both hands in salute. 'There's Mum, too, and Dad. Would you believe it? He's reading something!'

She made to move towards the waving figures, but Julio stopped her with an arm. 'Eve?'

Something in the way he said her name caused her to look up at him. 'Yes?' she said. Standing beside Julio at the top of the narrow pebble beach she waited, suddenly too nervous to smile, or to speak again.

Julio enfolded both her hands in his, smiling a little. 'Such tiny fingers,' he murmured, and then frowned, as if catching himself. Eve heard him take a deep breath.

'I hope to be a policeman in England,' he said. 'Does that please you?'

Eve's heart began to race madly. 'That you're thinking of coming to England? Yes, it pleases me very much.'

Julio let out a long breath of relief. 'Is it too soon for me to speak?' he said. 'I was going to ask you earlier this evening, but now I wonder. Is it too soon?

Looking round, still wary that even now they might be discovered, Eve was suddenly still. A tumult of pure happiness rushed through her as she guessed what he might say. She turned her fingers in his and squeezed his hand. 'You can say whatever you want to me, Julio. Whatever. However.'

Beside her, as if he had not heard her, Julio muttered something in Italian and then he said in a rush, 'I must speak. It will drive me crazy not to speak.'

He faced her and took her firmly in his arms. 'I love you, Eve Burnett,' he said. 'I would like you to be my wife. Would you please do me that very great honor? When we come to England, will you marry me, please?'

Eve stood on tip-toe again and said very clearly, 'Yes!' and then she kissed him again.

Julio kissed her heartily in return. Arm in arm, laughing happily together, they raced to the waiting boat.

HOLIDAY IN BOLOGNA

Chapter 1

Shading her eyes from a stiff breeze and the noon-day sun, Heidi stared through the high metal gates at an elegant stone tower and tiled roof. The rest of the villa was hidden by an avenue of pines, but somewhere within this grand Italian house were members of her family, people whom she had never met or known about until last month.

Standing on the pavement outside this imposing house on a warm, windy day in April, footsore after walking from her hotel in the center of Bologna to this villa on the rising outskirts of the city, Heidi felt her stomach fluttering with anxiety and anticipation. She was tempted to turn away. None of her relations knew who she was, or knew she was coming. She had ventured here out of curiosity, compelled to learn more about her father's family; driven too by a desire to belong, to be accepted by her own flesh and blood.

Her heart beating fast as part of her longed to push open these iron gates, Heidi swung her blue shoulderbag onto the pavement and glanced at the letter in her left hand. A letter handed to her, along with other documents and photographs, by her solicitor, Mr. Weaver, when she called in at his office three weeks ago, on her twenty-first birthday.

'This is from your father,' Mr. Weaver had explained in his dry, rather old-fashioned manner. 'He left it with me in the event of his death, with instructions that you were to receive it on attaining your majority.'

The bulky manila envelope had contained photographs and a letter in her father's familiar untidy scrawl – the letter she had gripped in her hand. She'd read it so often that she could remember everything he'd written.

'*My dear Heidi,*' she murmured, hearing her father's voice in her mind. '*I must ask for your kindness in this letter, and I hope for your understanding. I'd wanted to explain in person but must do my best through these poor pages.*

'*You have always known me as Ruggiero Manelli. That is not my original name, although to me it is my true name, the name I have become known by in my modest career as a photographer. I wanted any success to come as a result of my own efforts and not because of my family's name.*

'*I had another reason for changing my name, one even more relevant. I loved your mother, Sarah, with all my heart. She was everything to me. My cousin, Federico, never appreciated this, and at the time when we were still talking,* seemed to me to make no effort to understand. He and his wife, Rosa, opposed our marriage. They wanted me to stop "this nonsense" with photography and devote myself to the family business, in which I had no interest or aptitude.

'After many quarrels, I broke with my cousin and was determined to make a new life with Sarah in my newly adopted country. I changed my name as a further severing of any ties.

'I now regret that I broke so completely with my people, but I have never regretted marrying your mother. She made me happier than I had ever known it possible to be happy. Sarah often tried to persuade me to be reconciled with my family, but I suppose I was too proud – I always put it off. After Sarah's death, I could not bear the thought of my elder cousin's pity and so another chance at reconciliation was lost.

'Watching you play at my feet, little Heidi, I realize that I have deprived you of your heritage. Although I had no interest in the family business, you may wish to be involved. You may wish to make yourself known to the family.

'I have enclosed family photographs with this letter and papers proving who I am. Your true family name is not Manelli but Soleari, the name on these documents. Perhaps with you, Heidi, there will be reconciliation. If that is what you want, I pray that it occurs. With all my love, Papa.'

'Papa,' Heidi repeated, coming back to the present and her own dilemma. She had chosen to take her first holiday in five years in northern Italy. She had chosen to stay in Bologna where she now knew her family lived and worked. This was their house, the Villa Rosa. She could read the name on the whitewashed stone pillars of the main gate.

Should she make herself known? Should she go on, through the gate?

She had studied this view of these high iron gates before, in one of the photographs her father had left her. One thing the picture had not shown was the scale. The villa was far larger than she'd expected.

'I'll be the poor relation,' Heidi murmured. 'They might think I'm only here for what I can get, for money.' The idea filled her with horror.

Crouching on the hot pavement, her long black hair flicking against her shoulders in the breeze, Heidi dug through her bag with nimble fingers and brought out the old color photograph of her father standing before these gates, smoking a cigarette. *Papa* had never smoked in the time she'd known him. He looked impossibly young, grinning at the camera with his cigarette in one hand and his other arm hugging the shoulders of a pale, slender, dark-haired woman dressed in an elegantly tailored tweed suit and pearls. Not a cousin by blood but a cousin by marriage, perhaps?

With the tip of a finger, Heidi traced the

180

outline of the woman's face. This might be her cousin Rosa. The photograph trembled in her hand as a familiar ache of longing and sadness for her own lost family flooded through her.

'They did send a splendid wreath,' Mr. Weaver had told her, his mouth tight with disapproval, 'but when they made no effort to get in touch, your maternal grandmother concluded that they had no interest in you and never wrote to them again. She decided to say nothing to you to save you disappointment.'

Heidi could understand her grandmother Christine's reaction. Over the last few weeks she had been disappointed, sad and angry. She had come to this villa in Bologna partly as an act of defiance, to see and then to put her father's family finally behind her. Now that she was so close to their home, it was turning out to be not as easy as she'd imagined.

A sly gust of wind whipped the paper from her other hand and sent it tumbling through the slats of the iron gate and along the driveway.

'No!' Heidi started after the whirling, precious scrap, opening and slipping through the gates before she had even considered what she was doing. 'I'm not losing you, too!' Her reaching fingers closed around her father's letter.

'May I help you?' asked a male voice in English, a few meters off to Heidi's right.

'No, I'm fine, thanks,' said Heidi, rising to face whoever was emerging from the shadows of the pine trees. 'Just a piece of paper. I'm sorry to be a nuisance. I'm going now.'

Her voice trailed away as the man stepped onto the drive. He was smiling and, to her relief, not in the least annoyed at her possible trespass. 'That's quite all right. You don't have to hurry off,' he was saying. 'Are you lost? Would you like directions? Would you like me to call you a taxi?'

He walked past her, his long legs rapid over the flagstones, and opened the gate again to retrieve Heidi's forgotten shoulder-bag. 'I believe this is yours also?' he said, holding out the blue bag with another smile.

'Thank you.' Hoping she wasn't staring, Heidi took the bag from him. It was cool standing under the shade of the pine trees, but her face and the back of her neck felt hot. Whoever this man was, he seemed to have no idea of his initial impact on her and for that, she was grateful.

He was handsome in a lean, intelligent, patrician way, and very polite, but clever and charming men were not unknown to her. Perhaps it was the strange and immediate sense she had that he might be important to her, and that there was far more about him

182

than his blond good looks. He was older than her, somewhere in his early thirties, with long, narrow features and eyebrows darker than his wavy, straw-colored hair. Behind steel designer spectacles, a pair of bright brown eyes considered her amiably and frankly enough, though with a certain reserve. Aristocratic detachment? she thought, torn between amusement and exasperation. He was dressed in an old but neat pair of jeans and a navy shirt that set off his tan and carried several cut roses and a pruner. She did not think that he was the gardener.

'Are you lost?' He repeated his earlier question.

'I'm fine, thank you,' Heidi responded crisply. He was still looking at her in that considering way, as if wondering if they had met before. To her irritation she found herself stiffening, her head and shoulders very straight. She was determined not to check on her own appearance, not to fiddle with her long straight hair or her softly styled black silk trousers and loose fitting shell pink top. He made her feel like a nervous job applicant.

Taller than Heidi by almost a foot, he took a step towards her and Heidi's grip tightened on her bag.

'You're on holiday?' he asked. 'Is this your first trip to Bologna?'

'My first trip to Italy,' Heidi answered. 'I

183

like its history and culture. And the food – I love the food,' she went on, smiling herself as his brown eyes gleamed behind their spectacles. When he smiled, this man was easy to talk to. Could he be a second cousin? He was young. It wasn't his fault that Federico or Rosa hadn't tried to contact her. If she made herself known to him now, would he approve of her? Why did she want him to approve of her? Why was she glad they were not closely related?

Irritated by this defensive thought, Heidi sharpened her conversation a little. 'Why did you assume I'm English?'

She half-expected him to shrug, or make a joke about her pale skin, but he answered, 'You look English. Lively and shy together, and perhaps thirsty.' Heidi was still unsure whether to be pleased or aggrieved at his comment. His next statement surprised her still more. 'There is a café and *gelateria* a quarter-kilometer from here up the hill.' He pointed out into the sunny street. 'Would you accompany me there and join me in a drink and an ice cream? Our Italian ice cream is famous.'

'Thank you, I will,' Heidi replied. So much for aristocratic detachment! This man's initial reserve seemed to be disappearing fast.

'Good! I'll slip these flowers into the house and fetch my jacket.'

Heidi nodded and prepared to leave the

villa, telling herself that this innocent invitation would give her a breathing space. She would write to the family first, take care of her hotel, and not burst in on them unannounced. Her family had made no effort to get in touch after her father's death. They still might not wish to see her. However painful, she must respect that.

'I'm Heidi.' She extended her right hand, only then realizing that she was still holding the color photograph of her father.

'Stefano.' Long, sinewy fingers brushed against hers and were then abruptly withdrawn. Stefano's dancing eyes were suddenly still.

'What is...?' He sounded bewildered, strands of his blond hair blowing into his eyes and against his spectacles as he stared at the picture she was clutching.

Heidi had never felt more appalled and ashamed. She had done this so badly, so clumsily. 'I'm sorry, I was going to explain.'

Stefano's lean mouth soundlessly formed the word 'Who?' as he raised his head to Heidi's crimsoning face. 'Who are you? What is this? Are you a journalist?'

'No! I'm not here to pry.' Heidi held her ground as he came even closer. 'Can we go to the café you mentioned? I think it will be easier – for both of us – if I tell you as we're walking.'

Becoming more withdrawn again with

every second that passed, Stefano shook his head. 'We talk here,' he said curtly, and placed his cut roses and pruner at the base of one of the pine trees. 'I'm waiting.'

Who was he to order her when this family had never acknowledged her existence? Bitterness surged up in Heidi, and she raised her head to glare at Stefano's annoyingly patrician face. 'Don't you dare presume to judge me.' Hearing footsteps approaching along the flagged driveway closer to the house, the part hidden by the trees, she broke off.

'Stefano, is that you?' called a woman in Italian. 'Have you the roses you said you'd gather for me?'

It was Rosa. Heidi recognized her by her pale skin and straight brown hair, cut in a bob, a style that showed off her pretty, even features. She was as slender as she had been in the photo taken years ago with her brother-in-law and wore a tweed skirt, cashmere jumper and pearls.

As she walked towards them, her low heels drumming on the flagstones, Stefano lowered his blond head and said urgently to Heidi, 'Put that photograph away. Whoever you are, you will not upset her, understand?' Straightening, he went on in a falsely bright voice in Italian, 'Just bringing your flowers, Mamma. This young English tourist stopped to ask for directions.'

Heidi, who could understand Italian

better than she could speak it, was irritated at Stefano's deception but not about to dispute his version of events until he turned to her again and demanded in English, 'How long are you staying in Bologna? Two days, three?'

'I'm on holiday for five weeks,' Heidi said flatly, her blue-green eyes flashing as she saw through his crude hint to leave the city quickly.

'Five weeks? A young woman alone?'

'Who says I'm alone?' Stung, Heidi would have added more, but Rosa, who had just joined them, took in an audible breath beside her.

'Can it be? After all these years of waiting?' Rosa whispered in Italian, her hand groping for and finding Stefano's shielding arm. 'Stefano—' Her fingers plucked at his wrist. 'She wears grandmother's earrings!'

She turned paler still as Heidi stared at her in astonishment. Heidi knew that she looked nothing like her father, Ruggiero, but the news that her favorite pearl drop earrings were family heirlooms was a surprise.

'I didn't know,' she stammered in faltering Italian. 'I'd never have worn them today, given you such a shock...'

Her cousin Rosa – surely it could be no other – waved aside her apologies. She was recovering color in her thin, elegant features and now she stood away from the hovering

Stefano, her eyes taking in Heidi from head to foot.

'You're small and dark, like grandfather,' she announced in English. 'You have his eyes.' She shook her head. 'I can hardly believe it. Federico will be so pleased. You will stay a while? You will have dinner with us and meet the rest of the family? We have so much to talk about, so many changes–'

'Mamma, you must not over-tire or over-excite yourself,' Stefano broke in. Bending to retrieve the pale pink roses at the base of the nearby pine, he handed one to Rosa, his eyes softening as she took it, although his narrow, aristocratic-looking face remained expressionless and aloof.

His eyes narrowed as he turned to Heidi. 'Why did you not say at once who you were?'

Because I hadn't yet made up my mind whether I want to know this family, Heidi almost snapped back, but conscious of Rosa standing next to her, her slender, delicate frame as taut as a harp string, she answered mildly, 'I thought that a bald announcement might be tactless. I know that my father, Ruggiero, was away from Italy and this city for many years.'

A sigh escaped Rosa's lips, but she said nothing. Stefano threw Heidi another glowering look, removing his spectacles and vigorously polishing the lenses as he did so. 'You'd better come inside,' he told her grudgingly, hiding his expressive eyes behind their steel frames as he, Rosa and Heidi began to walk along the driveway towards the family villa.

Chapter 2

'Do you like this?' Rosa asked Heidi anxiously as the housekeeper-cook placed a plate of zuccotto in front of her. Whenever the courses changed, Rosa had asked her the same question throughout the long dinner. Heidi smiled as she had done before, thanking the departing housekeeper and saying to her cousin, 'Yes, indeed, very much.'

Conscious of Stefano watching her across the circular table, she waited until the other family members had picked up their silver spoons before doing the same. Every dish she had been given was delicious, but she found it hard to swallow and harder to relax. She felt on view and on trial, and she had so many questions for this family. Why had they never tried to contact her?

Nervous and a little resentful, Heidi covered her confusion by taking a sip of wine, glancing under lowered eyelids around the tiled, high-roofed dining room. With its softly gleaming terracotta walls and antique wall lights, its tastefully laid circular table loaded with fine china and Venetian glass on a beautiful, white cut-work tablecloth – Rosa's own work – the dining room was like the rest of the villa Rosa and Stefano had shown her – rich and well-bred.

Very much like the room's occupants, Heidi thought, glancing at the seated figures round the table. She had been introduced and knew their names now; their characters remained elusive.

She smiled at Rosa, sitting beside her, who wasn't eating her zuccotto either. Rosa was nervously plucking at her napkin with one hand and using her other hand to fan herself ineffectually. Studying the older woman's flushed complexion, tired eyes and drooping posture, Heidi was reminded of two of her regular clients and wondered if Rosa was affected in the same way. At around her mid-fifties, her cousin was old enough to be going through the menopause and her health might be suffering.

I can help you, Heidi thought, giving Rosa an encouraging nod before passing onto the family member sitting beside her – not the aloof Stefano, but an older man, small and stocky with curly gray hair, a pink rose buttonhole in his dark suit and a tie that was slightly askew round his neck. This was Federico, her father's older cousin.

He raised his glass to her. 'This wine is the finest moscato, opened specially to celebrate your homecoming!' he said in his gruff Bolognese Italian that reminded Heidi sharply of her father Ruggiero.

Federico, with his rolling sailor's walk and cheerful manner, had been a surprise. She kept puzzling through the meal how it was that he and her father had quarrelled so badly, although it was plain that Federico had a temper. When Rosa dropped in quietly, 'English, Federico,' her husband stiffened, one hand curling threateningly around the slender stem of a wine glass.

As there had been throughout this careful dinner, an awkward silence fell, this one broken by a new and not altogether sincere voice.

'Oh, I think our country girl understands us, Mamma,' observed the auburn-haired young woman beside Federico, in perfect English. 'Whatever you and Stefano have told her, I think she appreciates who we are.'

As she spoke, Artemisia touched the diamond choker around her neck, smiling at Heidi while trying to catch Stefano's eye across the table.

Heidi refused to be intimidated by her opulent good looks or her expensive designer gown or jewels. 'Yes, I do, Artemisia,' she replied swiftly in her rarely-used Italian.

Artemisia laughed, trying and failing again to catch Stefano's attention. Finishing his zuccotto, Stefano, who had been mostly silent, asked in English, 'Do you still keep the farm?'

'No, that's gone to another relative who

has a real feel for the land.' Heidi was surprised that Stefano knew about her maternal grandparents. He must have asked Federico or Rosa about her. 'Farming has to be a vocation in Britain. Although I loved the life, I have my own vocation,' she went on, adding before Stefano could interrogate her about that, 'as an aromatherapist.'

'Massaging men with oils?' Stefano asked with raised eyebrows. Beside Federico, Artemisia sat up, smoothing the flowing sleeves of the black and purple gown into a more elegant line and looking as if someone had dropped a shower of gold into her lap.

'Caring for men and women with chronic conditions such as arthritis, depression, eczema, migraine, stress, even bereavement,' Heidi countered. She had not expected such a crude misconception from Stefano, she'd thought him more intelligent. 'My clients are patients who have drawn as much as they can from conventional medicine. I can help them, too.'

Stefano gave a brief nod. 'My mistake.' His tanned, lean face remained impassive, and he seemed to be still staring down his long aristocratic nose at her, but his eyes registered apology and, to Heidi's surprise, a certain shame.

Artemisia knew no such self-consciousness or restraint. 'What a pity Marco isn't here!' she crowed, her perfectly made-up face glowing with malice. She helped herself to the last of the moscato. 'He adores anything alternative, especially when it involves a woman's touch.'

'Touch is important,' Heidi said steadily, 'and sensitivity.' To her inward triumph, she saw the woman's sultry black eyes flicker and knew that Artemisia had understood her full meaning. As had Stefano, who raised his eyebrows again.

'How long does it take to become an aromatherapist?' he asked.

'I'd say I'm still learning,' Heidi answered, glancing at her untouched plate of zuccotto. 'I suppose it's the same with your business. I understand you have a bakery and bread shop in Bologna. I looked for it today.'

'Soleari's isn't a just a bakery. It's not a "bread shop", as you put it,' snapped Artemisia, her pretty mouth turning down at the corners. 'That's like calling a painting by Botticelli a daub.'

'No, we are artists in bread.' Federico wagged a playful finger at Heidi for her apparent blunder. 'The creation of the staff of life, of beautiful bread and pasta, that's our passion. Stefano will tell you it's a serious matter.'

'Touch and sensitivity are important to us, too,' Stefano said with surprising lightness, a smile hovering in his brown eyes. 'But you're right about us always learning.'

'Not everyone can learn,' said Artemisia, giving Heidi a spiteful glare.

'I'd like to see Soleari's sometime,' said Heidi, wondering what to call the business, if not a bread shop. A confectioners?

'It will be my pleasure to be your guide there,' said Stefano, turning so swiftly in his seat to face his father that Heidi wasn't certain if he was mocking her or being sincere.

'Where is Marco?' he asked, in a harsher voice. 'He was supposed to be here tonight so that we could discuss the latest packaging designs.'

Marco, the younger brother, Heidi reminded herself, glancing at a gap in the table settings where Marco would have been sitting, had he been present.

'Relax, big brother, Marco will have it under control,' Artemisia said, checking her reflection in the back of a spoon. 'You know he's a superb designer. Wonderful eye and taste.'

Stefano became if possible even more still than he'd been for most of the meal. 'Where is he?' he repeated. 'Living up to his playboy image in Milan?'

With a scrape of her chair on the floor tiles, Rosa stood up abruptly. 'We'll take coffee in the sitting room,' she announced, nervously wringing her napkin between her hands. 'Heidi, if you've finished your dessert, would you like me to show you to your room?'

'What?' said Heidi and Stefano together, Heidi further distracted by Artemisia's throaty chuckle.

Rosa seemed to shrivel on the spot, but Federico looked up from the dining table's central arrangement of roses and said with blithe unconcern, 'I phoned your hotel and cancelled your room. They know me there, so it was no problem and no charge. Our gardener's gone to fetch your bags.' Federico bowed his curly head to inhale the scent of his rose buttonhole. 'You're staying with us, Heidi, your family, as is only right.'

This was too much. Resentment at the family's arrogance boiled in Heidi. 'You presume to know my plans, Mr. Soleari,' she said, leaving her zuccotto untouched and also rising to her feet. 'But that is not convenient.'

'Doesn't she look just like Ruggiero when she's annoyed?' Federico chuckled, appealing to the stricken Rosa.

'I think, Father, that Heidi is surprised, and with good reason.' Stefano walked around the table and drew back Heidi's chair. 'Please allow me to escort you to your hotel,' he said. 'I can help sort out this misunderstanding.'

'I don't need your help, thank you,' said Heidi.

'Please–'

'But she's family!' Federico broke into whatever Stefano was going to say, flinging

196

his arms wide.

'Then why have I never heard from you before?' Heidi demanded. She was going to walk out of this house in a few moments, and in her present mood of angry disappointment, she felt she had nothing to lose. 'My *English* grandmother wrote to you, and you didn't even reply. When my father died, none of you came to pay your respects.'

'There were reasons for that.' Suddenly Federico was no longer smiling. His shoulders slumped, and he looked much older. His reaching hand found one of his wife's, while Stefano stared at his parents as if seeing them for the first time and Artemisia leaned back in her chair with apparent casualness.

'It was my fault,' said Rosa, speaking to Heidi but with her eyes fixed on the cut-work tablecloth. 'I was ill for all of that year when we heard of Ruggiero's death.' She took a deep breath. 'I was in hospital being treated for a badly broken leg when we received your grandmother's letter. I'd fallen off a chair while dusting one of these wall lights. I was too ill and in too much pain to come, and Federico didn't want to leave me. But we did write back!'

Heidi shook her head. 'Grandmother told me she'd never had an answer.'

'We wrote,' said Federico bluntly. 'I wrote. When I learned about you, I wrote at once.

I could not believe Ruggerio would not tell me this.'

'Why should he?' Heidi answered, flaring up again. 'You made no secret of disapproving of my mother, of his choice.'

'We thought you and your family wanted nothing to do with us,' Rosa whimpered. 'Ruggiero had been so implacable before, so stubborn. Whenever Federico tried to phone him – and he did several times over several years – your father or grandmother always put the phone down on him.'

This was news to Heidi, but she understood *Papa's* reason. 'My father wanted an apology. My grandmother would, too. It was her daughter you disliked.'

'Not disliked,' Rosa pleaded.

Federico went red in the face. 'A man never says sorry!'

Heidi folded her arms and looked Federico in the eye. 'Then he should.'

A brief silence fell.

'I was bull-headed,' Federico admitted bleakly. 'I should have told him that we didn't care who he married, so long as he was happy, but by then neither one of us would willingly speak to the other.'

'Such a waste!' Pale again, Rosa sank back into her chair, raising despairing eyes to each of her family in turn while Federico patted her hand.

Fingers pressed lightly against her shoulder made Heidi start. She turned and found herself staring at Stefano's chest, raised her head and heard him say softly, 'I can still drive you to your hotel, if you wish. This must have been a terrific shock for you.'

'Rosa,' Heidi murmured, feeling dazed by the swiftness of these revelations. Two cousins' stubborn quarrel and a simple mis-directed letter had led to years of misunder-standings. It was both terrible and absurd.

'My sister will look after our parents,' said Stefano, still in that gentle voice. 'Let me see you safely back. You've gone whiter than our best flour.'

'I'd like to stay,' Heidi heard herself say. 'That is, if I'm still welcome.'

With a cry, Rosa broke free of her chair and cast herself at Heidi, who swiftly gathered the taller, sobbing figure into her arms.

'I'd love to stay,' she amended, feeling the prick of tears in her own eyes. 'I'd love to.'

Chapter 3

Stefano took another sip of his strong, bitter coffee and leaned against the jamb of the open kitchen door, staring out over the city rooftops. Closer in the garden were early foraging birds, and from farther off, the distant sound of a dust cart finishing off a night-time collection. The morning dew was burned off, but he had seen it settle, having been up through most of the night, supervising the first baking at the shop.

He stretched and rolled his shoulders. Over the years as a baker, he'd discovered he needed little sleep. He loved these post-dawn hours, when the rest of the family was asleep and the housekeeper-cook had not yet appeared. This was his thinking time, his time, when the villa was quiet, to prepare the family's own bread.

Stefano turned back from the open door and strode across the tiled floor to the large oak kitchen table. Making bread at home was always a pleasure, when he would try to devise new breads or pastas. This morning however, he was not himself. He was on edge, nervous about his proposed changes to the shop-come-bakery that he felt were necessary but which Artemisia and Marco opposed. And when was the last time either of them were up before dawn to fire up the bread-ovens? he thought, with a spurt of mingled amusement and resentment. They wanted the kudos of the business and the money rising from it, but neither wanted the work. That didn't matter to Stefano, but the way that his sister and brother voted at the twice-yearly family board meetings was vital. There would be another meeting at the end of this month, when difficult decisions would have to be made. Soleari's couldn't go on as it was.

Conscious of a lurking tension headache, Stefano had chosen to make a traditional bread that morning, the regional specialty of golden rolls made of *pasta dura* – literally 'tough dough' – that produced a dense, wheaty bread. Made with lard and olive oil, it was an extremely firm dough to work. He'd used his hands and a rolling pin to bind the stiff dough together, and now after rising, it was ready for his next attack. He tipped the dough onto the floured oak boards and began the next stage, trying to release his tensions through the highly physical, satisfying act of kneading.

Stefano frowned as his palms and fingers pounded and pinched. No doubt their newest family member would be able to soothe his headache away with some fragrant oil, but

Heidi seemed intent on avoiding him.

Or was he being unfair? In the three days that Heidi had stayed with the family, she had put herself at Rosa's and Federico's disposal. She had been shown round the villa and gardens by Rosa, been told dozens of family anecdotes by Federico, and pored over old photograph albums with both. She seemed eager to know about her family and keen to be pleased by them, so why was he now wary of her? Meeting her outside the garden gate, before he'd known who she was, he'd been tremendously attracted to her. She'd seemed to like him well enough, then.

'So why doesn't she seek me out?' Stefano muttered, deftly dividing the kneaded dough. 'We are not too closely related: we could have a relationship, so why not?' *She could ask the same of you,* an unwelcome inner voice reminded him. He was thirty-two, altogether too old to be afflicted by shyness. 'She's so self-contained,' he murmured. He was impressed, too, by her success in her chosen profession and touched by her losses. Both her parents had died before her tenth birthday, and her maternal grandparents had died when she was nineteen. Heidi was alone in the world, as he had once been, before he was adopted. He understood what that felt like. But what would she think of him, once she knew he was adopted? Would

202

she be wary of him, a man with no kin of his own to acknowledge him?

Heidi. Stefano found himself smiling as he pictured her, small and slim, with black hair spilling down her back and understanding blue-green eyes. She had a tiny gap between her front teeth that she was self-conscious about. She laughed often, as in spite of herself, but when she smiled, she rarely showed her teeth. He found that endearing. He wanted to know her better, an interest he'd rarely felt since the tragic death of his fiancée, Giulietta; killed by a hit-and-run motorcyclist five years ago, when she was just twenty-one.

Had Heidi anyone special waiting for her at home? At the thought, Stefano's fingers were stilled. He hoped she was free. He hoped that whenever Marco returned from wherever and whatever he was doing, that Heidi would be immune to his younger brother's easy charm and good looks. And of course he would need to tell her of his adoption.

Scowling, Stefano laid the last of the rolls onto the baking sheet and placed the rolls in a cool oven for a few minutes. As he took them out again and set them under a new cloth for their second rise, he had a sense of someone watching and turned towards the door leading to the main house.

Heidi came into the kitchen. 'You're an early riser, too. I was hoping you were. I've an idea I'd like to run past you.'

'Would you like some coffee?' Trying to hide his surprise, Stefano nodded to the espresso machine close to the sink. 'Or tea?'

'Tea, please,' Heidi answered, wondering if she should make it but unsure whether Stefano would consider that an impertinence. She had been watching him from the doorway, finding herself almost mesmerized by his clean, long-fingered nimble hands as they effortlessly shaped and molded the unyielding bread dough. For an instant she imagined the touch of those hands and felt herself blushing.

'Your room is comfortable?' Stefano asked, producing a small china teapot from one of the kitchen cupboards and setting the kettle to boil.

'Yes, thank you.' The villa, with its many beautifully tiled and wood paneled rooms and elegant furnishings, was far more exotic than her modest hotel room would have been. As she thought of that, Heidi decided to admit something else, which for some reason had been troubling her.

'I didn't plan to come to Italy alone, you know,' she said quickly, 'but Monica – she's my best friend who was going to come with me – got glandular fever less than a week before we were due to fly out and was far too poorly to travel. I'd arranged for my

regular clients to be seen by another aromatherapist and it wouldn't have been fair on
her or my patients if I'd suddenly cancelled.
This is the first holiday I've had in five
years.'

'You were coming with a girlfriend?'

'Yes.' Meeting his eyes, Heidi wondered if
he still disapproved, but then he smiled,
holding aloft a tray of tea.

'Where would you like to drink this?' he
asked.

They sat at the kitchen table, close to the
rising bread rolls, Heidi with a mug of tea
and Stefano with another coffee. He'd told
her how he'd always been fascinated by the
magic of bread, the way it changed, its wonderful smell, texture and taste. Heidi was
glad of this more approachable Stefano, and
she recalled too how considerate he'd been
on the night Federico had cancelled her
hotel room, offering to drive her back and to
help her.

'What is it you want to run by me?'

Stefano's question interrupted her reverie
and returned Heidi to another of her more
pressing concerns. 'That seems to be a
phrase I've heard a lot over these past few
days: "Ask Stefano",' she said, making a
small joke. 'So I'm asking. I think your
mother would benefit from a course of
aromatherapy, and I'd be very happy to treat
her, free of charge, while I'm here. I always

carry a small batch of oils with me, for my own use. They really do work, you know. So how would you feel about that?'

Stefano raised thick blond eyebrows. 'You think I'd be resistant to the idea?'

'Well, maybe,' Heidi said. 'But I think I can help your mother, and that's all that matters, isn't it?'

She saw his eyes soften behind his forbidding steel spectacle frames, but his answer was interrupted.

'If you're offering free trials, cousin, why not attend my fashion party this morning in our music room? The housekeeper and her husband are going to move the piano out of the way and bring in chairs – just a few. This is a select party.' Artemisia, in a black silk kimono, her auburn hair artfully tousled, paused in the doorway before continuing into the kitchen. 'Won't those rolls be ready to go in?' she teased, ignoring Stefano's taut response of 'Don't tell me how to bake,' as she homed in on the espresso machine.

'You could do a talk and demonstration in the use of essential oils for us,' Artemisia went on, helping herself to a demitasse of coffee. 'Mother will be there, hovering ineffectually in the background as always.'

'Artemisia, that's uncalled for and unfair.'

The redhead shrugged off her brother's remark, leaning against the sink as she studied Heidi with glinting malicious eyes.

'It will bring the gathering to a nice little close. The Contessa is always appreciative of light relief.'

Any more put-downs you can work in, Artemisia? thought Heidi, amused. 'I'll be very happy to give a demonstration.'

'I won't expect you to buy anything,' Artemisia drawled. 'The designs are very expensive, exclusive.'

'That's all you care about, isn't it?' Stefano broke in, his lean, handsome face rigid in frozen distaste. 'Exclusivity. Selectivity.'

With a casual, unconscious skill, he opened the wood-burning oven, checked the heat with his hand and placed the bread inside, his movements stiff but still agile and strangely graceful to Heidi.

'Excuse me.' He addressed her, his eyes meeting hers for a moment before he strode through the open kitchen door into the terraced garden.

'He'll be back to fuss over the bread.' Artemisia yawned, showing even teeth. 'I'd lend you a dress to wear this morning, but you're so skinny I don't have anything that would fit. Shall I translate at your *demonstration* for you?'

'No thanks.' Heidi shook her head, only too well aware of how her reluctant relative might twist her words. 'I'm sure the Contessa and your other guests will understand me perfectly. After all, English is the international language.'

Rising from the table, she too left the room, returning to the kitchen only when Rosa called her down from her bedroom to say that breakfast was ready and would she like tea or coffee with her fresh morning rolls?

Afterwards, Heidi felt that her talk to the Contessa and the other society ladies after their fashion show had gone well. She was used to explaining and demonstrating the benefits of aromatherapy, with its healing essential oils – the beautifully perfumed and powerful essence of plants and flowers such as rose and lavender, and resins such as frankincense – obtained by steam distillation. Even Artemisia's slightly off-color asides about the uses of oils in 'sensual' massage with a male partner did not put her off.

Halfway through her talk, the door to the music room opened and Stefano slipped inside to stand beside the harp at the back of the room. At the sight of him, Heidi felt her spirits unaccountably lifting, especially when she told her final story about lavender oil.

'This oil is a staple for aromatherapists,' she explained, passing round a small perfume stick of the oil for the listening women to inhale. 'It once saved Mr. Gattefossé, the French chemist who gave us the word aromatherapy, from the effects of a really bad burn. There was an accident in his lab where he burned his hand. He plunged his hand into the nearest liquid that happened to be a vat of lavender oil and discovered that the pain stopped immediately. Further experiments with lavender and other essential oils proved to Mr. Gattefossé that they accelerated healing. This is true not only of burns but of many other conditions.'

From the corner of her eye, Heidi saw Stefano straighten and unfold his arms and knew that she had convinced him. A glance at Rosa, sitting in the shadow of a huge arrangement of white roses, showed her looking interested and also – Heidi was sure of this – cautiously optimistic.

Feeling progress had been made, Heidi decided to leave it another day before she tentatively broached the possibility of treating Rosa. As she packed away her things, several of the fashion-party guests, including the Contessa, asked if she was coming with them to lunch at Notai, one of Bologna's more exclusive restaurants with its famous Art Nouveau decor. Heidi politely put them off, sure that Artemisia would not welcome her. As her talk had progressed, Artemisia, sitting on the front row, looked increasingly sulky.

Soon only she and Stefano were left in the room, Stefano moved the grand piano back to its place with an ease that told Heidi a great deal about his lean, rangy strength.

'That was fascinating,' he said, lifting the piano lid and trying a soft top A with his thumb. 'Thank you. I think Mamma especially really enjoyed it. Have you any plans for the rest of today? Lunch, for instance?'

'None that I know of,' Heidi said, her heart quickening as Stefano left the piano and walked towards her. His face was grave, but his eyes were warm.

'Would you have lunch with me? At Soleari's?' He lowered his blond head to her. 'I'd like to fulfil my earlier promise and show you 'round. You did say you loved food.'

'I do, especially bread,' Heidi admitted, glancing down at herself as Stefano's expression became quizzical. 'I know it doesn't show. I'm as skinny as a pin.' Her grandfather's nickname for her had been Stringbean.

'I'd say slender.'

'Whatever.' Heidi smiled up at him, happy that he'd remembered his promise. Intrigued and excited, she nodded at her small carrying case of oils. 'I'll put this away and fetch my bag.'

Chapter 4

Outside the villa, Stefano asked, 'Do we walk or drive?'

'Walk for me, please.'

'That's not like my sister or mother,' her companion grunted, opening the iron gate for her.

Heidi took advantage of the mention of Rosa. 'Stefano, I don't know how to put this without seeming to be intrusive, but I'm going to say it anyway. Rosa appears anxious, too anxious. You're very protective of her, and that's good, but does she need other help?'

'Medical help, do you mean?' Stefano picked up as Heidi faltered. 'I know she's seen our family doctor. When I asked her about it she told me, "Only women's troubles," but I think there's more. I know she's worried about the business. I think there's something about my father, too. I'm not sure what.'

They were out in the street by now, walking down the hill towards the city. Students milled round them, carrying armloads of books, and from across the road a middle-aged woman carrying a basket loaded with glossy purple aubergines called out a greeting. Stefano waved, saying softly to Heidi, 'One of Soleari's regulars. She'll be asking me about you tomorrow in the shop.'

Heidi smiled at the thought, then nervously checked the position of her shoulderbag as she wondered how Stefano would answer that question. 'Is your father not well?' she asked, returning to their earlier discussion.

'No, no, he's as strong as a horse. He's virtually retired and delighted to be so.'

'Glad to be out of the kitchen?'

'Yes, possibly.' Stefano nodded at another passing customer. 'With any other Italian man I might have thought "other woman," but I can't see that with my father. He's devoted to my mother. He even renamed the villa after her.'

I wonder if Rosa sees it that way. Heidi thought, saying aloud, 'Well, whatever's troubling your mother, I'll do my best to help if she's agreeable to my treating her. And if she chooses to tell me anything during her aromatherapy sessions, I promise you now that it won't go further. Our talks will be confidential. That's part of the therapist's professional code of conduct.'

'Like the confessional?' Stefano's somber face broke into a smile. 'Perhaps that's just what Mamma needs. She was very intrigued by your talk, I could tell.'

'That's good,' Heidi agreed, her spirits

lifting further as she mentally began to match possible treatments and oils to Rosa.

Meanwhile she and Stefano had begun threading their way through a jumble of medieval and Renaissance streets towards the heart of Bologna, the city of arcades and fresh pasta shops selling world-famous tortellini, the site of the oldest university in western Europe and still a place of culture and politics. Heidi saw several left-wing political slogans daubed on walls between the bookshops and posters announcing the forthcoming opera season. She wondered what it must be like to be brought up in such a bustling, thriving place and envied Stefano, who kept glancing her way, checking that she was not tiring, that there were no mopeds roaring up behind them through the arcades. Conscious of her shoe heels on the stone flags, she turned with him into one of the many squares in the city, close to the food market and the two massive, steepling military towers that loomed over the old center of Bologna, relics of the city's more violent past.

She and Stefano crossed the square, passing some workmen who were snatching a break from their drilling, smoking cigarettes and discussing something with animated hand gestures. Heidi found she could understand their rasping speech. 'So who *are* better at football – Italians or Brazilians?' one was saying, punching the air with a fist for emphasis.

'Football's close to a religion here,' said Stefano with a small grin. 'Not far now,' he added, his face taking on a look which Heidi could only describe as excited anticipation. She found his enthusiasm endearing. She was equally enthusiastic about aromatherapy.

They rounded a corner into another small square, Stefano's stride lengthening as they closed on an arcade draped in heavy purple awnings that would be drawn down in summer to shade the customers and visitors.

'Hi, Stefano!' called the barber from inside his shop.

'Good day, signore,' said the florist, coming to stand in the doorway as Stefano and Heidi wandered past.

Stefano acknowledged both greetings and waved at one of the waiters hovering under the gaudy umbrellas of the café opposite. 'That's Luigi's. They serve wonderful coffee and they buy a lot of our cakes. Very good customers,' he explained softly to Heidi, now pointing to the gleaming shop front just a few paces ahead of them. A hand-painted sign over the doorway read 'Soleari's' in curving gold script. 'Here we are,' he said, opening the door for her.

'Goodness me!' The exclamation burst from Heidi before she could even think to contain it, not that she wanted to. The large shop window, its frame painted a dark umber, contained a magnificent display, different from anything she had seen in Britain. In undisguised delight, she stared at the beribboned bags of pasta and bread-sticks displayed on brightly painted red, white and green racks. There were cakes on tiers, rich with fruit and dark with spices, and trays of savory vol-au-vents and other delicacies. Beside each kind of fresh pasta was a descriptive tag, written in a copper-plate script. Staring at a packet of tortellini, Heidi translated the Italian in her own head, 'Navels of Venus – for lovers,' – and felt herself blushing. Quickly, she glanced at the rising glass shelves in the middle of the window display, where Soleari's famous breads were laid out to admire: flat loaves, plaits and little rolls made in the traditional Bolognese shapes.

'We call that a *crocetta*,' Stefano explained beside her, pointing to a crusty X shaped cross of bread.

Heidi stared at the various sizes of *crocetta*. 'That one's tiny.' Her fingers briefly touched the window glass as she pointed to the smallest cross.

Stefano grinned. 'That's a *ragnino*, a little spider. How did you get into aromatherapy?' he asked, glancing at her hand.

'I suppose because of my grandfather.'

Heidi reluctantly tore her eyes away from the ribbons of the window display. 'Farming can be a tough life. Granddad suffered almost continually from backache and none of the conventional medical treatments worked for long. I read an article about aromatherapy and its uses in treating that kind of chronic pain and thought it was worth looking into. I started from there, really.'

She stopped, not wanting to admit that she'd been drawn to aromatherapy for other, possibly frivolous reasons. The scents and simple beauty of the oils had attracted her. 'It was very hard work on the farm,' she murmured. 'I'd have liked to make bread, but there was so little time.' The farm had taken all of her grandparents' and, as she grew up, her own energies. The aromatherapy, quite apart from helping her grandfather and later, when she'd begun to form her own client base, bringing in welcome spare money to the farm, had given her a break from a largely utilitarian existence.

Maybe that's why I feel so much at home here, Heidi thought, giving the bright, pretty window display another glance. *On our farm we were largely starved of beauty, because the living was so hard.*

'You're welcome to try your hand at baking while you're here. It would be my pleasure to teach you.' Stefano took her hand in his, the first time he had touched her, and added, in a deliberately lighter tone, 'Shall we go in before the staff and customers crick their necks with curiosity?' He guided her inside.

Even ahead of the wonderful scent of freshly baked bread, the number of customers struck Heidi. There was over a dozen people crowded inside this long, narrow shop, calling out orders to the three employees. At the very back of the shop were two huge brick-built bread ovens. 'The engine room,' Stefano said, pointing to each in turn. 'Cakes in this one, bread in that one.'

Closer to her was a long glassed-in counter, filled with cake racks and bulging with goodies. Near to the door were two small circular tables laden with yet more items for customers to browse and enjoy.

'Wizard bread – one bite and you're enchanted!' proclaimed a sign at one of the tables. Beside it lay Harry Potter phoenix cakes and Harry Potter pasta shaped like tiny broomsticks.

'I thought these might appeal to our younger customers,' Stefano explained, correctly interpreting Heidi's questioning look. 'Marco worked on that display last week.'

With so much to see and so many people, going through Soleari's took several moments. She and Stefano were assailed from every side by customers and staff members, the latter trim in crisp white bakers' uniforms and hats and wide-eyed in blatant curiosity as to who the boss's young companion was. Hearing their chatter and sensing their goodwill, Heidi felt accepted, the more so as Stefano introduced her as, 'My second cousin, Heidi. Ruggiero and Sarah's daughter,' acknowledging her and her mother.

'They're not exactly in awe of you, are they?' Heidi remarked as she and Stefano mounted a well-lit staircase leading to the upper floors. To her surprise, she'd just seen an older female member of staff rumple her companion's blond hair and jab him in the ribs.

'Emilia was merely asking when she should start preparing the ingredients for my wedding cake,' Stefano answered, brown eyes bright with mischief. 'We go through here, that red door.'

Wondering if her face was as vermilion as the paint, Heidi walked across the first floor landing and pushed the door open, entering an airy room with a small cooking range and sink in one corner and a long wooden table stacked with glasses, crockery and cutlery in the other. There was an espresso machine by the door and two scrubbed tables under the window.

'This is our self-service section for the employees,' Stefano explained, coming to stand beside Heidi as she wandered to the window to look out across the square. 'Fresh bread, salads and pasta from what's on offer downstairs. They have their lunches here before we close for the siesta. We're not reopening this evening, so they'll be having a late lunch today. They won't be up here for another hour.'

'I see,' Heidi said, selfishly glad that she and Stefano would have the place to themselves.

'Of course, it's free to them,' Stefano went on, a half-smile lurking about his mouth. 'I find their feedback on the new recipes very instructive. Now what bread and salad would you like? Shall I cook us some fresh pasta?' Quickly, he reeled off several different kinds of bread, pastas, salads and sweets until Heidi threw up her hands in mock horror, calling, 'Enough! Surprise me,' she said.

Chapter 5

Ten days later, at about the same time of day, Heidi was again upstairs in the staff lunch room, sitting at the table under the window and waiting with Alberto, one of Soleari's master bakers, as Stefano prepared their lunch. The grizzled, gray-bearded, stocky Alberto was having tortellini stuffed with Bologna sausage. Heidi was having a 'surprise'. It had become almost a tradition and part of her banter with Stefano. She had come to Soleari's for lunch with him every day and found herself vastly intrigued by the whole business. Unlike her father, Ruggiero, she was eager to learn more. She now knew for instance that Soleari's was a *panetteria,* and that here in Bologna and in contrast to other cities in Italy, businesses like Soleari's, specializing in bread, also sold pasta, the fresh pasta made by hand.

'Stefano tells me you know about scents and have a good nose. Smell that.' Alberto finished pouring her a glass of dark red wine and pushed it across the table to her. 'Smell. Taste. Tell me what you think.'

Heidi slowly swirled the wine in the glass, thinking about Stefano. In the two weeks she had known him she had discovered that under his rather shy reserve was a kind, good man. There was a sort of serious beauty about him, she thought, pretending to study the wine while watching Stefano. In profile, he was like a medieval woodcut, all long, clear lines. He'd broken off from tending his simmering pans to remove his spectacles and peer at the inside of Emilia's watch, which she said was losing time. While Emilia stood close by, her thin-plastic-gloved hands white with icing sugar, Stefano did something to the intricate mechanism with a small screwdriver and then returned the watch to her with a 'There you go,' as he replaced his spectacles.

Yes, I really like Stefano, Heidi thought, pleased to admit this to herself. She liked Rosa, too, and not only because she was now treating her older cousin. Rosa was still too shy for a full body massage with essential oils, but Heidi massaged her hands and feet, and today, after lunch, she would be working on her back for the first time. Rosa was not very talkative, but she had admitted to Heidi that she often felt 'poorly' and, in tones of deep apology, had confessed to a range of debilitating symptoms. After restocking her basic 'travel-kit' of oils in the city with Stefano's occasional help in translation, Heidi was treating Rosa with a mixture of essential oils for depression, lack of energy, palpitations and 'various problems with my monthly cycle', which Heidi had investigated further with several tactful questions. She thought that Rosa was beginning to look less strained and had already decided that she would try to persuade her to see her own doctor again and also to consider contacting a local aromatherapist.

'What do you think?' Alberto barked, breaking into her reverie and returning Heidi to the business of savoring her wine.

'Good balance between fruitiness and woodiness,' Heidi replied, almost automatically, still shy of using the language of wine. In the farm in Yorkshire, they had drunk copious amounts of tea, but no wine. Even one of these tall glasses was sufficient to make her faintly light-headed. Or was that due to the fact that Stefano had just looked up from his deft serving out to give her an encouraging nod?

'Not a very robust fragrance but a faint fizz,' Heidi went on, raising her glass and sipping the wine. 'You can taste the grapes. I like it.'

'Naturally you like it, that's Lambrusco from our region!' said Alberto, trying to scowl but failing. 'The word is bouquet, not fragrance. Ah! Our pasta!'

Stefano placed Heidi's and Alberto's dishes in front of them and came to join them with his own steaming plate of tortellini. 'Be honest in what you think of your surprise,' he told Heidi, raising his glass of Lambrusco to her.

Heidi ate one of the mysterious little parcels from her dish, aware of Stefano's frequent glances at her and of Alberto's vigorous exclamations.

'The finest food in the world!' the master baker was saying. 'Only to be compared with our bread!' He thrust his now empty fork in Heidi's direction. 'She has a good nose, Stefano, and I think she will have the touch. A baker is nothing without the touch, the feel for the dough,' Alberto explained, catching Heidi's puzzled look. 'I think you should tell her, Stefano. You need help from someone in your family.'

Heidi said nothing. She knew from various dark hints from the other staff members and from Stefano that all was not right with Soleari's.

'If Heidi tells me what she thinks of my latest pasta first,' Stefano replied.

'Be serious,' Alberto growled.

'No, it's all right.' Heidi found herself defending Stefano. 'If this is to be a possible new range of pasta for Soleari's then feedback is important.' She tasted again. 'I like the faint aniseed flavor mingled with that creaminess. It's refreshing and mouth-filling.' She nodded. 'It's good.'

'Tortellini with roasted fennel, garlic and

local goat's cheese filling,' Stefano confirmed. 'Glad you like it.'

'Not traditional,' muttered Alberto. He jabbed a thick finger at Stefano. 'Tell her what's happening. There's no one else up here now and I suppose Artemisia and Marco haven't graced us with their presence.'

'Not yet.' Stefano wiped his mouth with his napkin and looked at Heidi again as if sizing her up. 'Do you want to get dragged in?'

'One thing.' Alberto broke in before Heidi could respond. 'Why are you called Heidi? Is that a common English name?'

'No, Swiss. My mother loved the story of the little mountain girl and named me after her.' Heidi turned in her seat to face Stefano. 'I'd like to help, if I can.'

In a low, steady voice Stefano began to explain. 'Soleari's is a family business that has lasted over a hundred years. All members of the family down the paternal line have voting rights. Federico and Rosa are now retired. I look after the baking.'

'The creative side,' dropped in Alberto, finishing off his tortellini.

'Artemisia is in charge of the accounts and our younger brother, Marco, does the packaging and design. He arranges the main window and writes all the labels. Those have proved very popular.'

'Frippery!' Alberto snorted, and he

224

scratched at his gray beard.

Heidi thought of the witty, rather suggestive descriptive tags that she'd read in the window and wondered what she would make of their author when she finally met the elusive Marco.

'Recently, my brother has been very actively courted by the management of a massive international bakery who would like to buy Soleari's out,' Stefano went on. 'They are talking a great deal of money, but it would mean a fundamental change in what Soleari's would produce.'

'Plastic bread merchants! Pah!' said Alberto, slapping a massive palm onto the table.

'They have assured Marco that they would still produce some very exclusive handmade bread, and that has brought Artemisia round to the idea,' Stefano went on.

'Would this hand-made bread be very expensive?' Heidi asked, not in the least surprised when Stefano gave a grim nod. She thought of the other small bread shops and pasta shops that she had seen in Bologna, all proud to display their individually made, regional wares. 'Surely that kind of bland, international bread isn't what people want, is it?'

'No, you're right,' Stefano agreed. 'Marco's plan is against the history and tradition of Soleari's and even against modern trends in

225

the baking trade.'

'People want real bread,' said Alberto.

'Why does Marco want to change?' Heidi asked, eating more fennel and goat's cheese tortellini. She saw Stefano and Alberto exchange a look. 'Sorry, you don't have to tell me.'

'Marco has significant debts. Gambling debts that our parents, especially our mother, know little about,' said Stefano, in a hard, colorless voice. 'If the international bakery bought Soleari's out, then his share of that money would clear all his problems.'

'And he couldn't gradually pay off the debts?' Heidi asked, thinking about the number of times when money had been very tight on her grandparents' farm. 'You couldn't just leave the business as it is? It seems very successful.'

'It is.' Stefano drained off his glass of wine and poured another. Taking a deep breath, he said, 'The second oven has a fault in its stone base that's getting worse. It will soon need repairing, or better, replacing. But that will mean Soleari's closing for a time and a loss in revenues that neither Marco nor Artemisia will agree to. At the next family board meeting, they will propose that we sell the bakery.'

'Surely Federico and Rosa would never agree with that?'

'I don't know,' Stefano admitted. 'Marco

can be very persuasive. Rosa has never felt part of the business – Federico has been very old-fashioned and excluded her from any real decisions – and now he himself doesn't seem particularly interested anymore.' Stefano's thin features seemed to lengthen and grow haggard as he frowned. 'Perhaps Marco and Artemisia know their parents' true minds more clearly than I do.'

Heidi thought this a strange statement, but she was shocked by what Stefano said next.

'You can have voting rights at the next family meeting, if you wish.'

'Me?'

'Through Ruggiero your father. So far as I know you will still have full voting rights.'

'So use them well, little Heidi.' Alberto rose stiffly to his feet and headed for the sink with his plate.

'I'll wash up,' Heidi quickly volunteered, part of her still astonished by what she had just learned. She was alarmed at what was at stake, and just a little chilled. Was this why Stefano seemed interested in her – because of her voting rights?

Soon afterwards, Stefano and Alberto had to go downstairs as Emilia called up a series of questions from a regular customer that only they could answer. Alone in the staff room, Heidi gave herself a talking to as she washed up, recalling the first time Stefano had met her. Then, he'd invited her out before he'd even known who she was.

'Heidi? Are you ready?' Stefano called out from the bottom of the stairs.

'Coming.' Heidi sped off down the steps with a will. She found it hard to think badly of Stefano, and now, when he met her at the base of the staircase and held out his hand to her, she took it at once, glad of the contact.

'Thanks for lunch,' she told him.

'My pleasure,' Stefano said, with a smile. 'Shall we go?'

Arm in arm they walked through Soleari's, Heidi feeling proud of her tall, blond companion. They reached the door at the same time as a small, red-cheeked elderly man, smartly turned out in tweeds, who walked with a stick.

'Good to see you about again, after your operation, Signor Bartoli.' Stefano stood back and opened the door, but the old man made a shooing motion at Heidi with his checked shopping bag.

'Your young lady first, Stefano. I'm surprised at you!' he exclaimed, raising and lowering his walking stick. 'After you, my dear.'

'Thank you.' Heidi went ahead, stopping outside as the glare of the afternoon sun through the arcade struck her eyes. She heard the elderly gentleman's shuffling steps as he limped out of the *panetteria* and turned to guide him off the pavement if he needed it. Over his head, she caught a glimpse of Stefano also leaving the shop and then realized that Signor Bartoli was going the other way, towards a square black shadow that had appeared before Soleari's main window.

Except that it wasn't a shadow, Heidi realized, moving as she understood what she was looking at. 'Signore! Wait! Stefano!' She appealed instinctively to him as her reaching hand closed around the old man's upper arm, pulling Signor Bartoli back from the newly-revealed gaping drop in the pavement.

'I've got you,' she heard Stefano say and sensed rather than saw Stefano's strong, wiry arms enclose around the old man, lifting Signor Bartoli right off his feet as Stefano fought to draw him to safety.

For an instant all three of them hovered on the brink of the drop. Heidi saw the black hole in front of her seem to widen and deepen. She felt as if it was actually sucking her down, her and Signor Bartoli.

'No!' The protest burst from her. She stiffened, bracing her legs, and deliberately stepped backwards, keeping a tight hold of the man's arm. She felt a rush of air, a shift in her weight and then she and Signor Bartoli were standing safely on the pavement, with Stefano gripping them both.

'Are you okay?' she asked, as he asked her the same question.

Stefano nodded, saying, 'Are you?'

'Fine. A little shaken, but fine.' Heidi retrieved Signor Bartoli's walking stick, which had not fallen into the cellar but rolled into the gutter.

'Signore?' Stefano asked.

'Yes, yes! You can let go of me, Stefano. I'm not going to jump into the cellar today.' Signor Bartoli's red cheeks had paled slightly, but otherwise he was unhurt. 'Thank you, my dear,' he said, as Heidi handed him his walking stick, patting her hand.

'I think I will go the other way around the square,' he announced, and with an almost courtly bow to Heidi, he walked off in the opposite direction.

'That was lucky,' Heidi remarked, absently rubbing her smarting arm.

Stefano was closing the trapdoor. He didn't say anything until the wooden door was firmly in place. Then he looked at her. 'Are you sure you're all right?'

'Yes,' Heidi said gently, thinking that he looked strained. When he moved, he flinched, catching his breath and automatically rubbing his side.

'It's nothing,' he said, as Heidi came closer to help. 'I felt a twinge in my side when I caught Signor Bartoli. It'll go off in a minute. Can you wait here? I need to find out which idiot opened the cellar door and left it unattended.'

He was gone before Heidi could respond, disappearing back into Soleari's. She half-expected to hear furious shouting but instead Stefano seemed to be having a quiet word with each member of staff. He joined her a moment later, busily polishing his spectacles with his clean handkerchief.

'None of my people say they opened the cellar trapdoor, and I believe them,' he said starkly.

'But then who would do such a thing?' Heidi asked. 'Signor Bartoli could have had a very nasty fall– '

'–and Soleari's would have been respons-ible,' Stefano finished for her. Visions of law suits and crippling damages flashed in Heidi's mind. Shocked, for an instant she could not speak.

'That's the second time this month,' Stefano went on.

'What do you mean?'

Scowling, Stefano replaced his spectacles. 'Can I explain on the way home? This isn't something I want to talk about in the open square.'

'Of course.' Heidi stifled her questions as she and Stefano began to walk across the square, Stefano wincing for the first few steps until he realized that she was watching him.

'I'd like to take a taxi home,' Heidi said then. 'I'm still a bit shaken up. Look. There's a taxi rank just over there.' To her relief, Stefano did not protest and let her lead the way across the sun-bleached flagstones.

Chapter 6

Later, in the villa garden, after she had given Rosa her latest aromatherapy session, Heidi strolled with Stefano about the terraces and talked. Usually their talks were easy, with neither at a loss for conversation, but today, after the almost fatal 'accident' outside Soleari's, matters were very different. Walking with hunched shoulders and with none of his usual slim grace, Stefano spoke in a low rasping monotone.

He told her of several odd incidents and 'accidents' at Soleari's over the past two months that seemed too small and occasional to be sabotage but were nonetheless disturbing. Like Signor Bartoli, who could have fallen headlong into their cellar through the open trapdoor. Two weeks ago Signora Cardenli's beloved toy poodle, Nix, had been violently ill after eating one of Soleari's vol-au-vents, something the little dog had eaten many times before with no problem. The vet had told an anxious Signora Cardenli that the savory must have been tainted in some way, which an appalled Stefano could not believe. Their hygiene and methods were very strict. Luckily, the signora had accepted his explanation, and there had been no more incidents of that sort, but he was uneasy.

'What do you think it could have been?' Heidi asked at this point.

Stefano shrugged, a rare expressive gesture for him and one which starkly revealed his inner agitation. 'Perhaps the poodle was already sick. Or perhaps someone had spiked the pastry.'

'Who would do that? How?' Even as she spoke, Heidi was remembering how busy the shop was, how many customers there could be milling about both inside and out. Purchases were always elaborately bagged but perhaps someone had bought exactly what the signora had bought, slipped into a side-street, applied a few drops of weed-killer or another irritant and then resealed the bag and somehow swapped it with Signora Cardenli's.

Heidi scowled at the idea. It was too complicated, surely. But otherwise that would mean either that the pastry had been off – something she believed no more than did Stefano – or a member of staff had done it. 'That's terrible,' she murmured.

'There's more,' Stefano said heavily. Timers had been found mysteriously switched on or off and no one knew who had done it. On another occasion, a whole batch of olive focacce had to be thrown away, their crusts burnt and blackened beyond recognition.

'I've talked to Alberto, Emilia, and young Gina,' Stefano went on, naming the three regular members of staff. 'None of them remember seeing anything suspicious during these incidents and I can't believe they would have anything to do with them. Alberto and Emilia have been part of the business for years, and Gina is engaged and talks of nothing but her forthcoming marriage.' A tolerant light hovered in Stefano's warm brown eyes. 'I'd say baking is the last thing on her mind, but she's not careless.'

Heidi agreed. She was sure that none of Soleari's employees would be careless.

'What about–?' she began, and stopped, blushing at the thought of her own tactlessness.

'What about Marco and Artemisia?' Stefano finished for her.

By this time they had reached a terrace with a small fountain that blew a cooling spray over Heidi's scalding cheeks. Careless of the teasing spray, she stopped in front of the fountain, in the shade of a gnarled pine tree, twisted out of shape by the prevailing wind, and raised anxious eyes to her companion. 'I'm sorry. That was insulting and unfair, especially when I'm not even a member of this family.'

A curious look of shame and alarm shadowed briefly across Stefano's face, but it was gone as he took her hand in both of his. 'You are family, Heidi. We all think so. You are family far more – well, than some of us,' he finished obliquely. 'As for Artemisia and Marco, why should they sabotage the bakery? They may differ in their plans for the business, but don't forget they would lose out, too if Soleari's reputation suffered. The big international bakery might even withdraw its offer if these incidents became common knowledge.'

He was standing right in front of her, so close that she could see the definition of his lean, muscular frame through his crisp cotton shirt. 'Yes, I can see that,' Heidi said, exasperated at herself. She would never agree to massage a fully naked man but she dealt with male clients in her aromatherapy practice, treated their hands and feet, their necks and shoulders. Why should she be so flustered by Stefano? 'How's your sprain?' she asked, seizing gratefully on the change of subject.

'Better for this gentle walk,' Stefano said, in a voice of amused indulgence. 'But if you are offering to treat my aching shoulder and back...'

His smile deepened as Heidi was silent, torn between her professional life and this strange new shyness she seemed to have acquired while dealing with him. Perhaps it was because he had opened up to her a little and now, standing by this fountain, he was as close as her own shadow. Closer, because he was lowering that bright blond head and his clever, sensitive hands were encircling her narrow waist...

He kissed her lightly on the mouth and brushed a bead of fountain spray from her cheek. 'I've wanted to do that for a long time,' he said, kissing her again. He smelled of fresh bread and sun and his hands on her back held her tenderly, as if she was made of spun sugar.

'Don't you know how very pretty you are?' he said softly, laughing as she stiffened at the compliment. 'You are, you know. Like the little bride doll on top of a wedding cake.' Stefano blushed, clearly embarrassed at hearing himself say anything, so absurdly sentimental. 'Thank you for your help,' he said gruffly, taking a step back and releasing her.

It was only a thank you kiss, Heidi told herself. She'd known Stefano for only two weeks. *What does that matter?* an inner voice whispered, but Heidi ignored the voice and tried to control her rapidly beating heart, taking several slow deep breaths. 'Shall we continue our walk?' she said, grateful that her question was not a squeak.

Stefano stood back and pointed down the gravelled path. 'There you go.'

Moving first, Heidi set off along the path, scarcely conscious of the wafting spray from the fountain or the opulent red peonies and roses lining the terrace walkway. Stefano had kissed her. She touched her lips with her hand, feeling truly sensual for the first time in her life, registering that she was wearing a blue cotton button-through sundress and sandals, items that had just become her favorite outfit.

'Hey, wait!' Stefano overtook her in a few strides. 'It's usually you trotting after me,' he teased.

'Pardon me, but I don't trot.' Feeling more composed, Heidi took Stefano's hand in hers. 'Got you!' she teased in return. 'Where to now?'

Stefano's smile deepened. They could get lost in the garden for hours so far as he was concerned. 'You decide,' he answered, part of him astonished at how easily his serious concerns over Soleari's and his persistent, nagging doubts at his own place within the family seemed to have gone on holiday for the afternoon, ever since he'd kissed Heidi.

'This way.' Heidi pointed to a small grassy path that led farther down the garden, through a rockery and past several statues. As she moved, her long hair shimmered on her shoulders like black silk. I wonder what it feels like? Stefano thought, longing to touch it.

'Have you any ideas who might be behind

these incidents at Soleari's?' she asked, her question brutally reminding Stefano of his responsibilities.

He sighed and admitted the truth, 'I don't know. I was hoping–'

But the rest of his thought was interrupted by a new, cheery voice calling in charmingly Italian-accented English, 'Hello, my beautiful Heidi! How are you? Step away from gloomy Stefano there and come up into the sunshine with me!'

Inwardly cursing, conscious of an emotion that he would not admit was jealousy, Stefano fixed a smile upon his face and prepared to introduce Heidi to his younger, handsome brother, Marco.

Standing on a higher terrace above them with the sun outlining his sleek designer jeans and open-necked shirt was the most handsome man Heidi had ever seen, a dark Brad Pitt with a winning smile and expansive gestures. When she and Stefano reached this smiling individual and Stefano gave stiff introductions, 'Heidi, this is my brother Marco. Marco, Heidi–' Marco immediately swept her off her feet, whirling her about.

'Our sweet and dainty Heidi!' he exclaimed, so loudly that a roosting pigeon in one of the nearby laurels took flight in a noisy flutter of wings. 'Arte said you were tiny, but I'd no *idea* you'd be so enchanting.'

'Now that is too much!' Heidi said laughing, when her exuberant cousin finally set her back down on her feet. But Marco was not to be quelled. Dark eyes sparkling with mischief, he said, 'That's only my beginning, Heidi. Heidi. Have you an Italian name?'

'My middle name is Maria,' Heidi replied, glancing at Stefano for guidance but receiving no sign from him. He was wearing his frozen aristocratic mask again. The two brothers could hardly be less like each other, she thought.

'Maria.' Marco tapped his pursed lips with a finger. 'You are certainly dark enough to be a Maria, and my mother tells me you have our grandfather's looks.' He clapped his hands together. 'I shall call you Heidi Maria.'

'Marco, she isn't used to your ways,' Stefano said, but Marco brushed his protest aside with a muttered, 'Don't be your usual kill-joy,' in Italian.

'Should I call you Marco Federico then?' Heidi asked blandly, in perfect Italian. She was rewarded with a swift, hard-to-read look from Stefano and a shout of laughter from his brother.

'You are one of the family! Very much of the blood. And now you must let me take you to dinner at Roberto's. I insist,' he added, with a smile, as Heidi drew in a breath. 'In celebration of your prodigal return. What do you say?'

Again, Heidi looked at Stefano, who merely said, 'I haven't the time. I've lots of paperwork to get through tonight.' He shot a steely glance at his brother. 'You should be helping me with this. Packaging is your area. Where've you been these last few days anyway?'

'Computer conference looking at the latest digital design techniques. I did leave a note on your desk,' Marco said, utterly unabashed by Stefano's glare.

'Strange that I couldn't find it then,' Stefano said, and Marco agreed, 'Isn't it?' then turned to Heidi. 'What do you say? Don't let Stefano put you off.'

'Of course Heidi can go if she wants to,' Stefano said, in a dry, formal way that made Heidi want to yell at him, 'We kissed earlier this afternoon, or have you forgotten?' Perhaps it meant nothing to him. Or more likely, Marco was being deliberately provocative in that way of sibling rivalry that she'd seen so often amongst her friends in Britain and Stefano was reacting badly to that.

'I'm not sure,' she began, not wanting to seem a misery in the face of such obvious good humor. 'Your mother may have plans that involve me.'

'Oh, you needn't worry about Mamma. She knows I've booked us a table. Please say you'll come!' Marco exclaimed, dropping onto his knees on the path in front of her.

'Roberto would never forgive me if I didn't turn up at his restaurant tonight. He takes all cancellations as a personal insult.'

Embarrassed by this show, Heidi covered her shyness with a joke. 'If you stay on your knees much longer you'll take root. I'll be pleased to come with you. Is Artemisia coming, too?'

'No, no, just us,' Marco said, springing to his feet.

'Excuse me.' Stefano stepped back from both of them. 'I have work.'

He turned and was gone, vanishing between the bushy shrubs and brilliant flowers into the deeper tree shade.

'He's going the wrong way for the house,' Marco observed needlessly. Anxiously wondering why Stefano was acting as he was, Heidi said nothing.

The food at Roberto's brightly lit and expensive restaurant on Bologna's main square might have been delicious, but Heidi scarcely tasted it. Conscious of her simple black dress, she felt uneasy and out of place beside the gleaming gowns and smart bespoke casuals of Bologna's fashionable people. She missed Stefano, with a sharpness that surprised and worried her. As a dinner companion, Marco was spasmodically attentive and seemed reasonably eager to please, but she remained wary of him, perhaps because to someone as good looking as he was and as used to being stared at wherever he went, everything was a show. Heidi knew she was a novelty, another girl for him to be seen with as he chattered ostentatiously with Roberto himself and greeted and air-kissed several beautiful women coming into the restaurant with their older, Armani-suited escorts. Each time he did this, Marco seemed to recall who he was with and would slip deftly back into his seat to ask if she needed help in understanding the menu, or choosing the wine, or inquiring if she was comfortable. To all of which Heidi gave polite, neutral replies.

When their food arrived, Marco finally settled in his seat and began to tell her stories about the family. He told her about Rosa's first attempt to make a Sicilian-style pizza, which she overcooked and finished feeding to the birds. He told her about Artemisia's confirmation, where as his sister was walking about in the garden, proudly showing off her beautiful flounced white dress, one of the scarlet bows became entangled in a rose bush. 'Stefano cut her free with a pair of kitchen scissors, with Arte alternately shouting at him and crying because her dress was having to be cut,' Marco finished.

'My own confirmation the next year wasn't much better,' he went on. 'I managed to fall on my behind in my new trousers and went into church looking an absolute urchin.'

Heidi laughed at his story. When he grinned like that, Marco was very appealing and would have made a charming urchin. She guessed he was about her own age and briefly envied him his supportive and clearly indulgent family. 'What about your older brother's confirmation?' she could not resist asking, thinking how painstaking Stefano would have been in helping to free Artemisia from the rose.

Marco shrugged. 'I don't know anything about that,' he said dismissively. 'That would have been at the orphanage. Didn't you know?' His young, handsome face gleamed in the dazzle of Roberto's wall and ceiling lights, 'Has none of the family told you yet? Stefano's adopted. His parents were killed in a car wreck when he was seven, and he was at various foster homes and orphanages until he was nine. My parents decided to take him because they'd been told that Rosa was unlikely to conceive and they thought they couldn't have children of their own. They visited the orphanage soon afterwards and saw Stefano. Rosa thought he looked lonely and felt sorry for him and persuaded Federico to take him instead of a toddler or a cute baby. Life being what it is, one year later, Mamma had Arte, and then, a year after that, she became pregnant with me.'

Marco leaned across the table towards her, clearly relishing her silence and shock.

'Didn't you wonder why he was so different from us in coloring and looks?'

'Artemisia...' Heidi stammered, still trying to absorb what Marco had told her. Shocked by the casual, almost callous way he had described these tragic events, she was stunned that he'd said anything. It seemed almost deliberately cruel. 'Artemisia has auburn hair.'

'Skillful dyeing,' Marco told her, pressing the tips of his fingers together and looking at her over their table lamp. 'Arte's as dark as I am, or you.'

Marco waved a finger at her plate. 'Have you finished your antipasta?' he asked gently, referring to her half-eaten first course of shellfish salad.

'Yes, thank you.' Heidi put her fork and spoon together and pressed her damask napkin to her trembling mouth, hoping that Marco would not see how upset she was. There were two more courses to get through, and she did not know how she would manage. Following Marco's revelation, her appetite had deserted her.

'Yes, I'm sure that's why my good brother is so very serious,' Marco continued, raising a hand to alert one of the slim, sleek waiters. 'I remember when we were younger, how he was always trying to prove himself.'

Heidi said nothing. She now knew whom Marco reminded her of, Steve Todd, one of

245

the young farmers who had inherited a property close to her childhood home near Selby. Steve Todd was handsome and much sought after by all the young women of the area but Heidi had never liked him, especially after she had seen him striding about his fields with a gun, shooting rabbits and crows and kestrels. 'He's only being a good manager of his land and getting rid of vermin,' her grandfather had said, when Heidi had furiously protested, but she'd never forgotten the gloating, avid look on Steve Todd's face as he wandered around his property, carrying his gun.

Marco's movie-star face had the same expression as he added, just as a young bearded waiter began to approach their table, 'Of course, my parents are delighted with Stefano, and they'd be even more delighted if he and Arte would hurry up and announce their engagement. I'd say it's an understood thing, really. Now, what will you have as your main course?'

Chapter 7

Heidi struggled through the rest of the evening, and later she thanked Marco for a dinner which she would have done much to miss. Marco's words about Stefano and Artemisia were impossible to forget. No matter how many times she told herself that the evidence of her own senses proved that Marco's supposition was unlikely, her mind kept dwelling on their soon-to-be announced engagement. If nothing else, it would keep Soleari's securely within the family, and Stefano was certainly committed to the business.

That night Heidi slept badly. Her next shock was delivered the following morning by Stefano himself, during their pre-breakfast drink together in the kitchen.

'Sorry, but we can't have lunch together today,' he said, frowning at her through his spectacles. He dragged a hand through his wavy thatch of hair. There were rings of tiredness under his eyes. Heidi longed to comfort him.

'That's okay,' she said reasonably. 'There's always tomorrow. How's the sprain?' she added, irritated as she felt a blush rising up her face.

'Gone,' Stefano said tersely, but he didn't look pleased. If anything, he looked even more unhappy. 'No, I'm sorry, lunch together just isn't possible, not for all the rest of this week. So much is happening that I can't. I have to be places, somewhere else.'

Heidi waited, but he did not elaborate, just hid his drawn face behind his coffee mug. When she asked gently, 'Is it anything to do with what we've talked about earlier?' he leapt to his feet and left the kitchen table. 'I have to go now, back to Soleari's.

'Will you see to this morning's rolls for me?' He waved a distracted arm in the direction of the oven.

'I'll be glad to help,' Heidi told him, and she was. She was grateful that Stefano trusted her to look after the freshly-baked bread that she and the rest of the family would soon be enjoying for breakfast. All the family except for Stefano, who'd made them, patiently explaining each step of the process.

So if he could do that, why could he not tell me that he was adopted?

'Good luck,' she told him as he left.

He turned on the threshold and gave her the first genuine smile she had seen that morning. 'Thank you,' he said. Striding back into the kitchen, he leaned down and kissed her forehead. He seemed on the verge of saying something, but then he shook his head and walked away, back into the villa, possibly to retrieve the briefcase she'd seen him put ready to pick up as he left by the front door.

Alone, Heidi had only a few moments to dwell on her disappointment before a gentle cough alerted her to the presence of another family member. Raising her head from her lukewarm cup of tea, she saw Rosa standing on the kitchen threshold where Stefano had stood and forced herself to smile.

'Hello! How are you?' she asked, noting that Rosa seemed less pale than she had been and that there was a new brightness about her bobbed cap of sleek brown hair. Today, Rosa was dressed more colorfully than on previous occasions, in a tailored wool dress in a rich tangerine.

'I like the dress,' Heidi went on. 'Is it new?'

'Yes, it is.' Rosa plucked a soft tangerine pleat, adding in quiet Italian, 'Federico would once have noticed it was new,' before reverting to English, in a brisker manner, 'I am becoming well, thank you. Your treatments are helping me.'

'That's good,' Heidi said, pleased to have her instincts confirmed. Sensing that Rosa wanted to talk, she was keen to keep this spasmodic conversation going. 'Are you and Federico driving anywhere today?'

While she had been staying at the villa, Federico and Rosa had gone off on morning sight-seeing trips to various little towns and villages close to Bologna in the Emilia Romania region. Federico called it, 'Learning my own country,' and even if Artemisia scoffed and accused her parents of being the 'most unimaginative pair of retirees I know,' Heidi thought that what they were doing was charming.

'I-I think so.' Rosa started as the old timer that Stefano used to remind him to check the bread – not that he ever needed reminding, so far as Heidi knew – suddenly went off with a noisy buzz.

'Excuse me.' Hoping that Rosa would soon enter her own kitchen, Heidi switched off the timer and walked across the tiles to the oven. 'Stefano had to leave early this morning,' she explained over her shoulder as she opened the oven door and the fragrance of fresh bread blossomed in the room. 'He left me in charge of the rolls this morning.'

She lifted the bread out and tapped and tested each roll, piling them deftly onto a rack to cool. Behind her, she sensed a change of air as Rosa approached, heard her say in her low, diffident way, 'You move like Stefano around bread.'

'Oh, he showed me every step.'

'No, no. I mean you have the touch. You're not afraid of it.'

Heidi turned to stare at Rosa. She had sat down at the kitchen table where Stefano had been sitting. She was turning a teaspoon over and over on the well-scrubbed wood.

'I thought Federico would be right about you,' Rosa continued, still turning the spoon. 'I know what your hands can do.'

Embarrassed, Heidi plunged the empty baking trays into the cold water in the sink, where they sizzled and steamed. Strangely, as she grew shyer, Rosa seemed to become more confident, her voice becoming clearer.

'We have talked about it again, Federico and I, and we decided last night that it was the right thing; the just thing to do. We are resurrecting Ruggiero's old voting rights within the business and giving them to you.'

Suddenly Heidi discovered that she wanted to sit down. Stefano had mentioned voting rights to her as something she *could* have, but Rosa's statement made it clear that these rights were now something she *did* have. 'Are you sure?' She settled less than gracefully onto a stool. Her heart drummed inside her as she wondered how many other surprises this family would launch at her. 'What about the others? What does Stefano think?'

'Stefano knows, of course,' Rosa said. In contrast to Heidi's breathless state, Rosa seemed calm, pleased to have got the matter out of the way. 'Federico talked to him and Artemisia last night. Marco, too, after you had both come in from the restaurant.' Rosa laid the teaspoon down in front of her place and looked straight at Heidi with a gentle smile. 'Stefano approves.'

'I see,' Heidi said faintly. 'But I really know nothing about the business. I didn't even know that Soleari's is *a panetteria*, not a bread shop.'

Rosa's smile widened. 'But you are learning, yes?'

'I think so. I'm trying. Stefano really approves?'

'As do the others,' Rosa added swiftly, in a way that told Heidi that Marco and Artemisia – Artemisia probably – were less happy with this development. Still, she could not help rejoicing that Stefano was pleased. She valued his approval above all.

'You like Stefano, I think,' Rosa said, scrutinizing Heidi in a way that Heidi wasn't sure she felt entirely comfortable with. 'He is, as I am sure he has told you by now, adopted.'

'I know,' said Heidi. *Only not from Stefano.*

'But he is always very much a son to me,' Rosa went on. 'And of course, even if you were related, you would be second cousins, not so close by blood. Stefano's a good boy. Always very serious, although he can laugh.'

'Stefano? I can certainly make him laugh.' Artemisia entered the kitchen in another flowing kimono, this one in shocking pink silk. She claimed her mother for a kiss.

'Yes, *cara,* I know you can,' Rosa said fondly, staring up at her beautiful daughter with obvious pride and admiration. 'But then you and Stefano have such a special relationship.'

Artemisia smiled and kissed her mother again, declaring, 'Are those the breakfast rolls? I'm starving! Mamma, will you join me in having a coffee, some espresso before Papa and Marco come down and try to make us wait on them?'

'Excuse me,' Heidi said quietly, determined to slip away to her bedroom before anything else was said.

Mounting the marble staircase to the upper rooms, she felt she needed a moment to re-gather her composure as she wondered just how close Stefano and Artemisia really were. Had Rosa's mention of Stefano's adoption been meant as approval of her involvement with him? Or had Rosa's comment on Stefano's and Artemisia's 'special relationship' perhaps been Rosa's way of warning her off? If so, Heidi knew that any warning was already too late.

I'm falling in love with him, she thought, and a great sense of wonder rushed through her in a dizzying surge of joy. 'Stefano Soleari, the adopted son,' she said aloud softly as she entered her room, then walked to the window and looked down over the city, down into Bologna where Stefano was.

Feeling as she did, Heidi was torn between hope and dread that Stefano might notice how she now regarded him. Conscious of her spirits lifting each time she thought he might step into the same room or street as herself, she treasured the most fleeting glimpses of his tall, rangy figure.

Which was just as well, Heidi admitted wryly because she saw little of Stefano over the following days. No matter how early she slipped down to the kitchen, he was gone. Sometimes she doubted if he even returned from Soleari's after the night-baking. He did not return to the villa until late at night. Over the first couple of days, Heidi had walked down to Soleari's, but found that Stefano was not there. She had either just missed him or he'd not been there since the early morning. She did not feel she could impose herself on him during the night-time baking session, but she missed him very much, the more so because she wasn't certain that he ever thought of her.

As a further disappointment, Federico had taken over the ritual of the morning rolls. He was as good a bread-maker as his son, Heidi reluctantly admitted, and he always greeted her with a big smile, but unlike Stefano, he would not allow her to help. Perhaps he did not think she had 'the touch', Heidi thought sourly, and then berated herself for being so petty. This was the family she'd craved and longed to know about over the years, and they had welcomed her into their home. She should be grateful and happy. Besides, Federico had trusted her enough to agree to give her the old voting rights that had once belonged to her father and wasn't that something?

Even so, as the days drew on and Heidi walked about the city, chatted with the family and treated Rosa in her regular aromatherapy sessions, she began to wonder why she was staying. This was her first holiday for five years, and although Bologna was a marvellous city, filled with the wonderful arcades, markets and shops that she loved, Heidi found her eyes straying to the hills beyond. There was a whole region to explore, Venice and Parma and Florence, cities that she'd always wanted to see, and only a train ride away.

Rosa, meanwhile, had tentatively invited her to go with her and Federico on their morning drives, but Heidi had smilingly declined. She knew that whatever Stefano had said, Rosa was uneasy in her marriage, and she felt that Rosa and Federico might resolve whatever it was if they were left alone.

There was another, more sulky reason that Heidi only shared with herself as she scowled at her reflection in her bedroom mirror. If she was going to see Italy with any of this family, she wanted it to be with Stefano.

She appreciated that he was involved with the business, and she understood why. If he had been able to throw aside the lives of people like Alberto and Emilia and customers like old Signor Bartoli, she would have thought less of him. But day after day dawned, and she and Stefano scarcely spoke to each other. It was as if their lunches and that sensual, tender kiss in the garden had never been.

Had Rosa or Artemisia 'had a word' with Stefano, perhaps? Had they reminded him that he was supposed to marry Artemisia?

Heidi didn't like that idea, and honestly didn't think it likely, but Marco's mocking words haunted her. Marco and Artemisia themselves were equally distracting, in different ways. One morning, very early, Artemisia had appeared in the kitchen, dressed in a smart white cook's uniform and with her hair in a stunning French pleat and had proceeded to take over the baking of that morning's bread from her father, instructing Federico to go out into the garden to gather some roses for the table.

While her words reminded Heidi of when she had first met Stefano, Artemisia did not waste the chance of her father's absence to turn on her.

'I know what your plan is, Heidi, but it won't work,' she said bluntly, slapping her risen dough vigorously onto the flour-strewn table. 'Stefano isn't interested, Marco certainly isn't, and my parents will soon see through this caring-healing routine of yours. And I wouldn't feel too important about those voting rights, either. My father has a casting vote, so yours won't count.'

'So why are you so upset about it?' Heidi asked quietly.

'Who says I'm upset?' Artemisia snapped, kneading the dough with the palms of her hands. 'As far as I'm concerned, you're an irrelevance. You'll be gone in another three weeks, less if I have my way.'

'And that's what really eats at you, isn't it? Your lack of control,' Heidi said, knowing that her words would incense Artemisia further but unable to resist. Determined to say anything more – she had no wish to be drawn into an all-out argument in a house where she was a guest – Heidi swiftly left Artemisia to vent the rest of her spite in private and walked out into the garden to find Federico. Later, it should have amused her that Artemisia's bread, although acceptable, was not as outstanding as Stefano's or Federico's, but instead she felt no sense of satisfaction, only a regret that she and Artemisia could not be friends. She was aggrieved that the beautiful, cultured and rather spoiled Artemisia clearly saw her as nothing more than an upstart on the make.

'If she thinks bread is hard, she ought to try milking cows,' Heidi muttered, and was still grinning at the thought as she ran down the garden terraces.

Marco was as stand-offish as his sister, although less overtly hostile. Since inviting her for dinner, Marco had largely ignored her, which Heidi found a relief in some ways but hurtful in others. He made her feel dull. Clearly she had been found wanting at Roberto's, and her handsome cousin had decided that she was worth no more of his time.

What Marco and Artemisia did with their time remained a mystery to Heidi, since it was clear that they spent virtually no time at Soleari's. At breakfast, Federico always asked if they were going into the 'bread-shop' his new title for the *panetteria* and an indulgent teasing of Heidi – but when Marco and Artemisia said no or simply avoided answering, their father did not pursue it. Heidi could understand why Stefano felt that Federico had lost interest in the business and that saddened her, too, for Stefano's sake.

Another day slipped by, which Heidi considered note-worthy only because Rosa talked to her during her aromatherapy, hesitantly admitting that she was worried about Federico's regular absences on every Thursday afternoon.

'He won't tell me where he goes or what

he does, and he always takes the car so I can't follow,' Rosa said unhappily, her pale face pressed against her pillow as Heidi massaged her back and shoulders with a blend of fragrant and healing oils. 'Ah! That lavender scent takes me back to when I was a girl on holiday in Venice on the Lido! Have I ever told you about that?'

'I don't think you have,' Heidi said, going along with the change of subject. She longed to tell Rosa not to worry, but here, along with the mysterious 'sabotage' at Soleari's and the puzzle of when Marco and Artemisia did any work there, was another enigma. Where did Federico go on Thursday afternoons?

That evening, long before dinner, Stefano came home much earlier than he had been doing. He sought her out in the music room, where she was slowly playing through, 'Come back to Sorrento,' a tune she remembered her father singing to her.

'There have been no more unexplained "incidents" at Soleari's,' Stefano told her. 'I thought you'd be glad to know that.'

'Of course!' Heidi said, delighted that Stefano was here with her. 'That's great news!'

'What's that, Heidi-Maria, that you are coming to Venice tomorrow with me?' drawled Marco from the doorway. Ignoring his instantly grim-faced brother, he waltzed across to the piano to join them.

'Mamma told me how fascinated you were in her childhood travelers' tales and I thought that seeing I've been neglecting you,' – this said with a self-deprecating smile – 'that I would make amends by whisking you off to see Saint Mark's Square and all of La Serenissima's other glories.'

'La Serenissima?' Heidi was bewildered by Marco's sudden invitation.

'He means Venice,' Stefano said shortly, stepping back from Heidi and turning on his heel. 'I'll leave you two to make your arrangements.'

'Wait.' Heidi started up from the piano stool but found her path blocked by Marco, who took her hand in his and swung it to and fro.

'I think an early start will be best,' Marco said. 'I've so much to show you.'

But Heidi had decided that she'd had enough. 'I'm sorry, Marco,' she said as softly as she could. 'I'm afraid I can't go with you tomorrow. I'm meeting Gina in town,' she lied. She felt as if he had deliberately manufactured their day in Venice to drive a wedge between herself and Stefano, and while she was disappointed at his small-minded malice, she was also irritated at Stefano for not realizing what his brother was doing.

How can an intelligent man be so blind? she thought indignantly, striding away from the music room to her own bedroom. She could feel an anger headache building and abruptly decided that she would plead off joining the family for dinner tonight. She would have a bath and an early night and try to decide what to do with the rest of her time in Italy. Now that Rosa was improving and the business seemed free of sabotage, how much longer should she stay? She remembered her grandmother's adage about good guests not outstaying their welcome and admitted wretchedly that perhaps it was time that she tore herself away from the Villa Rosa. *And from Stefano,* her thoughts whispered, but she could see no other way. If he could not even admit to her the basic truth of himself, of where he came from and who he was, what chance had they of any lasting relationship?

The delicious scents of minestrone soup and roast lamb wafting up from the kitchen turned Heidi faintly sick rather than hungry as later she sat on her bed in front of the wardrobe mirror to brush her hair. She had warded off the worst of the headache with a judicious use of essential oils on herself after her bath, but she was glad she had given Rosa her apologies for tonight.

A soft knock at her door. 'Heidi? Are you okay?'

'Come in if you like, Stefano,' she called

out, her heart quickening as she heard his voice. She knew that her grandmother wouldn't have approved of her inviting him into her room, dressed as she was in her dressing gown, but she was after all twenty-one, and this was the twenty-first century. The dressing gown in question was one that enveloped her from head to foot in pale blue toweling so she was hardly immodest. Heidi felt strangely happy and rather reckless. 'Come in,' she said again, even as the door was opening.

'Mamma said you were unwell. What's wrong? Can I fetch you anything?'

Stefano's anxious face and questions soothed her more than her own healing oils. She drank in his concern like a thirsty flower accepting water but loved him too much to cause him grief. 'I'm feeling a little better, thanks,' she said, dropping her hairbrush on the bed and holding out a hand to him. 'Possibly a touch of sun. An early night will see me well again.'

'Is there anything you need? Here, let me brush your hair.'

Her hair was long, and felt longer still as Stefano's hands gently teased it free 'Is this okay?' he asked.

Heidi nodded, closing her eyes. The top of her head was tingling with a delicious tension, and the slow, gentle brushing of her hair made her feel stretched out and languorous. She wanted to ask him about himself, about his past, a way to show him that she was interested and possibly a way he would begin to talk about his adoption. Instead, before she even realized she was going to, she yawned.

'There you go.' Stefano dropped a kiss onto her forehead. 'Would you like anything else? No? Then I think I'd better leave. Sleep well, my Heidi.'

After he was gone, Heidi stretched out on the bed, closing her eyes and thinking of Stefano's smiling face. *My Heidi*. He had called her that.

'How can I think of leaving the Villa Rosa now?' she said aloud.

Chapter 8

The next day Heidi woke full of renewed doubts. Stefano's continuing absence at breakfast did nothing to reassure her, and the fact that he had left no message for her made her wonder if last night had simply been a moment of physical attraction that meant nothing to him.

Marco was not in the kitchen when she came downstairs in her newly favorite blue button-through cotton dress, but any guilty pleasure she might have felt at her handsome relative's not pursuing her further with suggestions of a day trip to Venice was short lived.

'Heidi!' Artemisia called from upstairs, her voice echoing down over the marble balustrade of the staircase. 'Will you come up here a moment? I want you to see something.'

Her face calm for Federico, who was listening with wide-eyed interest, Heidi retraced her steps upstairs to the villa's bedrooms. Artemisia was waiting for her on the landing, and Heidi braced herself for whatever revelation was coming.

'Here, I wondered if you might like to borrow this while you're still staying with us.' Artemisia held out a Mexican sombrero-style sun-hat. 'Stefano bought it for me. He bought this for me, too, but I'm afraid I can't lend it to you.' She tapped a wide silver bangle on her wrist.

'Stefano's generous,' Heidi remarked coolly, well-aware of what Artemisia was doing. 'Thanks for the offer of the hat, but I'll be fine. Gina and I will be undercover in town with all those arcades.' She checked her watch. 'I need to hurry if I'm not going to be late.'

Conscious of Artemisia watching, she walked along the landing to her own room, her thoughts remaining with that silver bangle. How did Stefano see himself within the family? As a brother by adoption or as an outsider? Was his gift to Artemisia that of a generous sibling or something else?

'Don't let her worry you,' Heidi said aloud. 'Don't.'

Leaving the villa soon after, she met Rosa in the street outside the garden gate, walking down from the *gelateria* where she and Stefano were about to go to have an ice cream on that first day, before her true identity was discovered. Rosa smiled at her.

'Off to town to meet Gina?' she asked.

Heidi nodded, feeling guilty at maintaining the deception which had only been a spur of the moment act on her part, born of irritation at Marco's assumption that she would instantly agree to his every suggestion.

Rosa gave her a penetrating look. 'If you get bored with shopping, you might like to try the walk along the portico of San Luca to the hilltop sanctuary of the Madonna of San Luca. There are some wonderful views of the countryside from there.'

'Thank you, I'd like that,' Heidi said. 'In fact I'll suggest it. The walk might help to clear my head.'

She was surprised when Rosa touched her arm. 'Are you still not well? Stefano was worried about you last night. He said you were very pale.'

'I'm fine.' Disconcerted by Rosa's genuine concern, Heidi was alarmed to find her eyes filling at the mention of Stefano. 'I'm just a little stale, I think. I need some exercise, get the blood pumping.'

'Of course.' Rosa looked uneasy at this idea but she politely agreed, adding, 'I hope you will like the sanctuary. It is very beautiful. Very holy and peaceful. It's a place of pilgrimage to the Madonna.'

'That sounds like just what I want,' Heidi said fervently.

From her guidebook, bought on her first day in Bologna, Heidi learned that the covered uphill walk from the city to the hilltop sanctuary of the Madonna of San Luca was the longest portico in the world. It was a popular place, but Heidi saw few people clambering the endless series of steps and slopes. Passing the florists, barbers, bars and ice cream parlors on the winding long portico's lower part, she felt the slope becoming steeper. Soon she was lengthening her stride and the secular shops gave way to religious frescoes and plaques recording the names of local dignitaries who had restored parts of the arcades.

She was trying to decide whether to remain with the family until this vital meeting about the future of Soleari's was over. Should she use her voting rights? Was she justified in doing so when she knew so little about the business? Perhaps she should tell Rosa this on her return from the sanctuary and then pack and leave. She would be lonely again, without family, but she was used to that.

'I am,' Heidi murmured, jogging defiantly up a few steps.

At first she thought the wail was her own sense of anguish perhaps bursting from her, then a police car down in the city. Stopping to listen, looking out over the grand houses and villas that were dotted here and there over the more open, hilly landscape outside Bologna, she heard it again – the exuberant swirl and drone of bagpipes.

'What?' Heidi began to chuckle with disbelief. Somewhere in one of those grand villa gardens someone was practicing the bagpipes. The sound made her want to both laugh and cry as a wave of homesickness broke over her. She had never felt more of a stranger and outsider than now, standing under one of the arcades listening to a haunting British folksong on bagpipes.

And that was how Stefano found her when he finally caught up after running most of the way from the start of the pilgrimage at the Saragozza gate. Mamma had told him where Heidi was going and had added that her young cousin had seemed pale and distracted.

'Heidi! Are you all right?' Stefano stopped, panting, beside a crumbling fresco. He thought she looked even worse than his mother had described – gray-faced, incredibly fragile. She was alone, too.

'Where's Gina?' he demanded, concern making his voice harsh.

'Gina couldn't make it.'

'Well, you can't possibly carry on as you are. Come back to the house.'

'Don't order me,' Heidi snapped. Any pleasure she'd had in seeing Stefano had vanished with his brusque greeting. 'I'm not your sister.'

The instant she spoke she regretted her

words, but when Stefano remained silent and impassive, Heidi's own confusion and pain made her lash out at him again, determined to provoke some reaction.

'I'm leaving today. That should please you, Stefano. I know the only reason you've left Soleari's or wherever else you've been spending most of your time these days is because you're wondering how I'll vote. But I'm leaving, so you and Marco won't have to bother trying to charm me 'round. I won't be at your precious meeting. Now leave me alone!'

The bagpipes rose to another crescendo as Heidi stormed off, striding up the slope. Bells and chimes began to strike the hour throughout the city and then, closer, she heard steady breathing as Stefano easily caught up with her.

'You can't leave,' he said urgently. 'I don't want you to leave.'

'Oh, go back to Artemisia!' Heidi quickened her pace but could still not escape Stefano's reaching arms. The next moment, she found herself caught and, as she whirled about to demand that he release her, only succeeded in trapping her small, slim body against Stefano's taller, more muscled frame.

'Is that what you think?' Stefano asked quietly, as she jabbed her forearm against his middle.

'I'm not discussing anything while you

269

man-handle me,' Heidi said, starting off again as Stefano instantly let her go.

He fell into step with her. 'Heidi, wait! Please! What are you talking about?'

'I would have thought that was obvious, but why not ask Marco? He was the one who thought I should know.'

'Marco told you that I was involved with my sister?' For an instant Stefano sounded disbelieving and then he cursed violently under his breath. 'Wait. No, stop.' He put an arm in front of her to prevent her moving forward. 'It's obvious that you know that I'm adopted, but you should know the rest.'

'Why didn't tell me you are adopted ? Didn't you trust me?'

'No! No, it was nothing like that.' A look of mingled pain and mortification slid across his face. 'I wasn't sure when to say anything. You seemed so pleased with the family that I hesitated to admit I was different. I wasn't sure what you'd think of me.' He sighed. 'I'm sorry.'

'And what about Artemisa?' Heidi flared up again, only slightly mollified by his halting explanation and recalling the silver bangle that she'd been shown by Artemisia only that morning. 'What does she think?'

Stefano's look of horror increased. 'Marco has a strong streak of mischief in his make-up. He knows that I think of Artemisia as my sister. She *is* my little sister by adoption, and for him to suggest I think of her otherwise... It's disgraceful. I'm ashamed of him.'

He found her hand and gave it a gentle squeeze. 'Artemisia is currently involved with a millionaire who lives in Milan. That would be more her style, wouldn't you say?'

Heidi instantly thought that was it, but she was given no chance to reply. Stefano wrapped his arm around her waist and lifted her off her feet.

'Let's go home,' he said.

'And your gifts to her?' Heidi persisted, feeling a tingling delight in his arms but determined to find out, once and for all, about that silver bangle.

'Gifts?' Stefano's face cleared as he nodded understanding. 'Ah, you mean her present! Artemisia likes jewellery, so I bought her a silver bracelet for her birthday. But that was months ago.'

His lips were brushing her forehead and when she did not protest, he lifted her higher in both arms to kiss her on the mouth.

'Stefano! This is a holy place!' Heidi protested when their long, sweet kiss had ended. 'Please, put me down. What if someone sees us?'

'I don't care,' Stefano said softly, kissing her again. He touched her hair and throat and shoulders with gentle fingers and then, as she struggled a little, playfully tightened his grip around her. 'Let's go home.'

At the end of the day Heidi sat up in bed hugging her knees, smiling as she remembered everything that she and Stefano had done. Once assured by her that she was really quite well, Stefano had told her that he'd taken a day off from the business that he wanted to spend with her. 'If that is acceptable to you,' he'd added anxiously.

Heidi had nodded, thinking of the contrast between his gallantry and Marco's arrogance and delighted at the prospect of spending so much time with him. He'd taken her sight-seeing around the city, going wherever she wanted to go, strolling with her round the colorful fruit and vegetable market, the bookshops, the massive cathedral of Saint Peter which, to her, looked more like a municipal building than a holy place, the Seven Churches and the church of San Dominico, where Saint Dominic was buried in an ornate marble tomb surrounded with tasseled incense burners and tall vases of white lilies.

That day at Heidi's request they had lunched at Luigi's, the café across the square from Soleari's where they had sat out of doors on the square under one of the café's colorful umbrellas and had cheerfully tried each other's dessert. Heidi had a spoonful of Stefano's spice cake, known by its local name of *certosino*, and she'd fed him a forkful of her own chocolate tartlet, moist with real chocolate and drenched with icing sugar.

'Working at Soleari's it's just as well for me that I never seem to put weight on.' Stefano patted his flat stomach. 'And you're obviously the same.' He leaned across the table and kissed Heidi on the cheek. 'My mother and sister are incredibly envious.'

Heidi smiled at him, no longer so self-conscious of the slight gap between her front teeth or her own slim shape, since Stefano seemed to find her pretty. Walking from Luigi's she'd been aware of admiring looks from other men and had felt astonishment and delight, although she thought that if she now realized she was reasonably attractive, it was because of the tall blond man striding beside her, who gave her confidence simply by his presence.

A lovely day, Heidi thought, wondering how many other such days there could be. What future realistically could she and Stefano have? In another ten days she would be returning to Britain, to her tiny flat in Selby and her aromatherapy practice and lack of family. She had plenty of friends, but it was not the same. And would she see Stefano ever again?

Scared by that thought and miserable, Heidi laid back in bed, pulling the covers up tightly over her shoulders. Tonight at dinner, Artemisia had flirted outrageously with

Stefano, complimenting him on his clothes, blowing him air kisses, and all the while, throwing Heidi searching glances, to see how she took it.

Artemisia can't help making a play for any man who's in the room with her, Heidi thought savagely, and then she was ashamed of her thought.

Marco meanwhile had been absent, and no one knew where he was. Heidi found Marco's behavior puzzling and malicious rather than Stefano's more generous interpretation of 'mischief, but perhaps her handsome relative saw her as a threat, especially if she decided to stay on for the family meeting about the future of Soleari's and used her voting rights. So far, she would vote for restoring the *panetteria* and not for any sale of the business and presumably Marco knew this.

Why could Marco not sort out his gambling debts? Heidi wondered. She remembered how Stefano had told her that in the past bread had been used to smuggle goods. A loaf would be hollowed out and a message or money or jewels placed inside, then a bread 'lid' would be replaced and the whole loaf repackaged. Was Marco perhaps involved in smuggling?

'Smuggling what?' Heidi scoffed aloud. She was allowing her imagination to go wild.

What was that? Heidi froze as she heard

the door handle to her room being softly tried for a second time. Had she locked it? Should she put the light on and demand who was there. She drew in a soft breath, listening intently. She could hear nothing but the sound of the wind in the pine trees, but she sensed, with every taut nerve of her body, that someone was still lurking outside her door.

Thank goodness that she had locked it.

Still undecided whether to challenge who-ever it was or simply to yell and wake the whole villa, Heidi heard a soft padding of footsteps moving away from the door and along the corridor.

Stark awake, she waited another half an hour before moving out of bed to jam a chair under the door handle and then returned shivering to her bed, where she did not sleep much for the rest of the night.

Chapter 9

When she rose and dressed the following morning, Heidi was determined to act. She did not suspect Stefano of anything, but she had decided that she would not mention the incident to him alone. She wanted to catch the family together, confront them with what had happened and see how they reacted.

To her surprise, Rosa and Artemisia were already in the kitchen with Federico when she slipped downstairs. The big tiled kitchen, with its dark oak central table, was filled with the deliciously mingled scents of coffee, yeast and fresh bread – smells of family life, Heidi thought, the breath stopping in her throat. Soon she would have to leave this and Stefano, and the idea of tearing herself away made her want to rush weeping into the garden.

Someone had tried to enter her room last night, Heidi reminded herself. Stiffened by this, she answered Artemisia's over-sweet, 'And how did you sleep, Heidi?' with a bracing, 'Excellently, thanks.'

'You do look much brighter this morning,' Rosa remarked, taking a sip of her espresso.

As do you, Heidi thought, smiling at her.

Standing by the coffee maker, slim and elegant in another new tailored suit, this one in a flattering burgundy, Rosa was a different woman from the pale, apologetic figure Heidi had first met. Maybe I had some part in the change, Heidi comforted herself. If so, it perhaps went a small way to repay her debt to her relatives' generous hospitality.

'Little Heidi-Maria!' Marco came in behind her, pressing a button on his mobile phone before placing it on the oak table. 'You slept well, I trust?' This said while giving her his best movie star smile.

They were all in the kitchen now, everyone except Stefano, whom Heidi wanted to protect from this unpleasant mystery anyway. Smiling in return, Heidi admitted clearly, 'I would have slept better if whoever it was who tried my door last night had knocked first and had asked to come in. Was that you, Marco?'

'You were dreaming,' Artemisia scoffed, while Marco held up both hands.

'Not guilty!' he said. 'I never go where I'm not invited. Or were you hoping, perhaps, that I would?'

'Marco, you forget yourself,' said Federico sharply, turning from whatever he was doing by the oven to shake a finger at his youngest. 'Really!'

'Marco, please,' pleaded Rosa in a small voice.

'She was dreaming,' Artemisia repeated, her dark eyes flashing dislike.

'Oh, I'm sure that's what it was,' said Marco smoothly, registering Heidi's scalding blush with another wide smile. 'But these English girls, you know.'

'That's enough, Marco.'

Stefano stood framed in the open doorway leading to the garden. Marco took one look at his harsh, unyielding face and was instantly silent as Stefano stalked into the kitchen. 'What's going on?' he demanded. 'Heidi, did I hear you correctly? Did you say that someone tried to enter your room last night?'

'"Enter your room",' Artemisia mimicked. 'Don't be so stuffy'. The silly girl was dreaming.'

'No, I wasn't!' snapped Heidi.

'Perhaps Stefano is so self-righteously indignant because he has a guilty conscience,' Marco went on, recovering fast and now offering a new, and to Heidi, an altogether more disturbing suggestion. 'You remember, Arte, how our Stefano used to sleepwalk around this house, especially after he'd told lies? I used to wonder if it was because he was afraid he might be sent back to the orphanage.'

'Marco, that's unfair!' Federico protested.

'Stefano hasn't sleep-walked for years,' Rosa said, her hands visibly shaking. She looked close to tears, and Heidi moved to comfort her.

'I used to sleep-walk as a child,' she said, praying that her face would not give away the fact that she was lying. After Marco's studied unkindness, she was determined to offer Stefano her public comfort and support. 'In fact that's why I lock my door at night,' she went on in seeming cheerfulness. 'So if that's all it was there's no harm done. Is there?'

Her question challenged both Marco and Artemisia, neither of whom replied.

She had tried to show Stefano support, but the incident saddened and embarrassed Heidi. After eating a small bread roll that she found almost impossible to swallow and drinking a hasty cup of tea that burned her mouth, she made an excuse and left the kitchen. Glad to be escaping the strained, frozen silence where none of the family were even glancing at each other, she decided to walk down into the city. She had no plans of where to go, but her absence might give Stefano and the others an opportunity to speak freely.

'I can't possibly stay on for the meeting,' Heidi murmured, opening the garden gate into the street. She was horrified by the tension and disruption that her presence had obviously provoked within the family. Whatever her hopes and feelings for Stefano, she couldn't remain at the villa. It would be selfish. It might not even be safe.

Why can't I fit in? The question haunted her as she pounded along the pavement, the more so because she knew that her dream of finding her father's family had in the end turned into both dream and nightmare.

'Heidi, wait for me.' Stefano caught her arm, and she swung round.

'What? Can't I go for a walk now?'

'Heidi, I'm sorry, really sorry about this morning. I should have told you about my sleepwalking, I know, but there's been no time and I honestly thought I hadn't done it for years. Years!'

Stefano stopped on the pavement in front of her, his face racked with shame. Alarmed that he should blame himself when to her there was only one person who should feel guilty, Heidi put her arms around him.

'Did you really think Rosa and Federico would send you back to the orphanage?' she asked softly, hugging him as she felt a shudder run through his strong figure. 'I can understand that. For months after Papa died, I used to lie awake in bed listening for my grandparents. If I couldn't hear them I used to worry that they'd perhaps gone away in the night.'

'And left you. Oh, God, Heidi. My poor Heidi.' Stefano's arms were encircling her, hugging her tightly in return. Oblivious to the passing students and shoppers, they clung to each other.

Heidi glanced at her untouched ice cream and then stared out of the window of the *gelateria,* watching a man on an old black trike attached to a dustbin full of brooms and mops pedaling furiously uphill. She and Stefano were sitting in the ice cream parlor that he'd wanted to take her to on the first day they met. He had just been telling her about Gina, the youngest assistant at Soleari's, whom he'd escorted home first thing that morning after Gina had received a phone call in the *panetteria* and become very upset. Stefano had no idea who telephoned Gina or what the caller said, but Gina had been trembling and tearful. Stefano had swiftly taken her home, away from prying eyes and over-curious customers, but he had been uneasy about her ever since.

'I wish none of this was happening,' he said.

'If Gina's still upset tomorrow, perhaps I could help?' Heidi asked tentatively.

Stefano shook his head. 'I couldn't ask that of you, Heidi. That should be Marco's job, or Artemisia's. It wouldn't hurt them to work at the business for a change.' He frowned. 'I have to go away for a few days.'

Meeting Heidi's inquiring look, he took a deep breath and confessed, 'I have to leave

Bologna this afternoon. I've a long-standing business meeting in Palermo in Sicily that I can't afford to break.'

This was a shock, and a bitter blow to Heidi, but she determined not to add to Stefano's problems by showing how upset she was. 'How long will you be gone?' she asked, pushing her ice cream to one side across the tiled table.

'Two, three days. No longer than that, I promise. Why not take the opportunity to have a change yourself? Stay at a local hotel in Bologna and pamper yourself. I'll pay.' The sudden brightness in his face faded as Heidi shook her head.

'I'll be perfectly all right at the villa,' she told him gently, telling herself she was only slightly hurt that he had not invited her to go with him.

'But someone tried your door last night! Marco says it must have been me sleep-walking, but I'm sure it wasn't. So, who was it?' Stefano struck his palm on the table for emphasis, rattling their empty cappuccino cups. 'Stay at a hotel. I'll pay,' he repeated.

'I'm not letting Rosa down by making her feel I don't trust her family. I can take care of myself.' Heidi gave a teasing grin when Stefano looked as if he would argue again. 'Don't you trust me?'

'Of course I do,' he said. 'But you *will* be careful?'

'I will,' Heidi promised. She was horribly disappointed that Stefano was leaving but perversely glad of his anxious concern for her. He'd not said anything about his feelings, but surely he cared a little for her? Why else would he worry?

Perhaps because of your voting rights, a nasty inner voice reminded her; a voice she resolutely ignored.

That night, with Stefano gone, Heidi did not expect to sleep, but when she next opened her eyes on a beautiful dawn morning, she felt as relaxed and refreshed as if she had treated herself to aromatherapy. Marco and Artemisia were both missing at breakfast, and when Rosa hesitantly asked her if she minded doing a little shopping, Heidi was happy to oblige.

'Will you be home for lunch?' Rosa asked.

'No, thanks. I'll pick something up while I'm out,' Heidi said easily. She had her own plans, and since these involved Soleari's, she decided not to mention anything to Rosa or to anyone else. She wanted to take another look at the *panetteria*, partly to savor that delicious window display, partly to reassure herself that there had been no more incidents of sabotage.

Rosa's shopping took longer than Heidi expected, but only because she found the people and the colorful market stalls and the arcaded Bologna streets endlessly fascinating. Pausing to admire an old religious fresco at one of the street corners, she realized with a start of surprise that it was mid-afternoon and the shops were closing for the siesta. She could hear the sound of clinking knives and forks from the shuttered first floor apartments of the Renaissance buildings she was passing, and the only creature moving across the small square ahead was a feral, fawn-colored cat.

A cat and now a stocky, gray-haired figure with a red rose buttonhole, striding with a bustling purpose she knew well. Her cousin Federico, obviously going somewhere.

'It's Thursday,' Heidi breathed, as she set off after him. She knew she shouldn't follow, that what the poor man did on Thursday afternoons was nothing to do with her, but curiosity won out over guilt. Why not? she thought, stealing after Federico across the square as lightly as the cat. No one need ever know.

Another street and another row of terra-cotta-colored apartments, with iron bars across the shuttered windows on the ground floor and walls covered in political posters. Federico pressed the door pad beside one of the anonymous, paint-peeling doors and after a few moments, was allowed inside.

Heidi hurried to read the names on the door pad and almost laughed out loud when she realized where he had gone. There was only one name on the door pad, written in fine calligraphy.

'Studio Fra Lippo Lippi – Learn to paint like a master!' she read aloud. So this was Federico's grand passion! Not another woman but art classes.

The door to the studio clicked open, and with a definite twinkle in his crinkled brown eyes, Federico beckoned her inside. 'And now that you've tracked me down, niece, you might as well know the rest.'

The studio was large and airy and full of students of all ages at a drawing class. Federico showed her his easel and regular workspace and then, with permission from the tutor, brought Heidi to a smaller room whose walls were gradually being filled with pictures.

'For our summer exhibition,' Federico told her proudly. 'Here's my section of wall.'

There, hanging in pride of place, was a newly-finished portrait of a softly-idealized Rosa, sitting on a wicker chair holding a posy of pink roses.

'I've painted it for her birthday in August,' Federico explained. 'Do you think she'll like it? Do you think it does her justice?'

Heidi smiled. 'I think she'll love it,' she said.

'Rosa is very fond of you, Heidi. She says you've made a real difference to her life.' As

Heidi blushed at this lavish praise, Federico patted her arm. 'For me, having you here is like having Ruggiero back. Marco and Artemisia will see that, too. You just need to give them time.

'It's strange, really,' Federico continued. 'I'm the one who wants to learn to paint, but it's Artemisia who has the talent. She has a real eye for shape and color, you know, so you'd expect it would be her who'd be responsible for the packaging side of the business. But Marco wanted it, and since he's a real whiz with computers and graphics, he got it.'

'Do you like his designs?' Heidi asked.

Federico shrugged. 'Call me an old traditional baker, but sometimes I think his stuff is a bit too way-out. Still, it's what's inside the cake and bread boxes that matters, and Stefano handles that.'

'Does Marco resent that?' Heidi asked carefully.

'Marco? No! He doesn't want to get up at three in the morning to bake every day!'

Chapter 10

Thinking back to their conversation as she battled through the afternoon heat to reach Soleari's before it closed for the siesta, Heidi wondered what Federico and Rosa would make of Marco's extensive gambling debts, if they knew of them. With the late spring sun scorching the back of her neck, she sped along the main square, avoiding the cars and mopeds. Bologna's last two remaining medieval towers loomed above the Palazzo Del Podesta and emotion rose in her throat as she saw the names and photographs of the resistance victims on the memorial plaque in the square. Slowing to read more, she realized in horror that in one tragic case five brothers from the same family had perished in the Second World War.

Perhaps it was because she was standing so still and quiet that the men's laughter issuing from a nearby arcade seemed brazen, almost callous. Glaring across the square at them, Heidi gasped and shaded her eyes, convinced she must be mistaken.

But she was not wrong, and Heidi knew it as she whirled about on the spot, turning her back on the two men and walking swiftly into the sheltering shade of the nearest tall building. She did not stop until she had turned a corner, and there, she leaned against the peeling ochre-painted wall and tried to collect her shattered wits. Although now in shade, she felt clammy and feverish as disbelieving tears pricked at her eyes.

She could not ignore what she'd seen and now she admitted it. One of the men laughing on the edge of the square had been Stefano. 'He said he'd be in Palermo,' Heidi mumbled through trembling lips. 'Perhaps he was able to come back early.'

But she couldn't quite believe that, or rather it seemed naive to do so. The simple facts of geography, distance and times of air travel were against that idea. Much more likely was the shocking thought that Stefano had never left Bologna, that he'd deliberately deceived her, and the rest of the family, and his own loyal employees at Soleari's.

Why should he do that? Heidi asked herself desperately, as other questions crowded her mind. Who was the man he was with? Why was he not in Palermo?

Harder than the questions was her own sense of disillusionment. She had believed Stefano when he told her about Soleari's and what he thought was best for the future of the *panetteria*. But had he told her everything? Had he told her the truth? Did he perhaps want to keep Soleari's frozen in

288

time and small-scale not to preserve the excellence of its bread and fresh hand-made pasta but for more sinister reasons?

Thinking furiously, Heidi raced across the path of an accelerating scooter to dart along another arcaded street, ignoring the scooter driver's furious volley of curses. Perhaps for 'special customers' Stefano provided prettily-wrapped bread and cakes with missing centers that held drugs or other illegal items. Who would suspect a family bakery?

It's Marco who likes the good life, Heidi argued with herself, but it was Stefano who wanted to keep the business as it was, not Marco. Over and over, in her mind she replayed the sight of his distinctive blond hair and the sound of his laughter ringing across the square until she felt that he was laughing at her. How could she have ever imagined that they were close? In truth, she hardly knew Stefano, knew nothing of the possibly illegal acts he might be capable of, once pressed. He had not even told her of his adoption until forced to do so by others. A snippet of Marco's conversation with her in the restaurant at Roberto's drifted back into her memory, 'He's very competitive. Stefano likes to win at everything he does.' What if Marco was right, and Stefano had been sleepwalking because he had lied?

'That's absurd,' Heidi told herself, but she did not feel reassured. Clutching her shopping bags tighter, she quickened her pace even more. Soleari's itself should hold the answer to her questions, she thought, but she must reach it before it closed.

Gina, the youngest assistant, was closing the shutters on the window display at Soleari's when Heidi crossed the square. A plump, cheerful young woman, Gina's usually glowing complexion looked blotchy and her brown hair seemed to have lost its natural chestnut highlights. Her white chef's uniform was as spotless as ever but she moved with none of her usual bounce. Greeting her and asking how she was, Heidi inwardly prayed that nothing had happened to Gina's fiancée, that the wedding was still on.

'I'm fine,' Gina said, careful not to look at Heidi directly. 'Everything's fine now.'

Even as she spoke, tears sprang into her eyes. 'I'm just tired,' she murmured.

'What is it, Gina?' Heidi asked softly. She dropped her shopping bags onto the floor, leaving them where they lay, and approached her.

'Nothing.' Gina began to tremble.

'I know you were upset after your phone call yesterday. Can I help you now?' Heidi went on, gently shepherding Gina through the door and away from the few remaining customers who lingered along the shady pavement outside.

'No, it's nothing.' Gina's pretty face twisted in her effort not to cry, and Heidi felt dreadful at having provoked this response. But then Gina leaned into her sheltering arm and added in an urgent whisper, 'I must talk to you!'

'Come on,' Heidi encouraged. 'Let's find somewhere private.'

Swiftly, she drew Gina through the shop, past Alberto who was wiping down shelves, moving at a smart pace towards the ladies' cloakroom.

'Emilia will be putting on her make-up in the rest room!' Gina warned, her breath catching as she fought down sobs. She was on the verge of tears.

'This way!' Heidi pointed to the staircase. Beside her, Gina was now openly weeping, trying to mop her streaming eyes with a tissue. Climbing the stairs, Heidi turned out her pockets until she found a clean handkerchief. 'Here.' She handed it across before pushing open the door to the staff lunch room where, only recently, she and Stefano had so enjoyed each others' company.

Except that it wasn't the staff room. By mistake she had brought them to an office with two large desks and computers and, standing beneath the window and its closed blinds, a water cooler.

'Sit down a moment, catch your breath.' Heidi gave Gina a brief hug before releasing her, longing to tell her that it would be all right but hardly daring to speak in case she made things worse. Was poor Gina distraught because of a lovers' quarrel, or a family tragedy, or was it, as Heidi increasingly suspected, something to do with the place where she worked?

She fetched Gina a glass of water and made a deliberate act of walking slowly around the two desks, giving her companion time to compose herself. Both desks were modern, in a simple Swedish-style design, and with no distinguishing marks. The computers on these desks were similarly anonymous, without so much as a single sticker or cuddly toy.

Beside the desk with a large swivel chair, Heidi's attention was drawn to a scrap of print-out paper in the nearby waste bin. She was alerted chiefly by the faint charred scent, because the paper was badly scorched. Crouching to examine the print-out, she made out the word 'difficulties' and then there was a gap where the paper had completely burned away, and then 'enable a sexier offer,' and, after another gap in the scorched paper, 'worthwhile'.

You shouldn't be looking, Heidi's conscience scolded, but her curiosity was stronger. Glancing up from the waste bin, she noticed a handsome print of Botticelli's *La Primavera* hanging on the wall immediately opposite the other desk. She remembered Artemisia's scornful comment, 'Soleari's isn't just a bakery. It's not a "bread shop" ...... that's like calling a painting by Botticelli a daub.' Was the desk opposite the Botticelli's painting of Springtime Artemisia's? If so, to whom did this second desk belong? It's very plainness made Heidi wonder if it was Stefano's, which quenched her spirits further, since presumably Stefano had been the one who had received and then burned the email print-out mentioning 'a sexier offer'.

Sitting on a spare chair, Gina finished her water and began to talk. 'It started a couple of weeks ago as a joke,' she said, her voice hesitant at first, becoming stronger as Heidi said encouragingly, 'Go on.'

'I did something silly with one of the oven timers. I won't bother trying to explain what because that isn't important. What matters is that he suggested it as a joke, and I did as he asked because I thought it would be amusing.'

'And it wasn't?'

'No!' Gina began to sniffle again.

'Who asked you?' Heidi prompted, when Gina fell silent. 'Who was it, Gina?'

Gina took in a long breath and clutched her empty water glass more tightly. 'He wanted me to do it again with the oven. I told him no, that it hadn't been that funny, but he said that I should do as he said because otherwise he would tell everyone else – Alberto, Emilia, everyone. He said I'd lose my job. And I love my work, I really do.' Gina began to cry again, very quietly.

'But who told you to do these things?' Heidi asked again. A name rose slowly and hotly in her throat, threatening to choke her, but she forced herself to say it. 'Stefano?'

Gina broke down completely, sobbing so loudly that Heidi could hardly hear, much less understand what she was saying. She caught the words 'shame' and 'sorry,' before Gina gasped out, 'He ... he does not like it when people say no to him.

'After a batch of olive focaccie were burned to a crisp and then old Signor Bartoli almost fell into the cellar, I became really scared,' she went on, wiping her eyes with Heidi's handkerchief. 'That open trapdoor certainly wasn't me. It must have been another of his people, but I guessed who was behind it. I refused to have anything to do with him.'

'That's good, Gina, but you must tell me his name.' Heidi could not believe it was Stefano who had bullied and threatened in this way – she was desperate not to believe it.

'Who is pressurizing you? And did he telephone and threaten you yesterday?'

Gina nodded and began to rock to and fro

on the chair. Her heart full of pity, Heidi walked across to the young woman and knelt beside her.

'Gina, it will be all right. You're not going to lose your job for something that you did as a joke, but you'll have to come clean and admit what happened. Otherwise this man, whoever he is, will keep on blackmailing you.'

Could Stefano really be doing this? Surely that was impossible!

'No, no!' Gina wailed now. 'I can't say anything! I can't afford to lose my job, especially now. My wedding dress cost over two thousand euros!'

'Let me help you,' Heidi pleaded. 'I'll talk to the others, but you have to tell me. Gina, who is it?'

Behind her, she heard the rapid footsteps on the stairs. Straightening quickly and placing herself between the opening door and the sobbing Gina, Heidi prepared to meet whoever was coming into the office.

Chapter 11

Marco strolled into the room, glanced at Gina and said easily, 'Hello, Heidi-Maria, I see Gina has been telling you about Stefano.' He smiled and then added in a more serious tone, 'Do you understand now? Stefano will do anything to keep Soleari's in the dark ages. Isn't that so, Gina?'

Heidi stared with horror as Gina nodded her head. 'But that would mean–' Heidi stopped as her stomach turned over within her. Gina had just been telling her about the mysterious 'him' who had threatened and blackmailed her. Now Marco was suggesting that 'him' was Stefano, and Gina had agreed!

Gina, threatened by Stefano? Stefano, harming his own people? Did Gina really mean that?

It isn't possible, Heidi thought. She felt stunned with disbelief. This was worse than incredible. It was a living nightmare. Stefano had told her nothing about himself, not one story of the time he spent in the orphanage or if he remembered his natural parents. Why did he not want to share? Now he was lying to her, telling her he'd be in

Palermo when all the while he was here in the city, bullying Gina. It was a horrifying, sickening betrayal of trust.

What do you expect? drawled a voice in her mind that sounded eerily like Marco's. *He's the adopted son. He's not one of us by blood.*

I don't believe that nonsense, Heidi thought, and she rallied. Stefano would tell her more when he was not beset by problems, when they had more time to relax together. For an instant she had been thrown off-balance by these seeming 'revelations', but how real were they? Gina was still distressed, ready to agree with any stronger personality, so of what value was her account?

But she was losing concentration and her grasp on events. Marco was talking, and she'd better pay attention.

Leaning against the desk opposite the reproduction of the Botticelli painting, Marco was holding forth, clearly enjoying this moment.

'Yes, and if our potential buyers learned about the troubles at Soleari's they might easily pull out.' He smiled at Gina, who seemed rooted to her chair.

'Or demand the business for a cheaper price?' Heidi dropped in, determined to put forth an opposing point of view.

Marco waved aside her objection. 'Unlikely,' he said. 'That might happen in Britain, but not here. In Italy, we do business properly. A solid reputation is everything. Stefano clearly hoped to undermine our reputation so that our buyers would vanish away like mist.'

Inwardly raging at that insult about Britain, Heidi rearranged her face into what she hoped was a convinced expression. 'That's terrible.' She reached out and gave Gina a comforting squeeze on the shoulder. Gina had stopped crying in the last few moments, but she was still upset. 'Can I telephone anyone for you?' Heidi asked her gently, thinking that Gina might welcome the appearance of her boyfriend.

'No, I'll be all right.' Gina rose to her feet and tottered to the door, saying without looking at either Heidi or Marco, 'I'll see if Alberto and Emilia need help clearing up.'

She was gone, and Heidi was glad to hear Gina's footsteps heading safely downstairs. 'So what now?' she asked, speaking to Marco but really addressing herself. Stefano, a liar and a blackmailer? She could not bear to think of him in those terms. Had she been mistaken about him? Could she have fallen in love with such a man?

Staring after Gina, a fleeing figure in white, Marco said quickly, 'I realize this has been a huge shock for you, Heidi. I know you liked Stefano, and I'm sure you won't want to run into him again, not on this trip, at least.'

Heidi was silently staggered at Marco's glib assessment of her feelings and also of her character. She very much wanted to talk to Stefano, to give him the chance to explain what he had done and why. Why was he here today in Bologna, when he had told her – and the family – that he would be in Palermo?

'It's probably best if you leave quietly to-day, while Stefano is away. It's obvious that he's an obsessive sort of character, possibly even dangerous.' Speaking, Marco held the office door open for her to go first. 'I've got my car nearby, so I can take you back to the villa and you can pack, say your farewells and then I can drive you to the station or wherever you want to go.'

Marco was trying to rush her, wanting to hustle her off. Heidi was already aware that he didn't want her at the rapidly approaching family meeting, where the future of Soleari's would be decided by vote, but she wondered at his haste today.

Why don't you want me to talk to Stefano? she questioned him in her mind as she walked down the staircase and back into the *panetteria*. Noting the muted greetings that Emilia and Alberto gave Marco, she found herself asking why Gina had seemed to freeze like a rabbit in the headlights of a car whenever Marco smiled at her.

Still dazed by Marco's claims, Heidi

turned and waited for her handsome cousin to catch up. He was talking quietly to Gina, he smiling, Gina nodding. Waiting again, Heidi could not help thinking about Stefano. Her sense of him was very strong here, amidst the glass shelves and small tables with their displays of cake boxes and streamer-trimmed bags of fresh pasta.

In a series of frozen tableaux in her mind, she remembered him. How sensitive and concerned Stefano had been on her first night in the villa, when Federico had cavalierly cancelled her hotel room and Stefano had instantly stepped forward to help, offering to drive her back to the hotel. She remembered him brushing her hair and how careful and gentle he'd been. He had come rushing up the longest portico in the world, over half the length of the covered four kilometer uphill walk from the city to the hilltop sanctuary of the Madonna of San Luca because he'd been worried about her. She remembered the tender urgency of his kisses.

Stefano had shown her nothing but good. She remembered him with others, too, his saving of Signor Bartoli; his indulgence of Emilia's teasing; his protectiveness towards Rosa. He had escorted Gina home because she was upset. Was it really believable, Heidi thought, that Stefano had been the one to upset her?

I trust him, she thought. Despite the dreadful shock of seeing him in town today, she still trusted Stefano. In contrast, and in a basic, fundamental way, Heidi realized that she could not trust Marco at all. On the heels of that realization came another, that it would not be prudent to get into Marco's car.

What had Gina said? 'He does not like it when people say no to him.' Did that description not fit Marco, the spoiled younger son, absolutely?

As she left Soleari's, she wordlessly practiced what she would say and do. On the pavement outside, she spoke to Marco, her voice light. 'I'm sorry, Marco, but I need to go to the chemist's. It'll be quicker if I walk. It's right in the middle of town, by the food market.' She was backing slowly away as she spoke. 'I'll see you back at the villa, okay?'

Marco was following her. He was smiling but silent, matching his steps to hers, as if they were involved in some kind of dance. A shiver of fear iced its way down Heidi's back as she watched this tall, good looking man prowling after her in his designer jeans and black cotton-silk shirt.

He does not like it when people say no to him...

'I have to go.' Heidi knew she was still backing away along the arcade, but she wasn't too proud to admit that she was scared to turn her back on Marco. Her hesitant feet found the edge of the pavement at the end of the square, and she knew that before she moved further, she had to find a means to distract him.

'Look!' She pointed behind Marco's shoulder towards Luigi's café, forcing her taut mouth into a large smile. 'Isn't that... Hey! Hello!' she called out.

Marco turned, and Heidi was off, walking quickly down the pavement, across the narrow street at the end of the square and then immediately a hard right down another alleyway. Her light sandals pounding the hard flagstones, she ran, skirting wildly around a parked Mercedes that filled most of the alley, ignoring any raised voices or the usual car horns and building drills that were so much a part of the daily sounds of Bologna. Tasting the salt of tears in her mouth, she ran on, allowing the prevailing wind to blow her along the street like a piece of thistledown.

Careering into a new alleyway, narrowly missing a startled-looking woman pushing two toddlers in smocked gingham dresses in a double buggy, Heidi pushed herself to go faster, faster.

Missing her footing once, her legs scissored widely and she tumbled, a cry escaping from her as she realized she was falling.

Strong arms caught her, and she screamed,

shuddering from head to foot, terrified for an instant that Marco had seized her.

'It's all right,' Stefano said softly against her ear, easily supporting her as her legs buckled. 'I won't let you fall. It's all right, my Heidi. I can explain.'

'Well done, Stefano. You do have this irritating knack of being in the way.' Marco, breathing heavily, stepped up to his taller, leaner brother and chuckled as Heidi turned her face away from his, resting her head in the crook of Stefano's shielding arm. 'That wasn't very well-mannered, Heidi-Maria, rushing off like that. Now, why don't you come away from him?'

Marco made a grab for her, but even as Heidi shied away, Stefano had turned his own body so that Marco's reaching fingers scraped down his shoulder and arm and did not touch her.

'Let me go!' Heidi whispered, disliking the feeling of being trapped between the two brothers, one very fair, one very dark, one she could trust, one she was increasingly afraid of.

Glowering at Marco, Stefano instantly released her. For Heidi, his immediate acknowledgement of her wishes provided the final proof of both her hopes and her darkest suspicions. Realizing the truth, she gasped as everything else fell into place.

Marco gave a rueful grin at her reaction.

'It's over,' he drawled, addressing Stefano over her head. 'You've been found out, Stefano. And why aren't you in Palermo, as you told us? You do realize that Heidi has been incredibly disappointed and–'

'You were the one behind the sabotage,' Heidi interrupted him. Sensing that here and now would see a final confrontation, she stepped forward to face Marco. 'Do you deny it?'

She glanced at Stefano. 'Is that what you suspected? Did you allow us to think you were away so that you could watch Soleari's and finally see how Marco was bullying and blackmailing Gina and others into doing his dirty work for him?'

'That's absurd.' Marco smilingly denied it, tapping the side of his head with a finger. 'I think you've had rather too much sun again, Heidi-Maria.'

'And in the office, that was your desk,' Heidi continued, throwing Stefano a glance of apology for ever suspecting him. Of course the desk near the Botticelli print was Artemisia's and the completely plain desk was Marco's. He was hardly ever there to add any personal touches. If the desk was Marco's, then the half-burned contents of the waste bin were his, too.

'I saw you at breakfast with your mobile,' Heidi countered, more and more convinced that what she was saying was right. 'You'd just finished a call to Gina, hadn't you? She's afraid of you. That's why she agreed with you upstairs in the staff office when you said it was your brother who was organizing those "accidents" in the bakery.'

Marco put up his hands. *'Panetteria*, please,' he said.

'You were working at the *panetteria*, arranging that "wizard bread" display when Nix was taken ill with one of Soleari's vol-au-vents,' Heidi said, part of her deeply relieved now that she understood that Stefano had played no part in poisoning the little dog.

'Nix? Who on earth is that?' Marco blustered, but Heidi cut across him.

'Soleari's is very busy. There are always people milling around the counters. It would have been easy for you to spike part of Signora Cardenli's order.'

'And alter the timers,' broke in Stefano, his face hardening. 'But why? I really hoped I was mistaken in my suspicions of you, and I kept hoping I was wrong, but I wasn't. But why Marco? Why do this?'

Marco shrugged and refused to answer, brushing a speck of ochre paint off his black shirt and glancing hopefully to the end of the alleyway as a Vespa trundled across the top of the street from one arcade to another. When the driver did not turn down towards them, he smirked and turned back to Heidi.

'Are you going to say next that it was me who tried your door a couple of nights ago? Believe me, you're not so attractive–'

Stefano cursed and shot across the cobbles towards his brother, but Heidi grabbed his arm. 'Don't!' she said urgently. 'It doesn't matter. He didn't hurt me, and he only did it to encourage me to leave the Villa Rosa before the family meeting.'

Marco sighed and straightened as he realized that Stefano was not going to launch himself at him. 'Excellent thought. Pity you didn't act on it.'

'But you've acted, haven't you?' Heidi went on. 'You went so far as to have someone open that trap-door and leave it. Did you tell whoever did that for you that it was for a joke, as you told Gina? Were you hoping to obtain a more competitive price for the *panetteria* for its potential buyers? Were they going to make it more "worthwhile" for you if you could give them the chance to present "a sexier offer"?'

She hurled the terms of the mystery email printout back at Marco. Beside her, standing in the middle of the narrow alley as if in defiance of any passing moped and Vespa drivers, Stefano looked coldly furious at the revelation of his brother's treatment of Gina, then puzzled.

'Sexier offer?' he repeated. 'You mean you did this for money?' he asked Marco, his bright brown eyes shining with pain and confusion. 'Simply for money? I'd hoped I was mistaken, that the odd hints Gina gave me that made me dread it might be you behind these "accidents" were going to turn out to be groundless. Marco, why couldn't you have come to me for help? Or to Artemisia? We wouldn't have stood by and let you sink under a mountain of debt. You only had to ask.'

'Give you another chance to play patronizing older brother? No way. As for Arte...' Marco snapped his fingers so hard that Heidi flinched. 'She's bailed me out twice but no more. Why does this pathetic little *panetteria* mean so much to you, anyway? My scheme would have seen us all rich.'

Stefano clenched his fists by his sides. 'What about the tradition? The people like Alberto who've served us faithfully over the years? The pleasure and joy we bring to others, the pride in our work, in what we produce. Do these things mean nothing to you?'

Marco said quietly, 'You're wrong. You're both making a huge mistake, but I suppose that's your privilege.' He turned in the street, just as a moped driver skidded round the corner and bore down on them, blowing her horn as she swerved around Stefano. 'I'll see you around, maybe.'

With a wave and a final dazzling smile,

Marco was gone, striding off in the same direction as the moped driver. Building shadows hid his tall, blackshirted figure and then, a few moments later, Heidi heard the roar of a car pulling away in a screech of tires. Torn between relief and a kind of shocked numbness, she leaned back against the alley wall, feeling the chill bite of metal against her shoulder from one of the building's iron window grilles. Silent and still, she and Stefano stared at each other, feeling no sense of satisfaction at their unraveling of the mysterious 'accidents' at Soleari's, but only a resigned sadness.

Finally, Stefano crossed the narrow alleyway out of the path of passing mopeds, joining Heidi in leaning against the alley wall as he took off his spectacles and gave them a long polish on his jeans.

'I'm sorry,' he said, looking at Heidi without his glasses, his gaze holding hers. 'I deceived you, and I shouldn't have done. I was trying to keep you out of danger, but instead I brought you closer to it.'

Heidi shook her head. 'No, you didn't,' she said, reaching out and clasping his arm as he put on his spectacles. 'But you should have told me what you were doing. When I spotted you today in Bologna I wondered if I was seeing you or your double.'

Staring up at him, she had the rare experience of seeing Stefano visibly discomforted, the more so as a slow blush swept over his face.

'I wanted to keep you out of it,' he growled. 'You're the last person to stay on the sidelines if there's trouble, and I didn't want you involved.'

Heidi refused to be distracted by Stefano's implied compliment, if compliment it was. 'Who was the man you were laughing with today, close to the Palazzo Del Podesta? And for how long have you suspected Marco?' she asked gently, reluctant to pry but sensing that these hard questions must be settled between them.

Stefano smiled at her as a troop of elderly Italian tourists walked slowly past them, led by their gesturing guide. 'Would you believe that man was a policeman?' he told her under cover of the tourists' shuffling footsteps. 'He's an old school friend whom I joined at one of the local bars for a drink. I was chatting to him about his surveillance work, trying to draw him out about clues and signs when you must have spotted us. I suppose I was thinking I'd be my own detective.' He sighed. 'When the "accidents" first started, I wondered about Marco and remembered how he loved to play tricks when he was a little boy. But then I told myself he was an adult, that he would not be so petty. I suppose I did not want to think of my brother in that way.

'I didn't tell my friend Pietro anything about Soleari's, or what I was afraid might be happening there. It would have sounded too bizarre. I was too ashamed.' He lowered his head.

That was Marco's talent, Heidi thought, his ability to make members of his own family feel guilty. Impulsively, she touched Stefano's arm. 'It's not your fault.'

Stefano ran a distracted hand through his wavy blond hair. 'I knew Marco had the strongest reasons for wanting the business sold, but I didn't want to believe that he would actually sabotage it. Gina was white and trembling when I took her home after that phone call. As I said earlier, the little she would tell me about her mystery caller made me think of Marco again, made me determined to stop him, to unmask his filthy campaign of dirty tricks. And then there was his treatment of you.'

'Me?'

'His insolence, his unkindness.' Stefano folded his wiry arms across his chest, tightly gripping his elbows. 'I was so jealous of Marco when he took you out to Roberto's restaurant and asked you to go to Venice with him. So jealous and so afraid that you'd fall for his easy charm.'

'I suppose women usually do?' Heidi asked, thinking that this explained Marco's invitations. He'd been trying to charm her into doing whatever he wanted, especially with regard to the family business.

'Usually, damn him!' Stefano kicked the wall with the back of his heel. 'And there you were, so pretty, and second cousin to him, nothing to stop you both...' His voice trailed away and he would not look directly at her.

So here was the reason Stefano had been so brusque with her whenever he'd seen her with Marco! Heidi's hopes and spirits began to lift, to almost soar. Jealousy was not the result of indifference, or caring solely about how she used her voting rights. 'He is good looking,' she said in a considering way, 'But we're not really suited. We don't have anything in common and I'm pretty serious.'

Stefano unfolded his arms. 'That's what Artemisia is always saying about me,' he said, his voice tense with barely suppressed emotion.

'Serious and caring,' Heidi agreed. *And with hair as golden as the bread you bake and wonderful warm brown eyes,* she added in her mind, too shy to speak her thought aloud.

Perhaps something of her feeling showed in her face because the next moment she was in Stefano's arms, being whirled off her feet.

'Lord, Heidi, I've been so worried about you!' he exclaimed, lifting her high in his arms, oblivious to a passing disapproving priest. 'When you cannoned into me today, you looked so pale, so scared. I went through hell, wondering what was wrong, what had happened to you. When Marco came after you, I wanted to kill him.'

'I'm all right,' Heidi swiftly reassured him as his arms tightened around her waist. She felt to be floating away, buoyed up by his concern. 'Nothing happened, Stefano. I was never in any danger.' She said nothing of her sudden reluctance to go with Marco in his car. Stefano, she sensed, had already been badly torn by family loyalties and family responsibilities because of his younger brother. Trying to keep it light, she asked quizzically, 'Are you always this protective?'

Stefano gave her a long kiss that made her feel even more light-headed. 'Of you, my Heidi? Oh, yes,' he said, kissing her again as he set her down gently on her feet. 'I like to look after you.'

'Isn't that rather old-fashioned?' Heidi teased as they turned and began to walk hand in hand back towards Soleari's, their family business.

'Maybe.' Stefano swung her hand up to his lips and kissed her fingers one by one. 'I don't care.'

Neither do I, Heidi thought, as they strolled into the sunlit square. Above her head and around her, she could hear bells ringing, a joyous sound, driving away the last of the shadows that had hemmed them both in since Marco had tried to set his devious plans in motion.

'I wonder if we'll see Marco at home,' she said aloud.

'That's unlikely. My brother likes to avoid reckonings if he can. I imagine he'll be on his way to Milan or farther. We'll probably hear from him in a few days' time.' Stefano gently squeezed her hand. 'I know you care for all the family and your coming amongst us has certainly transformed my mother's life, but you really mustn't worry about Marco. He always lands on his feet.'

'Even with his gambling debts?'

'Even with those,' Stefano answered.

Stefano was right. When he and Heidi returned to the Villa Rosa later that afternoon, Marco was nowhere to be found. A few days' later, on the morning of the family meeting to consider the future of Soleari's, Marco emailed a proxy vote to Artemisia with the instruction to, 'Do exactly what you want with it.'

Stefano insisted that the meeting take place at Soleari's, in the staff lunch room next to the plain office. There, within the sounds and mouthwatering smells of the *panetteria*, Stefano explained how the ovens need to be repaired and modernized and for long how the business would have to close

313

while this work went on. Federico and Rosa sat side by side, holding hands as they listened to his intense, careful account.

Watching them together and seeing Rosa's increased aura of peace and serenity, Heidi wondered if Federico had decided to show his wife the birthday portrait he had made for her a little early. Rosa glowed with life.

'What's wrong with you two?' Artemisia snapped, as Federico and Rosa smiled through her presentation about the advantages of selling Soleari's. 'We could make a great deal of money here, and you're hardly listening to a word I'm saying!'

'Money isn't everything, is it?' observed Federico, nodding to Stefano across the table. 'I think it's time we voted.'

Heidi voted with Stefano to restore the *panetteria,* but she was glad that her vote was not needed. Rosa and Federico both voted with their adopted son, and Federico even used his casting vote on that side. Faced with a five to two split, Artemisia took the result in surprisingly good part, saying that she wasn't entirely surprised and that neither was Marco.

'In fact he told me to tell you that he's giving up his share and interest in the business,' Artemisia announced, with the air of a cat with a freshly-captured mouse. 'He's going to devote himself to his new wife-to-be, the Contessa Donna Maria Eugenia of

314

Palermo. They met recently in Milan and are going to announce their engagement this weekend.'

'See what I mean?' Stefano remarked in a low voice to Heidi as Rosa and Federico broke into starts and exclamations of mingled surprise and delight. 'Marco always lands on his feet.'

Later, Heidi and Stefano slipped away into the garden of the Villa Rosa to walk and talk. Heidi was returning to Britain in two days' time to pick up her old life. Strolling along the terraces towards the small fountain where Stefano had first kissed her, she realized that the thought gave her scarcely any pleasure. Stefano had said that she had transformed Rosa's life. Federico had told her that having her around was like having his brother Ruggiero back. The staff and increasingly the customers at Soleari's greeted her as one of their own. She would be leaving all that behind, leaving this new family, leaving Stefano.

Had she transformed Stefano's life? she thought, stealing a glance at his reserved, aristocratic-looking profile as they wandered side by side along an avenue of ferns and pines. Would he be able to return to Soleari's in three days' time with no more than a few memories and perhaps the odd regret? Was their brief time together to be no more than a holiday romance?

'I will write to you,' Stefano suddenly announced. 'Every day.'

'It will be nice to keep in touch.' *Nice?* Heidi asked herself, while tears threatened. Only her pride stopped her from snatching hold of Stefano's arm and demanding that he say something to her.

Into her mind swept Gina's extravagant wedding dress, which Gina had shyly shown her only yesterday. Running a fingertip over its frills and flounces and its satin bodice, Heidi had shamelessly put herself and Stefano into Gina's and her fiancé's places. Did she want that? Did she and Stefano know each other well enough for such a commitment?

'I hear Gina's invited you to her wedding,' Stefano said, and hope flared in Heidi again. If he was thinking of weddings... 'We'll see each other then, of course.'

'Of course,' Heidi agreed, lowering her eyes to stare blankly at a row of flowers whose names she had forgotten and whose colors and shapes were blurring with the treacherous pricking of her tears. How could he be so cheerful?

'But I'd like to see you much sooner. Every day. I can't stand the thought of not seeing you every day.' Stefano nervously drummed his fingers along the edge of the small marble fountain where he and Heidi had first kissed. Did she remember? Dare he say more about his feelings?

She was determinedly not looking at him. Watching her small, dark-haired figure peering through the fine spray of the fountain, Stefano felt a surge of love punch through his chest and middle. 'Do you know how you've changed all our lives?' he burst out. 'Because of you, I now feel that I truly belong to this family, like a full son.'

She raised her beautiful blue-green eyes, her face haunting in its bewilderment. 'Did you not realize that, Stefano? They chose you.'

Her words gave him a chance that he seized at once. 'As I would choose you, Heidi. I would like there to be more between us than the friendship of family. I would like to visit you in your home town and spend as much time as possible with you, learn everything about you.'

'Why?' Heidi asked, feeling for an instant like a gambler, risking everything on a single result. She trembled as Stefano took her in his arms, lowering that bright blond head closer, closer...

He kissed her, murmuring endearments in Italian and English, saying that he loved the little gap between her front teeth, that she smelled like wine and roses and honey to him. 'I love you, my Heidi. I love you so much. I want us to be together. I want to learn aromatherapy from you and teach you all I know. I want to show you where I was born. I want to show you the orphanage. I want to come to Selby, where you live. When can I come? When?'

'Soon,' Heidi promised. 'Very soon.' Giddy at the confirmation of Stefano's love, she blushed with pleasure at the thought of finally learning more about him and of his seeing where she lived. 'I love you,' she said simply, feeling herself coloring more deeply at the delicious idea of teaching him, of learning from him.

'Good!' said Stefano, kissing her again. 'I would like you to be thinking of rings, my Heidi. An engagement ring, a wedding ring–'

'You will choose a wedding ring, too?' Heidi asked. 'I'd like that.'

'Of course! I want to show the world that you have chosen me!' Drawing back from her only a little, Stefano wound an arm tenderly about her waist. Listening to the midday bells ringing out again over the city of Bologna, he and Heidi continued their walk past the fountain, along the gravel path bordered with red roses, and so back to the villa, to tell the family their news.